BODY
HEAT

Doctor Hughes hunts a deadly arsonist in this murder mystery

CANDY DENMAN

Paperback edition published by

The Book Folks

London, 2020

ISBN 978-1-913516-33-8

www.thebookfolks.com

BODY HEAT is the second standalone title in a series of medical crime fiction novels featuring medical examiner Dr Callie Hughes. Look out for the first book, DEAD PRETTY, and the subsequent books, GUILTY PARTY and VITAL SIGNS, available on Kindle and in paperback.

Prologue

He was driving carefully, making sure he didn't attract attention, although he hardly saw another car once he had left the town. He had driven this route several times in preparation, knew all the bends and dips, the houses and driveways, every potential threat.

What he hadn't accounted for was the excitement and tension of doing it for real and the effect of all that extra adrenalin. He thought he was driving exactly as he had in the practice runs, but in fact, he was driving considerably faster. A little too fast for a corner that came up sooner than he expected. He braked hard, and panicked as the rear wheels drifted and hit the grass verge. He overcorrected and the car lurched onto the wrong side of the road, throwing his passenger from side to side as he struggled to straighten up and regain control of the car. He was lucky the road ahead was empty.

He pulled over to the side of the road and rested his head against the steering wheel, waiting for his heart rate to come down to something near normal. He couldn't afford to have an accident. Not now. He took a deep breath to calm himself and then turned to check that she was all right. He had taken care to strap her in with the seat belt when he put her in the car, even though she wouldn't sit up straight to help him. Couldn't. She looked fine; slumped in her seat, her head lolling to one side, seemingly asleep, but then she mumbled something incoherent. He felt it was critical in tone. Bitch.

"Sorry," he said as he looked at her with disgust.

She gave a little smile that could have been a grimace, or wind, and mumbled again.

He thought it might have been: "S'okay."

That was better, he thought, more respectful. She looked as if she might be sick. He hoped not. He hated the smell of vomit, and he didn't want her to spoil the moment. If she only knew what he had planned for her. He smiled to himself, feeling instantly better as he thought about what lay ahead, excitement building in his gut again. He started to drive, but more carefully this time. Slow and steady.

At last he pulled into a deserted parking area. It was ideal – remote and surrounded by trees. He had chosen well. He opened his window and the fresh air seemed to wake her up a little. She blinked, trying to work out where she was, and then noticed her skirt had ridden up slightly leaving her lacy panties on show. She giggled. The whore.

"Just getting a rug out of the boot," he explained as he got out of the car. "Don't want you getting cold." He smiled to himself at the irony, then quickly checked she hadn't noticed. But she was too busy pulling her skirt down, trying to make herself look respectable again, to worry about what he was doing.

He hurried to get everything out of the boot. The folding bike was awkward to handle. It caught on the lip of the boot and he had to wrench it clear. He stopped, listening in case she realised what was going on. He heard her try and open her door. He needn't have worried. In her befuddled state, it took her a while to realise that she couldn't. She didn't seem to understand why it wouldn't open and kept trying. He smiled. He had plenty of time.

He carried the bike to the edge of the trees and returned for the rest of his equipment.

She stopped banging the door when she saw him return to the driver's window.

"Can't seem to get out," she said, her voice slurred with drink and drugs, "don't feel well."

She started to climb towards the driver's side, but her tight skirt made movement difficult and it took her a moment to understand what she had seen in his hand. A petrol can. She looked up at him, puzzled, just as he started to splash the liquid inside the car, and over her.

"What the fuck?" she shouted, trying to shield herself from the petrol with her hands, suddenly sober.

But it was a futile attempt to stop the inevitable, and he didn't bother to answer her, just emptied the can and threw it behind him, towards the trees where he had left the bike. He took out a book of matches, tearing one off, lighting it and then using this match to light the rest of them. He threw the flaming match book into the car quickly before it burnt his hand, grabbing the petrol can as he scurried back. Fast. He didn't want to get caught out by being too close, but he didn't want to move too far either, he wanted to see. He wanted to see her burn. He wanted to see her punished for her sins.

It took a moment for her to realise what had happened. What was happening. The first flames danced, prettily, and she tried to pat them, put them out with her petrol-soaked hands. He almost laughed out loud as she waved her burning hands in the air, hoping the wind would douse the flames. Panicking now, she tried her door again and then started to climb across to the driver's side, through the flames. She was shouting something, but he couldn't hear her over the roar in his ears. Was it the roar of the fire taking hold or excitement? He thought she might have been shouting "help", but he couldn't be sure.

Her hair was on fire now, her carefully styled and coloured hair was crackling and burning, leaving nothing but a blackened, blistered scalp, and she hadn't even got across to the driver's side yet. There was a sudden whoosh as the back windows blew out. Despite moving away from the car fast, he felt the rush of hot air on his face, not enough to burn or scald him, but a warning that he was too close. He would remember that in future, when he did this again. It was a shame, but he needed to keep his distance. He wouldn't want to have to explain away any injuries later.

As he backed away from the car, dragging the bike and picking up the discarded petrol can, he watched as her attempts to escape waned. He unfolded the bike and put the can in a plastic bag and stowed it safely in the back pannier. Her hands, already like claws, were still moving in a futile attempt to put the flames out, a scream frozen on her open mouth, her skin charring before her vaporizing eyeballs. And then she stopped. There was a pause as the fire really took hold, followed by an explosion as the petrol tank blew. Not as dramatic as in the films, but satisfying all the same. Was she dead before the explosion? He would never know, but he hoped not. He took one last look to make sure he had left nothing behind before pedalling away, burning leaves floating down around him. He smiled at a job well done.

Chapter 1

It was early on a Sunday morning and Callie was wishing it would rain. What she wanted was a deep, cleansing downpour, to wash away the terrible, overpowering smell of burnt flesh, despite knowing that it would also destroy any evidence. The awful odour emanating from the car in front of her was making her heave, even with the liberal dose of vapour rub she had applied just inside and under her nose and she knew the smell would remain with her for hours if not days, as particulates would be lodged in her fine nasal hairs.

Dr Callie Hughes, part-time GP, part-time forensic physician for the Hastings police, had been called out to pronounce death and confirm that it was unlikely to be due to natural causes. That was going to be the easy part: whatever the cause – suicide, accident or murder – this death would need a full forensic work-up. She looked around; the car park was little more than a clearing in the woods at the end of a muddy track. The trees, which were showing signs of new spring growth with pale green leaves just appearing, had been scorched by the flames and hot gases, but had not fully caught alight and the fire had burnt itself out without needing help from the fire brigade. No need for hoses meant that the ground wasn't a quagmire, but it also meant that nothing was keeping down the smell, either. Already dressed in the obligatory gloves and paper suit, Callie slipped on a mask to further protect her from the foul odour and moved to take a closer look at what was left of the body in the burnt shell of the car.

The remains were badly disfigured, the blackened skin cracked in places to reveal waxy, white, avascular flesh below, the intense heat having coagulated the blood and cauterised the blood vessels. Nothing much seemed to remain of any clothing, although they might find something in the debris or under the body, and there looked to be some lumps of melted plastic on the floor that might have been a handbag or shoes. Something that might possibly be the remains of a stiletto, but equally might not. Hopefully, there would be enough left to help identify the victim, but for now, Callie wasn't even sure if it was a woman or a man in stilettos.

Callie had read somewhere that those who had survived being engulfed by flames said that it was surprisingly pain free and even induced an ecstasy-like state, but she didn't believe it for one moment. It seemed more likely that the brain blocked out the memory and was helped in this by all the painkillers given to burns victims after the event. As she looked at the open-mouthed grimace of the corpse in the car, even knowing that the expression was called a rictus and was caused by the contraction of muscles and tendons in the intense heat, the body seemed to be shrieking in fear and pain, and she found it hard to imagine this person died in ecstasy. Very hard indeed. She closed her eyes and shuddered. What a horrible way to die.

After her moment of weakness, Callie opened her eyes and got back to work. The size of the body was hard to estimate because the arms and legs had been pulled up as the tendons contracted in the flames, pulling the body into the position sometimes described as foetal, or as a boxer's crouch, hands in front of the face, or rather, where the face had been, balled into pugilistic fists and with knees drawn up to the body, except that, in this case, one leg seemed to be straighter, stretched out behind the body, but she couldn't quite see why.

A shout broke her concentration.

"No, not that one, it's too close, use that tree over there."

Callie turned to see Colin Brewer, the short, muscular crime scene manager, doing what he did best: organising. He was supervising the uniformed officers who were taping off the area, and clearly hadn't approved of their choice of trees to use as anchors. He looked at his watch impatiently, willing the rest of his team to arrive soon so that they could start collecting evidence and then, with a small sigh, he carried on doing what he could. He designated one officer to guard the way in and keep the sign-in sheet, telling the others to keep back and not trample on any evidence. They scuttled back to the designated perimeter, happy to keep their distance. The smell of charred meat was hanging in the air, and the grotesque remains in the car was the stuff of nightmares. Working a 'death by burning' case was never easy to forget.

Callie looked around the small parking area. It had been a well-known haunt for lovers and doggers alike until a recent raid by the police had scared them off, and anyway, she didn't think they usually torched the car afterwards, but what did she know? She shook her head and she resumed her examination of what was left of the car.

Whilst the driver's door was fully open, the passenger door was about an inch ajar. The body was leaning towards the driver's side, lying half across the skeletal remains of the passenger seat and with one foot in the driver's well. The leg that hadn't contracted into the crouch position was still in the passenger side of the car. She changed her position to see better and saw that the foot had caught under the frame of the passenger seat, and had been partially protected by its position. Callie walked round to the passenger side where she could see that the car was parked up against a row of wooden posts that delineated the car park boundary and that it was impossible to open the passenger door enough for an adult person to escape. This seemed to explain why the victim had been trying to get across to the driver's side.

Callie crouched down, and gently pulled the door open the two or three inches that it could before hitting the post, and looked into the car. The foot trapped under the passenger seat appeared to be small, with the remains of a high-heeled strappy sandal attached, indicating to Callie that the victim had probably been female. It looked as if fumes and flames had overcome her before she had managed to climb over the gear stick, let alone get out. The poor woman must have been terrified. Callie could only imagine her last moments as she realised she was trapped, on fire, in terrible pain, but still led by the instinct to survive to try and escape. To try to live. Callie paused, and then pushed the door back to its original position, in order to look more closely at the charred wooden post. It was difficult to see if the victim had pushed the door hard enough to mark either the door or the post, such was the damage from the flames.

"Mmmhmm, I love the smell of crispy bacon in the morning."

Callie stood up quickly. There was only one person she knew who would say something quite so gross and insensitive.

"What're we doing here, Col?" the voice continued, "one of the stupid twockers hurt himself?"

A man in his fifties, with thinning hair and a thickening waistline, was walking from the road towards the car park entrance, swearing under his breath as he struggled to put on his purple nitrile gloves. Detective Sergeant Bob Jeffries. His body shape was not enhanced by the white coveralls he was already wearing over his clothes. Callie knew that the police referred to joyriders as twockers because they were usually charged with the offence of 'Taking Without Consent' or 'TWoC', but she hated the derisory way it was used, particularly by DS Jeffries.

"Bit more than hurt himself," her cool voice admonished him. "Perhaps you'd like to show a little respect?"

"What's up, Doc?" Jeffries grinned as he signed the log and pulled on his mask.

Callie was distracted as a second man approached from the road, where DS Jeffries went, Detective Inspector Steve Miller was likely to follow. Or vice versa. Younger and taller than the man who had been speaking so ill of the dead, he was a dark, good-looking and solidly built man in his late thirties, with the slightly bent nose of a rugby player.

"Dr Hughes," Miller said with a nod to Callie, as he also signed the log before entering the scene. "I take it you've pronounced?" he continued as he pulled up his facemask, settling it comfortably over his nose, and walked towards the wreckage that had once been a car. And a woman.

"Yes, Detective Inspector, I have pronounced life extinct," she told him. "Although you probably didn't need a doctor to tell you that."

He barely broke stride as he responded.

"No, I think we can all see that this man is dead." He was standing on the opposite side of the car to her now, peering in through the driver's door.

"As a dodo," Jeffries added as he came around the car to the passenger side.

"Woman. This woman," Callie corrected them, "if I am not mistaken." She had hoped to see a reaction from Miller, but was disappointed. "And it's clearly not from natural causes." She was finding it hard to hide her irritation at Miller's cool and offhand manner.

"Quite." Miller looked at her expectantly. "Anything else, Doctor?"

"The passenger door can't open because it's blocked by a post, and the victim seems to have been trying to climb across from the passenger seat to get out, which would suggest it wasn't suicide."

"Unless it was a last-minute change of heart. She could have parked deliberately against the post to stop that exact eventuality, couldn't she?" He looked directly at her for the first time since he had arrived. His hazel eyes had a hint of amber and Callie struggled to concentrate as they locked on hers.

"Of course, but—" Callie stopped because Miller had already turned away and was talking to Colin.

"We'll need to alert the pathologist to organise the PM and get the fire investigators out, too."

"Fire investigator's on his way, Guv. The fire crew alerted them."

"Fire crew?"

"They left as soon we got here, Guv." Colin explained.

"The fire was already out and they were needed elsewhere." The voice came from behind them and they all turned to see who was speaking.

"Chris Butterworth."

The newcomer held out his gloved hand as he introduced himself, and Miller shook it.

"Fire Investigation Unit," he said. "I can give you all the fire crew details so that you can interview them later, but there was a bit of a rush on. Warehouse fire over in Bexhill."

"No problem." Miller nodded his acceptance of the situation. "As you say, we can take statements later."

Butterworth stopped and looked around at the scorched trees before continuing towards the burnt-out shell of the car. Both policemen followed behind him. Miller seemed surprised that Callie was still there.

"Have you finished here, Doctor?"

"Yes." She couldn't believe he was dismissing her like this. "All finished."

Miller returned his attention to the fire investigator.

Callie walked slowly back towards the crime scene perimeter to sign out and get out of her crime scene clothing. Once done, she looked back at the remains of the car where Butterworth was walking carefully round the outside, taking a look at the damage, peering into the open boot and through the blown-out windows before he crouched down beside driver's door and took a look at the body. She listened carefully, keen to hear what was said.

"I'll take samples to confirm, but I'm pretty sure an accelerant has been used," he said as he looked carefully round the site.

"From the fuel tank exploding?" Miller queried.

Butterworth pointed to some scorched grass and some faint marks still visible across the rear floor of the car.

"I'll need to have a more detailed look, but, for what it's worth, my initial impression is that it's not from the fuel tank exploding. See those lines there?" he pointed at some marks in the scorched grass. "They're called pour patterns, and are from when the accelerant was splashed about."

"But the victim could've doused the car before getting in and setting it alight, right?" Jeffries asked.

Butterworth gave Jeffries a pitying look and called across to Colin Brewer.

"Have your guys turned up a container yet?"

Brewer shook his head.

"No," Brewer paused, before adding with a look at Miller, "and we've completed the preliminary search of the area."

Butterworth turned to Miller.

"Can't see the remains of anything that could have been used to hold the accelerant in the car, so, unless it's been thrown quite a distance or someone's nicked it—"

"It's not suicide." Miller finished for him and looked across at Callie who tried not to look triumphant to have had her view confirmed.

* * *

"He was being a completely arrogant—" Callie struggled for the right word.

"Sod." Kate happily supplied it for her furious friend, knowing her dislike of using even the mildest of swearwords. "Prick. Bastard. Wanker. Take your pick, so to speak."

It was ten o'clock on Sunday morning and Callie was recovering from her early morning call to the scene of the burnt-out car by having coffee with her best friend. They were in Kate's sitting room, a room of rich jewel colours and textures. Deep red velvet curtains, a purple patterned throw on the burgundy plush sofa. It was too early for Kate to be up and dressed after her usual Saturday night social life, so she was wrapped in a soft and comfortable robe, patterned with swirls of pink and purple. Not something that Callie was ever likely to wear. The two friends' taste was different as their characters. If Kate was an overflowing bowl glass of Merlot, warm, dark and full-bodied, then Callie was a precise 175ml measure of Pinot Grigio in a champagne flute, cool, light and crisp.

"There we were, at the crime scene, and he treats me like I'm something he trod in. Didn't acknowledge me or, or what happened, at all."

Callie brushed a speck of dust from her immaculate jeans, the clothes she had been wearing at the crime scene had gone straight in the washing machine as soon as she had got home and she had spent a long time in the shower, washing herself and her hair in a mix of shampoo and lemon juice in an attempt to get rid of the smell before coming to see Kate.

"Perhaps he was waiting for you to say something, after all, he did save your life a few months ago," Kate countered.

"I would have, but he made sure I didn't get a chance." Callie was still seething. "He hasn't been in touch since the last case was closed and when we do meet, over this poor woman's body, he completely ignores me."

"I think the relevant point there is 'over this poor woman's body'. He was probably just keeping it professional."

Callie wasn't about to be pacified that easily.

"And as for Jeffries describing her as crispy bacon, well that's hardly professional, is it? In fact, it's just plain disrespectful."

"You know what he's like. Policemen's black humour, it keeps them sane. Or comparatively sane, anyway."

Kate was a solicitor, specialising in criminal work and so had a better than passing knowledge of the policemen at the local station in Hastings where both of them worked and lived. Like Callie, the majority of her clients were low-level cases of drink driving, drug possession and drunken assaults. As a forensic physician, or police doctor as she was sometimes called, Callie would take their blood samples, assess any injuries and declare them fit for interview, or not, and Kate would represent them legally during their interviews.

Kate's practice, Harriman Sydenham and Partners, actually consisted of just her and her long-dead partner, Neville Sydenham, and no one could quite remember who Harriman had been or if he had ever existed at all. She had kept the firm's name after Neville's death from cirrhosis of the liver because she couldn't be bothered to change it and because getting all their stationery reprinted would have cost an arm and a leg. Now there was just Kate and a succession of temps to answer the phone and she longed for the day when she would have enough work to afford a legal clerk to send to the police station and support clients in the middle of the night, rather than having to go there herself.

"So, what do you think happened? How did that poor girl die?"

Callie sighed and took a sip of her coffee.

"Well, it looks like she was still in the car when it was torched and that they didn't wait for her to get out."

"What an awful, awful accident and a terrible way to go." They sipped in silence as they thought about the victim's last few moments of life.

"I can't help thinking that it wasn't accidental," Callie said at last.

"Why's that?"

"Because the car was parked up against a wooden post, so the passenger door couldn't open, and they must have known she was still inside."

"That's terrible. You don't even want to think about what must have been going through her mind when she realised."

"No," Callie responded thoughtfully. "You don't."

Callie blew her nose, hoping to clear the last of the smell that was probably now only inside her head.

"Do you think she was a specific target or just random?"

"There's really no way of knowing that yet."

"I suppose not." Kate thought for a moment. "I sincerely hope she was targeted, I'd hate to think there was someone out there doing it for kicks."

"Yes," Callie agreed. "Because that would mean he might do it again."

Kate gave a shudder and quickly changed the subject.

"How's your dad since whatsisname the pathologist died?" Kate asked, reaching for another biscuit. Callie was thankful for the chance to discuss something other than the horrible death.

"As well as can be expected, considering he and Ian were such good friends," she answered.

Ian Dunbar had been the local pathologist, her father's oldest friend and Callie's godfather. In fact, she believed he was to blame for her being named Calliope. Now that Ian Dunbar was dead, killed by the man who had so nearly killed Callie a few months before, it was a name used by a dwindling number of people, for which she was very grateful.

"Speaking of good friends, how's the love life?"

"Very subtle." Callie smiled. "And non-existent."

"Not even any blind dates or one-night stands?"

"Nada."

"That's a shame. I always love hearing about them afterwards. The rich merchant banker who liked to be spanked or the academic who insisted that mealtimes should be silent so that his digestion wasn't disturbed."

Callie smiled.

"At least that date was quite peaceful, but he really couldn't understand why I didn't want to see him again." She sighed. "So, come on, if your love life is so successful, tell me all about it."

Kate curled up on the over-stuffed sofa like a cat who had got the cream.

"I thought you'd never ask. I've been dying to tell you." She settled herself comfortably. "I met him at the gym."

"You went to the gym? Without me dragging you there?"

"Well, only to the café, it's a such great spot to ogle the talent. All those muscles. All that sweat."

Kate giggled and Callie gave an exaggerated sigh again, but sat back to enjoy the story of Kate's latest conquest, happy to forget her troubles: her own lack of a love life, the arrogance of Detective Inspector Miller, the insensitivity of his sergeant and the awfulness of the burnt corpse in the car. For the moment, at least.

Chapter 2

Monday mornings are always the busiest time for a doctor's surgery and all the staff were expected to pull their weight and see extra patients. No sickness was allowed either, amongst the staff that is, and Callie knew it was the one time of the week when Dr Hugh Grantham, the senior partner at the practice, would not tolerate her taking time off for her police work, so she had to fit it in during her breaks.

Callie wanted to find some time get to the mortuary, not only to find out what was happening with the woman who had died so horrifically in the car, but also to get the post-mortem report on one of her patients who had recently died unexpectedly. The latter reason being the one she would use if questioned by Dr Grantham. She was speeding through her patients as quickly as she could, not even stopping for a coffee break, and was irritated when she noticed that an extra had been added to her list, and even worse that it was Mr Herring, her least favourite patient. A fussy little man, and a hypochondriac, he persistently refused to believe Callie's assertion that there was nothing seriously wrong with him and it was her constant fear that one day, simply to spite her, he would be proved right.

Knowing that it was best to get it over with, she pressed the buzzer to call him in, and seconds later the door opened. He must have been standing at the waiting room door, ready to rush to her room the moment the buzzer went.

"Hello Mr Herring, do take a seat. What can I do for you today?"

"I must congratulate you, Doctor. One minute early. First time that has ever happened. Perhaps we will be able to get through a few of my outstanding complaints."

Callie tried not to show her dismay as Mr Herring brought a piece of note paper with a list written in his small and precise script covering the whole of the page.

"Number one. Bowel actions. Now these have been less regular of late…"

* * *

Once she had finally persuaded Mr Herring to leave with a completely unnecessary prescription clutched in his hand, Callie leant back in her chair with a sigh. She was now running late despite her good start and desperately needed a break, something to eat and a cup of coffee, but she knew she would have a mountain of paperwork waiting for her in the office upstairs and if she ventured up to use the kitchen she wouldn't be allowed to leave it until later.

Callie sighed; just thinking about how busy she was made her feel tired. Running two part-time jobs, as a GP and a police doctor, was supposed to give her variety and flexibility but, more often than not, just meant that she worked long hours and satisfied nobody, including herself.

She closed her eyes for a moment and leant back in her chair. If it came to choosing just one role, GP or forensic physician, which would she pick? Her mother would tell her that her reluctance to accept a full partnership and give up the police work was simply another way of avoiding commitment, like she usually did, particularly where men were concerned. Callie yawned delicately.

She was startled awake by a knock on the door and looked up at the clock as Linda Crompton, the practice manager came in.

"Taking a nap, were we?" she asked.

"Just closing my eyes for a moment." Callie was relieved to see that she really had only been asleep for a minute or two.

Linda put a cup of coffee on the desk and added a couple of chocolate digestives beside it.

"I thought you might need these after Mr Herring," she said.

"Thank you, I do, even though I am deeply suspicious that you have an ulterior motive." Callie gestured at the bundle of prescriptions Linda was holding.

"Always," Linda agreed. "Dr Brown feels he has done enough this morning and has left without doing these urgents. I thought if you could just check and sign them for him?" Linda hesitated slightly because she knew it wasn't Callie's job, but equally she knew Callie wouldn't let patients go without urgently needed medication just because someone else didn't care.

"Oh, for the luxury of being a locum and not feeling any sense of responsibility."

"I don't think Dr Brown would feel any sense of responsibility even if he was substantive." Linda harrumphed. "The man's a royal pain in the you-know-what and the fact that he's still here is simply a measure of how desperate we are. Last week he left a baby clinic dead on four when there were still two patients waiting."

"So I heard," Callie said as she started signing the forms. "Gauri told me all about it. At length." Dr Gauri Sinha was one of the full-time partners at the practice and had been incensed when she had been called in to see the last two babies for the locum.

"There," she said as she handed the last of the prescriptions to Linda. "Can you call down my visits and let me know if there's anything urgent I need to deal with now? I'll do the rest when I get back."

She smiled at Linda, who knew full well what Callie was trying to avoid, but reluctantly agreed to help.

* * *

Callie was walking fast as she approached the mortuary, which had been built on the far side of Hastings General Hospital and was some distance from any of the visitor car parks. A row of leylandii had been planted in a poor attempt to screen the building from public view. Callie entered by an unmarked side door. The corridor it led to was windowless and led only to the lift that took her down to the mortuary.

As Callie stepped out of the lift, she was struck by the silence. Ian Dunbar had often played music as he worked, but now there was nothing. She shuddered slightly and wondered if she would ever be able to enter this place without remembering how she had found Ian Dunbar's body in the autopsy suite. She had been here since, of course, speaking with the stream of locum pathologists as the hospital struggled to replace Dr Dunbar. It was sad that they hadn't found anyone permanent, but it seemed that nobody wanted to take a post in a mortuary known for the horrific murder of its pathologist, and who could blame them? She gave herself a mental shake, hurrying along the corridor to the main office and saw with relief that the door was open and Lucy Cavendish, the current locum pathologist, was in there, speaking to Mike Parton, the coroner's officer.

"Hello, Mike," Callie said and he nodded, giving her a small, dignified smile and looking for all the world like a funeral director.

"Good morning, Dr Hughes."

"Lucy, glad to see you are still here," Callie continued.

Lucy scowled. She was a thin colourless woman in her thirties with a pointy face and a permanent look of discontent. She was completely swamped by her hospital scrubs and their dingy green colour did nothing for her pale and rather sallow complexion.

"Why?"

Callie had to admit it was a good question. Lucy was miserable and angry that she had ended up in a backwater like Hastings when she considered she was worthy of a much better position. Unfortunately, a minor professional mishap in her past had left her with little choice.

"Well, it's nice to have a bit of continuity," Callie managed to say, and looked to Parton for support.

"Absolutely, yes."

Callie knew he missed Ian Dunbar almost as much as she did.

Lucy pursed her lips and returned to her computer screen, ignoring them both.

"What's happening to the burns case from yesterday, Mike?" Callie asked as Lucy pounded on the keyboard, taking out her frustration on the inanimate object.

Parton cleared his throat and looked uncomfortable and Lucy snorted with derision.

"The great Home Office Pathologist has decided to work from a better facility," she said, despite the question having been directed at Parton. "Apparently this humble workplace isn't good enough for him."

"It was decided to transport the deceased to the Brighton and Sussex Mortuary as it is better equipped to handle the more delicate requirements of a badly burned corpse." Parton responded tactfully, totally ignoring the pathologist's outburst.

Lucy finished typing and the printer by her side whirred into action. She grabbed the sheet of paper as soon as it was spewed out by the machine and handed it to Parton.

"Thank you, Dr Cavendish. Much obliged." He tucked the paper into his briefcase, gave Callie a solemn nod and left.

Callie gave Lucy a nervous smile.

"Brighton again?"

She was well aware that most of those working in Hastings felt that the money, and kudos, always went to Brighton, but it was a bigger hospital, attached to a university and medical school, serving a larger population and Callie had no doubt that it was reasonable for it to be better equipped. Lucy scowled at Callie again, managing to convey that, like the burnt corpse, she was better suited to the facilities provided in Brighton.

"Have you come here for a reason? Or are you just being nosy?"

Callie didn't quite know how to respond to such rudeness and couldn't think of any other reason to be there, so she just shook her head and left the office.

Disappointed not to have got anything useful from the pathologist, Callie stopped by the autopsy suite to have a word with the mortuary technician who was the direct opposite of the man he had replaced. Small and thin, with more tattoos than teeth, he was, nonetheless, helpful when she needed information or results.

"How's it going, Jim?" she asked, adding, "anything of interest happening?"

"Did you go out to that burning job, Dr Hughes?" he asked in return, as interested in it as she was, it seemed.

"Yes, I understand the body was taken to Brighton?"

"Odd, that case," Jim continued, with Callie's full attention now. "I heard that preliminary findings were that she was old, well, older than you'd expect, anyway. Late twenties to early thirties."

"Not a textbook joyrider, I agree, but hardly a pensioner," Callie admonished him gently. After all, that was her age, and she wasn't old, was she?

"Mother too, well, at least there were signs she'd given birth at some point," Jim continued.

Callie was impressed with the high standard of his information. She knew he was likely to know someone in the Brighton pathology department; after all, he'd worked there previously and had been brought in, temporarily at first, to cover the unit after its troubles and had decided to stay. She had thought that, with Ian Dunbar's death, she would no longer be in the loop, but it was pleasing to find that he was happy to pass news on.

"Just what on earth was she doing in that car?"

They both silently gave that some thought before Jim shook his head and started to prep the autopsy table, straightening the instruments as he checked they were all there, and whistling tunelessly.

* * *

It started to spit with rain as Callie walked to her car, and she broke into a run, holding her handbag over her head to protect her hair with one hand and cursing the fact that firstly, she had left her umbrella in the car; and secondly, that she was wearing a white cotton blouse beneath her jacket and it would undoubtedly go see-through when wet.

She reached her midnight blue Audi TT and threw herself inside just as the rain began in earnest and her mobile phone began to ring.

Pulling her phone out of her bag, Callie saw that the call was from the surgery and answered it, whilst checking her hair in the vanity mirror.

"Hello, Callie here."

"Hi Callie," Linda Crompton replied, in a whisper. "We've had a call from the police, can you pop in there on your way back? They've got a suspect they want you to look at and say if she's fit for detention."

Callie sped towards the police station, happy to have a reason to go there and see if she could find out anything more.

Chapter 3

Whenever she entered the large modern building that was the Hastings Police Headquarters, Callie felt a buzz of anticipation. She could never really know what she was about to face and whilst most of her work for the police was mundane, there was always the possibility of something more interesting, something other than the seemingly endless parade of drunks, drug addicts and the aftermath of petty violence.

She knew most of the uniformed sergeants and many of the constables by sight if not by name and, being a regular visitor, Callie was recognised by the civilian on the front desk and was quickly buzzed through the door into the body of the police station. She made her way briskly to the custody suite, stopping at the desk to let them know that she had arrived and was ready to see the patient, before heading to the treatment room to wait.

The custody suite treatment room was slightly smaller than her consulting room, but felt much more spacious as it had less clutter, as well as a somewhat different array of equipment. Here there were syringes and tubes for taking blood samples from drunk drivers in one cupboard, along with swabs for taking DNA samples. Another cupboard held first aid equipment such as dressing packs, plasters and steristrips, to patch up both prisoners and policemen. Plus, there was a sink to wash her hands, complete with the obligatory notice reminding her to do so frequently. As if she needed reminding.

Callie sat at the desk and read the custody notes for the prisoner she was about to see, quickly realising the information was superfluous. Marcy Draper was a long-time patient of Callie's; a prostitute and a drug addict, she was a regular at both the surgery and the police station.

There was a knock at the door, and it was opened by the custody sergeant.

"Come on, Marcy, don't keep the doc waiting," he said as a woman who looked about fifty, but who Callie knew to be only thirty-two, shuffled into the room.

"Sorry, doctor," Marcy said, misery oozing from every pore, "I've messed up again."

Callie sighed, some things never change, and Marcy, it seemed, was one of them.

* * *

Once she had dealt with Marcy, giving her enough medication to keep withdrawal at bay and certifying her fit for detention while she waited to go up before the magistrates, Callie headed for the canteen. She needed to pick up a sandwich to eat on the way back to the surgery, as there was no time to stop and eat elsewhere if she was going to get her paperwork done before evening surgery.

The canteen was busy with a mix of people having a late lunch and others an early tea break. Callie looked round, spotting Penny Davidson, a uniformed constable she had met before, sitting at a table with two other uniforms. It looked as if they were about to leave, so Callie grabbed a chicken salad sandwich and a bottle of water and headed for the till.

"Hi Penny, have you got a moment?" Callie asked, slightly out of breath as she caught up with her at the canteen door and thinking that she really ought to find more time to get to the gym, and, unlike Kate, not just to pick up buff men.

"Sure," Penny replied and turned to her colleagues who had also stopped when Callie approached. "I'll catch you guys later." They left with a wave and Penny came back into the canteen and indicated a table by the door. "Have a seat. What can I do for you?"

"Nothing majorly important, it's just that I pronounced death for the body in the car and wondered if you knew anything about the case? I heard that it was a mature woman, not some teenage joyrider."

Penny shifted in her seat and looked at something over Callie's shoulder. Too late, Callie realised that somebody had come into the canteen after them and was standing just behind her.

"Constable Davidson, I trust you're not being asked that because you are the station gossip."

Callie knew the voice all too well and leapt to her feet and faced Detective Inspector Miller.

Away from the crime scene and out of the unflattering protective clothing, Miller was dressed in a smart, conservative blue suit and a crisp white shirt. Callie was standing uncomfortably close to him and could smell the faint scent of his sandalwood aftershave as well as an undertone of something soapy, as if he had just got out of the shower.

"Can't have you leaking information to members of the public, Constable," Miller continued. The shower image disappeared in a puff of smoke and the look Callie gave Miller was blatantly hostile.

"I am hardly a member of the public, Inspector. After all, I was involved in this case from the beginning, and so I am bound to have a professional interest in it."

Miller hesitated briefly.

"Well, why don't you come up to the incident room and I'll give you an update, Dr Hughes? If it's just a professional interest." He looked pointedly at Penny. "Better than hanging around the canteen trying to pick up bits and pieces of inaccurate hearsay."

Before Callie could explain that she was in a rush, DI Miller turned and left the canteen.

Callie made a quick decision and mouthed a "Sorry" to Penny, who waved her away with a smile and gesture that suggested, all too eloquently, what she thought of her superior officer.

As Callie hurried after Miller, she attempted to defend the constable.

"Penny didn't say anything she shouldn't have."

"I know," he said with a little smile as he opened a door for her, "she doesn't know anything." He ushered Callie through the door and closed it before he continued. "I am far more interested in how you heard that the victim was a mature woman."

"Oh, you know, I do have my sources elsewhere." Callie was pleased to see the look of irritation cross his face as they walked along the corridor.

"I am sure you are aware of the need to keep information like that quiet, Dr Hughes… Callie. We haven't identified her yet and I wouldn't want this to get out to the press before we had a chance to speak to her relatives."

"Of course. I'm not stupid, Inspector, just curious, and you never know, I might even be able to help." He might have decided to relent and use her first name, but she wasn't sure if she was ready to do the same just yet given his frostiness at the crime scene.

As Miller ushered Callie into the Incident Room, she could sense the atmosphere of excitement that was part and parcel of a major enquiry, at the start at least. As the investigation progressed, that excitement would become tinged with anxiety, particularly for Miller, the Senior Investigating Officer or SIO.

There were eight desks in the room and Callie was pleased to see a familiar face in Sergeant Nigel Nugent, whom she knew in his usual role as custody sergeant, realising that he must have been borrowed to set up and run the incident room. He was busy directing the people connecting up computers and phones, crawling under desks trailing wires. Nigel would be sticking the wires in place with hazard tape once they were finished, she was sure, as he was that sort of person. Sometimes called Nerdy Nigel, even to his face, Sergeant Nugent had excellent IT skills and was methodical, thorough and pedantic, which didn't win him many friends but would make him an ideal person to be in charge of an incident room. He gave Callie a small wave of acknowledgement before a hapless constable dropped a box of equipment and Nigel hurried over to sort out the mess.

Miller was leading Callie towards his office, which was at the end of the room where a whiteboard with a few photographs of the scene was already in place. Two men were moving a second board into place next to it. Callie paused by the whiteboard and looked at the photographs. Close-ups of the car were beside a handwritten note of the make, model, registration details, including details of the owner and the info that it had been reported stolen at 10.30 pm, and last seen in Ebenezer Road at approximately 8.30 pm.

The photos of the car in situ at the car park, or rather what was left of it, illustrated how closely it had been parked to the pole, making it impossible for the passenger to escape. There were also some pictures of a match and what looked like a burnt-out match book.

"Is that what the killer used to start the fire?"

"Yes, the first match was used to light the rest and then discarded. We're hoping to get some forensics off it, but…"

Callie could imagine that it wouldn't be easy to get anything off a single match, particularly if the killer wore gloves. Miller waited patiently as Callie moved on to look at pictures of the corpse both in and out of the car. An arrow pointed to the photos with a question mark and the name Sarah Dunsmore.

Callie approached the board for a closer look.

"Is this who you think she is?" she turned and asked Miller.

"It's possible. She's the only misper who fits the profile from the post-mortem," Miller confirmed.

Callie knew that he would have been checking reports for any missing person who had not been seen since Saturday in the hope of identifying the body as early as possible. With most victims being known by their murderers, if not actually related to them, knowing who they were could quickly lead to the culprit, or at least narrow the list of suspects.

"The PM has been done already?"

"And I have the preliminary report." He led her into his office, picked up a file from the cluttered desk and held it out to her. "Strictly not for sharing."

Callie glanced at her watch briefly and saw that it was gone three o'clock. Her evening surgery was due to start at four. Silently apologising to all her patients who would be seen late, Callie took the file and quickly opened it.

Cause of death was given as smoke inhalation; the superheated smoke had pretty much destroyed the lungs. That this had happened before the fire had managed to do anything more than superficial damage to the rest of the body was strangely comforting. At least the worst of the burns had happened after death.

Callie went on to read the more detailed report on the body. No gross abnormalities, the presence of erupted wisdom teeth, fusion of epiphyses, structure of the skull, condition of the pelvic bones and more besides, had led the pathologist to conclude that it was the body of an adult Caucasian female, approximately twenty-six to thirty-five years old. The pathologist had added that further microscopic examination of the osteons, the minute tubes within bone that contain blood vessels, might enable a more accurate estimate of age. Jim the mortuary technician had also been right in that evidence of pelvic bone scoring suggested the woman had given birth at some point in the not-too-recent past.

Miller asked her to explain one or two things from the report and she realised that he had asked her up there for a reason, other than just to satisfy her curiosity, and what's more, that she might be able to help him in a small way at least. Not that he was likely to admit he needed help, or that she had been any use.

She explained that the report suggested the woman had been alive when the car was set alight, the burning gases searing her lungs, which then flooded with fluid, effectively causing her to drown. A horrible way to die. Callie could only begin to imagine the fear that must have passed through the victim's mind as she realised what was happening. She was being burnt alive, and her escape routes were either blocked or too difficult to reach in the short time she had left.

"What on earth was she doing in the car?"

"Looking for excitement, maybe?" Miller suggested.

A new voice broke in.

"Well, she got that, didn't she? Only, I think it was probably more fucking thrilling than she expected. Nice to see you again, Doc. Come to look at our pretty pictures?"

Callie turned to glare disapprovingly at Jeffries who was standing in the office doorway, but it was like water off a duck's back. He was munching a biscuit and had a mug of tea in his hand. Callie saw Miller look at the newly set up refreshment station which Nigel had furnished with a kettle and mugs borrowed from the canteen and a supply of tea, coffee and biscuits. It already looked as if it had been hit by a tornado, with the lid off the coffee jar, sugar spilled across the surface and a solitary teaspoon left beside an almost empty packet of custard creams. No doubt the tin for people to contribute to the cost of supplies would be empty, as it was generally considered the SIO's responsibility to pay for it.

"The fire investigator from the crime scene is downstairs, boss. He insists on speaking to you. Do you want him brought up?"

Miller nodded and Jeffries called out to a young woman, "Tell 'em to bring him up then, Tracy love."

What Tracy thought about being called 'love' was hard to tell, but she did as she was asked all the same.

Callie handed the post-mortem file back to Miller and turned to leave.

"Are you using dental records to identify her?" she asked as he walked with her towards the incident room door.

"Initially, yes. We've got the details of Mrs Dunsmore's dentist and he's emailing her records and recent X-rays to us and the pathologist for comparison. Obviously, we'll have DNA too, but that will take longer."

They both looked up as the door opened and Chris Butterworth the fire investigator was shown in. Now that he wasn't wearing crime scene overalls, Callie could see that he was a lean and muscular man in his forties, with his dark hair cut very short. Completely ignoring the policewoman who had shown him in, Butterworth spotted Miller and quickly walked over to him.

"Good of you to bring the investigation report over in person," Miller said holding out his hand, whether to shake Butterworth's or to take the file he was holding from him it was unclear, but either way the fireman ignored the outstretched hand.

"Inspector, I wanted to let you know as soon as possible that I think I know this arsonist. From his MO. I thought I recognised it this morning and wanted to go back and check my files and I was right. He's a regular and always starts fires this way."

At this point he thrust his file at Miller who took it eagerly, as Jeffries tried to take a look at the name on the front. The three men retreated into Miller's office and Callie found herself left outside with the door being firmly closed in her face.

Any thawing in her feelings towards Detective Inspector Steve Miller vanished. He hadn't even bothered to thank her for the information she had given him about the cause of death. She glanced at her watch, forgot all her frustration at being ignored and ran down the stairs. Being this late was going to need a lot of explaining.

* * *

Evening surgery had been every bit as bad as Callie had expected it to be. Starting late meant that every patient came into her consulting room already cross and determined to be heard. Now she was in the office, doing all the paperwork she should have done before surgery began, trying to complete it before all the receptionists left, and she ended up with the additional job of locking up the building when she finally finished. She didn't mind locking up, it was working alone in the building that worried her. Not because it was spooky or frightening, but because there were always people knocking at the door, wanting a doctor or a prescription and unable to understand that they needed to come back in the morning. They seemed to think that as she was there, that she should deal with their problem right then, however petty or unimportant it was, or however easily it could wait until morning. And then, of course there were the cases which actually couldn't wait until morning. Callie had once been stopped, just as she was leaving to go home, by a man wanting to see a doctor urgently. It quickly became clear that he was right, he did need to see a doctor urgently as he was having a heart attack, and Callie had to wait with him, praying he wouldn't go into cardiac arrest before the ambulance arrived. She knew her limitations and wanted to get him to the heart attack centre as quickly as possible as they would be so much better equipped to help him.

Callie was just getting to the last report and the receptionist hadn't even looked at her watch or started muttering about time to close up, when Gerry Brown, the locum, came over to her. She was surprised he was still there, given his reputation for leaving strictly on time.

"Hi Callie, had a patient of yours earlier, only needed a repeat prescription and seeing as you were running late, Linda asked me to deal with it."

"Thanks, Gerry, who was it?"

"Can't remember the name, needed Thyroxine. Anyway, you know me, always happy to do you a favour." He hurried on, seemingly oblivious to Callie's look of disbelief. "I'm sure you'd do the same for me. Speaking of which, could you take a couple of patients for me tomorrow morning? I have to finish early for my half day. I've sorted it on the lists for you. Cheers."

He didn't wait for a reply, which he probably sensed wouldn't be polite, but grabbed his bag and hurried out of the office, leaving Callie irritated and wondering why he thought that doing one repeat prescription constituted such a big favour that he could dump a couple of patients on her tomorrow. She checked her list and saw that he had actually moved a total of five patients across to her list, meaning that he would finish at eleven and she would probably still be there at two. Silently seething, she had to admit it was probably Karma for the many times she had got colleagues to see patients of hers whilst she rushed off to do police work. She just hoped whatever Gerry Brown was up to at lunchtime was worth it.

Callie looked round at the receptionist who nodded towards the doorway Dr Brown had just left through and mouthed the word "Tosser" before looking pointedly at the clock, prompting Callie to hurry up and finish so they could all go home.

* * *

33

Later, once she was home, Callie picked up her post and the copy of the Hastings Advertiser from the hall and ran up the stairs. She lived in the penthouse, taking up the whole top floor of a large, brick-built, Georgian house situated in a commanding position high up on the East Hill. At some point in the past twenty years it had been converted into flats, or apartments as the estate agent had insisted on calling them when Callie went to view it. The house had surprised her with its tall windows and graceful lines. It stood out as being different from the Victorian villas more usual in this part of town. Although it consisted of just three rooms, a bedroom, a bathroom and a living room with a kitchen area along one wall, the rooms were large and well-proportioned, the conversion having been sympathetic and the period features left intact. But it wasn't the corniced ceilings, the sympathetic conversion or even the balanced proportions of the house that had sold it to Callie the moment she walked into the main living room, it was the views.

Through the two large windows, the coast was visible from the funfair on the far left, along almost to the new town until the West Hill blocked a view that would otherwise include St Leonards, and Marine Court, the block of flats built to look like a majestic liner sailing towards the Old Town. Down and to the right of her was the Old Town nestling in the valley, crowded and compact, and further, across to the West Hill, the castle ruins, and the swathe of green parkland crested by a terrace of white houses. It was a view that never ceased to impress her, whether it was early morning with the rooftops floating on a sea mist, the castle back lit by a setting sun, or with the streetlights in the valley twinkling invitingly below. She had bought the flat for these views, paying more than she had planned, but they had been worth every penny.

Callie made tea and then leafed through the Hastings Advertiser. The story of the body in the burnt-out car had made the front page, as expected. They had used a picture of Sarah Dunsmore in a strappy evening dress that revealed a large amount of décolletage, and the suggestion of a nipple underneath the thin fabric. She looked a lot more attractive in this photo than the charred corpse that Callie remembered all too well. She took a sip of tea and read the accompanying text:

> The body found in a stolen car, early Sunday morning, has been named by police as being that of Sarah Dunsmore, 31, of Ashburton Close, Hastings. Forensic experts used dental records to identify Mrs Dunsmore. Her husband, Brian, a salesman, said he had no idea why she was in the car and that he had thought she was on a girls' night out. He then asked to be left alone, so that he, and his two children, Molly, 5, and, Alfie, 3, could grieve in peace.

A girls' night out? Callie wondered who 'the girls' were and if Miller had asked them why Sarah hadn't been out with them. She was sure he would have done. It was possible it was an innocent mistake and that they knew nothing about it, of course, but Callie was willing to bet that at least one of them knew where she had really been. That this night out was an alibi to cover whatever Mrs Dunsmore had been doing, or who she had really been seeing.

Chapter 4

"It's just not right, Hugh." It was Wednesday lunchtime before Callie managed to get Dr Hugh Grantham, senior partner at the practice, on his own. "He skives off at the drop of a hat, and even when he does do something helpful like a repeat prescription for my patients, he expects something in return."

They were standing in the tiny kitchen, Callie effectively blocking Dr Grantham's escape by standing in the doorway. During her morning surgery, Callie had checked which of her patients had been seen by Dr Brown the night before, only to discover that he hadn't actually seen any, all he'd done was dealt with a repeat prescription request over the phone.

"He's a locum, Callie, what do you expect?"

"I expect him to behave like a decent doctor," Callie responded angrily. "He brought up Jill Hollingsworth's records to print the prescription, so he would have seen that she was well overdue for a medication review. If it was you or I, we would have added a note to that effect, and printed out a blood test form for her as well, but no, just because he's only here temporarily we have to put up with a job half done."

Hugh sighed.

"I agree, but you know how difficult it is to find anyone in the current climate. It took us three months to find Gerry."

Callie knew he was right. Hugh looked pointedly at the corridor, clutching his mug of coffee and hoping she would let him get away.

"I'm just saying we need to keep on trying to find someone permanent."

"Well, we haven't given up hope that one of our part-time GP contractors will decide to give up her work on the side and join us as a full-time partner." He gave her a meaningful look and slipped past her into the corridor and the office beyond.

Callie sighed. He had a point, just not one she wanted to consider at the moment.

She opened the biscuit tin, nothing but some broken rich tea fingers were left, but she took one anyway. When in need…

* * *

Benji the pug settled down next to Callie and refused to take any notice of her subtle efforts to show that he wasn't wanted. The more she delicately pushed him away, the more he lovingly leant up against her and slobbered, covering her with slime and hair equally. Her suit would have to go to the cleaners. Finally, deciding that a more direct approach was needed she gave him a shove. He yelped as he landed on the floor.

"That's right, dear, be firm with him," Mrs Tomkins said as she hobbled back into the room carrying a plate of biscuits in one hand and using a stick with the other. Callie was embarrassed to have been caught, but Benji didn't seem to be worried. He was much more interested in the biscuits.

"Do you want a biscuit, then, my love?"

For a second Callie thought the old lady was talking to her but Mrs Tomkins picked Benji up and sat him next to her on the sofa and wriggled to make herself more comfortable, her short, fat legs not quite reaching the floor. She had the biscuit plate between her and Benji as she chose three or four for them both while the dog sniffed and slobbered over most of the rest. Callie had a moment of disorientation as she realised how alike they looked. Flat round faces, noses so small they were almost non-existent and slightly bulging eyes.

"Help yourself to a biscuit." Having chosen theirs she held the plate out to Callie.

"No, no, I just ate lunch. Thank you." There was no way Callie was going to eat a biscuit that had been anywhere near the dog. Mrs Tomkins put the plate down on the table.

"Please yourself." She turned to the dog. "All the more for us, eh Benji boy?" And she gave him a custard cream which he swallowed pretty much whole.

"It's good of you to drop in, Doctor. I've been a bit more out of breath recently and wondered if I needed something a bit stronger."

As she could hear both her patient and the pug wheezing from across the room, Callie knew she was right, although fewer biscuits and more walks for Benji might help them both more than another course of steroids. Realistically, Callie knew that Mrs Tomkins was coming up for ninety and Benji was pretty old for a pug, so perhaps it was a bit late to be putting them both on a diet and exercise regimen. So, Callie sat back and drank her tea, hoping that the dog hadn't been anywhere near it and listened as the old lady listed her symptoms, the man next door's symptoms and some long and involved story about an Aunty Mabel, long dead.

It was clear she didn't really expect her doctor to do much, other than write a prescription before she left, so Callie sat and listened periodically and allowed her mind to wander. This was her final visit and Wednesday being her half day, her time was her own once she had finished. Callie was making a mental shopping list and Mrs Tomkins was recounting a story about a badly behaved poodle when her phone started buzzing. Once she had fished out her phone, Callie saw that it was Helen Austen, a local social worker and sort of friend. Callie couldn't think why Helen was calling but it was possible that it was something urgent to do with one of her patients.

"I'm awfully sorry, Mrs Tomkins, but I have to take this." Callie answered the phone and stepped into the kitchen to speak to Helen.

"Hi, Helen, how can I help?"

"Oh, Callie, thank goodness. The police picked up Mark Caxton this morning. They want to interview him about that awful car fire and he needs an appropriate adult. I'm pleased they realise he needs one, but angry that they didn't give me more notice."

"Mark?" Callie knew the young man Helen was referring to because both he and his mother were patients. Both had mental health problems. The mother was an alcoholic who had struggled with the stress of being a single mother once Mark's father had died of heart disease, and Mark himself had learning difficulties and had been in trouble on many occasions for arson. Callie closed her eyes. Of course, the fire investigator had recognised the method used to start the fire.

"I know. Completely mad to think Mark had anything to do with it but the police are pushing for someone ASAP."

"You don't think he's the person who did this, then?"

"No way. I mean, I know he sets fire to cars, but that's a big leap to killing someone, isn't it? And you know what he's like, liable to admit to anything if he thinks he'll get left alone."

"What about his mother?"

"Not in a fit state and before you ask, I can't go because I have a vulnerable child conference starting in five minutes. It seems they've even tried to get a volunteer in but no one is free; thankfully, because you know what Mark's like with strangers. He gets so frustrated that he can't articulate his needs and he sometimes comes across as aggressive."

"Yes, but—"

Helen didn't give Callie a chance to think of an excuse.

"Look, you are his doctor and I know you have Wednesday afternoons off, so it couldn't have worked out better, could it?"

"Well, I'm not sure I'm the best person—"

"I understand your concerns, believe me I do, but to my mind you are the absolutely perfect person. You are Mark's doctor and he trusts you, plus you have experience of the way the police work."

"It's because of my work for the police that I might not be the right person. What if there is a conflict in my role there and being Mark's appropriate adult?" Callie finally managed to say.

"All you have to remember is that Mark is your patient so he comes first. Simple."

"I wish it was that simple, Helen. I mean, I am employed by the police—"

"For the care and welfare of their staff and those in their care. Like Mark." Helen clearly wasn't prepared to listen or, at least, she wasn't prepared to take no for an answer.

"I'd need to check that they are all right with it first."

"For goodness sake, Callie, you need to get off the fence and decide whether you are a doctor or a policeman first and foremost. It's decision time."

Callie had to concede. Like Hugh earlier, she had a point.

* * *

Miller was sitting very still, outwardly calm, and waiting for an answer, whilst the good-looking lad across the table from him sullenly and silently glared at him. Callie had tried to explain her role to Mark, but she wasn't convinced he understood the subtlety of her position and he kept looking to her, expecting her to answer for him and he seemed to be getting more and more irritated that she wouldn't.

Miller himself had been angry when he had come down to the interview room to discover that Callie was there as Mark's appropriate adult. He was sure that it couldn't be right for a police doctor to also be present as an appropriate adult and had rung through to his superior officer and even to the CPS advisor to check that it was in order. Under the Police and Criminal Evidence Act 1984, a child under seventeen or any adult that could be considered vulnerable, such as someone with learning difficulties like Mark, had to have an appropriate adult with them when interviewed under caution. Miller didn't want any information he gained as a result of the interview to be thrown out because Callie's relationship with the police prevented her from being considered appropriate.

Needless to say, this was not a situation that had much in the way of precedents and the CPS advisor had taken ages to consider his answer before reluctantly telling Miller that he thought it was probably okay. Probably was hardly definitive, but with the alternative of having to delay the interview further whilst they waited for Helen to be free or Mark's mother to sober up, Miller decided to press ahead. If the interview was thrown out, he would blame Callie and the CPS advisor equally. Callie, meanwhile, had been getting more and more irate herself. What a colossal waste of time this would have turned out to be if she had spent her free afternoon cooling her heels in an interview room only to be sent home. An afternoon when she should have been doing something useful like her shopping and laundry for the week.

Finally, once it had been agreed to go ahead with Callie sitting in, Miller insisted on explaining her role, making sure she realised that she was not there to interfere with the interview, but simply to support Mark, as if she didn't already know that, but perhaps the re-iteration would help Mark understand it. A legal executive from one of the local firms that specialised in criminal law and who had represented Mark before had already spoken to him and advised him to make no comment as he knew that Mark was not competent to answer questions without the risk of incriminating himself. He intended to be present for the interview as well as Callie and, she felt, was best placed to interfere if interference was needed, quite frankly.

And now the interview had been going on for almost an hour, going round and round in circles, with Mark constantly answering "no comment" to every question, apart from denying that he had anything to do with the car fire, or the body inside it.

"Why did you torch the car with the woman still inside it, Mark?" Jeffries asked bluntly.

"No comment."

Jeffries leaned forward as far as he could, trying to intimidate the boy, whilst continuing with a barrage of questions.

"Did you enjoy it? Did you enjoy watching the woman burn? Get a kick out of it, did you? Get a hard on?"

"No. I didn't!" Mark was horrified but Jeffries was delighted to have finally got a rise out of him.

"Did you like it as she screamed? Or the smell as her flesh sizzled and burnt?"

"No! No! No! Stop it!"

Mark put his head down and covered his ears with his hands, anything to get away from this onslaught from Jeffries.

Callie put her hand on Mark's arm and turned to Miller for support.

"Inspector, I must protest. Mark's—"

Mark snatched his arm away from Callie's touch and raised it as if he might hit her. Miller jumped to his feet with a face like thunder and there was a tense silence for a moment before Mark lowered his arm and went back to staring at the table. Once he was convinced the threat was over, Miller sat down again.

"I'm sorry, Mark." Callie tried to sound normal, although her heart was pounding. She had been convinced he was going to hit her. "I didn't mean to alarm you. Just try and stay calm. Okay?"

Miller glowered at Mark but the legal executive was nodding, approving of Callie's intervention, although she was thinking that perhaps he should have stopped the interview earlier and glared at him to get her point across.

"Perhaps you could move on. My client is clearly upset by the tone of your questioning," he finally said.

"Not half as upset as his victim's husband or her children," Jeffries said, but the legal advisor heeded Callie's look and waded in.

"He has already told you several times that he knows nothing about the car that was set on fire at the weekend, Inspector."

"Let him say it again then."

Miller watched as the boy looked at Callie.

She was surprised that he seemed to be asking for her approval despite his anger at her a moment before. She nodded at him encouragingly, knowing that the interruption had done what was needed and given Mark time to recover a little.

"Go on then, Mark, once more for the tape."

"I don't know nothing about the car. I was at home Saturday night from early. I didn't torch anything, honest. I don't know nothing. Can I go now?" Mark Caxton almost pleaded to Miller, looking out from under his long floppy fringe, all aggression gone.

One more push and he would confess just as Helen had predicted, Callie was sure, and she was sure that Miller and Jeffries knew it too. But Miller would also know that Mark would recant his confession as soon as he was out of the room and that Callie would almost certainly stand up in court and tell the jurors he was pressurised by the police into confessing. Callie felt there was a good chance she would be believed because she was a professional who worked with the police and Mark had the sort of endearing looks that would make the jury want to mother him. The prosecution would need to have more evidence than just a confession if there was to be any hope of a conviction. Callie could see all this going through Miller's mind as he debated with himself whether to press on or not. Jeffries was chomping at the bit, wanting to make the final push. It was decision time and Miller had made his decision.

"Have you got a girlfriend?"

Jeffries looked disappointed by the question, knowing that Miller was backing off, and Callie was suspicious. Only Mark accepted it as just another question in a long and seemingly never-ending interview, and at least it wasn't about the dead woman.

"'Course."

The legal exec mouthed "no comment" to Mark.

"Tell me about her."

"Inspector–?" the legal exec started to interrupt, but was silenced by a look from Miller.

"What's she called?"

Mark looked at Callie again, but she wasn't sure what to do; should she tell him to listen to his advisor?

"Mel," Mark said as Callie hesitated.

"Is she pretty?"

"She's all right." Mark thought for a moment. "Have you got one?"

Jeffries tried to hide a smirk and Miller ignored the question.

"It's nice having a girlfriend, isn't it? Do you see her a lot?"

Mark nodded and looked at Callie again. It seemed a pretty harmless line of questioning, so Callie looked at the solicitor, he was making notes and hadn't told Mark not to answer again, so she didn't interfere.

"For the tape, Mr Caxton nodded," stated Jeffries.

Miller was annoyed by the interruption, however much he knew it was important for when the tape was played back. He had been gaining Mark's trust but now, he was distracted again.

"So, did you see her that night?" he asked. Callie looked at Mark's legal advisor, uncertain whether to remind Mark again that he should say no comment. It was clear that Miller was trying to find out if Mark had an alibi which could work for or against him, depending on his answer. In the end, neither stopped Mark from answering.

"What night?" Mark was confused by the change in direction.

"Saturday night?"

"Erm…" Mark was trying to think back.

"That was three nights ago."

Mark thought some more before answering.

"Dunno."

Three nights ago was clearly a long time to Mark.

"Well, did you see her last night?"

"Yeah," Mark smiled at the memory.

"And the night before?"

"No, she was at her nan's, I think. We don't see each other when she's at her nan's, 'cos it's too far to walk."

"And the night before that? Was she at her nan's then?"

"I don't remember."

"So, had it been a few days since you last met up when you saw her last night?"

"I dunno. Might've been." Mark struggled to think, then shook his head. "I just see her when she's around, you know?"

Mark genuinely didn't seem able to remember.

"We'll need her full name, Mark," Miller said with resignation. He sighed and looked at Jeffries, who was clearly irritated. They both knew this wasn't going to be an easy conviction after all, they were going to have to do it the hard way, by collecting the evidence and building the case.

Much to Callie's relief, Miller ended the interview.

* * *

"I'm not sure this is right," Callie told Miller. He had caught her just as she was about to leave. Mark was being released whilst they checked his alibi and tried to find further evidence against him.

"I'm pretty sure it's wrong for you to be his appropriate adult, but you still did it." Miller was still angry about that, it seemed.

"I know you have some circumstantial evidence linking Mark to the murder, but, I mean, look at the boy, why would a mature woman get in a car with a young lad like him?"

"I can think of a number of reasons, and it's more than just circumstantial evidence. You saw what he was like, for goodness' sake, he almost hit you for just putting a hand on his arm, what would he have done if you had put your hand on his knee or something?"

Callie had to concede he had a point. She had been shaken by his violent reaction, just as much as Miller had been, and if the victim had come onto him? Touched him somewhere intimate? Perhaps that might have been enough to provoke him into killing her.

"The boy's a powder keg, so I don't want you to see him alone in surgery or anything like that. Get one of your colleagues to be his doctor, if needed."

Callie looked at him in amazement.

"You have no right to tell me which patients I can or can't see, Detective Inspector."

"I'm just trying to protect you—"

"I do not need your protection. I am not stupid and I will take suitable precautions, but I will see whoever I need to see and I certainly don't need your permission to do it."

She turned on her heel and left.

Chapter 5

Callie arrived for work bright and early. She planned to park her car in one of the 'doctors only' spaces in the small adjacent car park.

The surgery had been built in the 1980s, and was moderately user-friendly but far too small and Callie knew that Hugh had recently been looking at the possibility of relocating to other premises in the Old Town as there was simply no possibility of them being able to extend anywhere apart from into the very small car park which only provided two spaces for patients and three for doctors on a strictly first-come, first-served basis. Except for Hugh Grantham's of course. As Senior Partner, his space was sacrosanct. Callie usually left her car at home and went back to pick up her car if she was doing visits or was called to the police station, but today she wanted to fit in a quick visit to the supermarket between surgeries and she had a baby clinic as well, so she had driven.

Arriving at the car park, Callie was surprised to see that even this early both of the general doctors' spaces were full. She recognised one of the cars as belonging to Gauri Sinha but the other was unknown to her. Now she had a dilemma, Hugh's space was definitely out of bounds, but he was also adamant that the two patient spaces should be left free for those who needed them. Many of their patients were elderly or infirm and were unable to walk far. Parking spaces were few and far between and it took Callie twenty minutes to find a free one, so far up the East Hill she was almost back home, and then walk back down to work.

As Callie collected her basket of paperwork from the main office, Linda was sorting through the list of calls made to the out of hours service during the night.

"Good morning, Linda, anything interesting?" Callie asked her.

"No, not that I can see."

Callie started for the door, but turned and asked as an afterthought, "Who else is in?"

"Just you and Dr Sinha."

"So, whose is the other car in the doctors' space?" Callie was indignant. There was a chain across the car park entrance overnight to stop locals from using it after a time several years ago when Hugh had regularly arrived at work to find his space taken. The car turned out to belong to a particularly rude man three doors along who felt he had a right to use it when the surgery was closed, but equally didn't want to get up early to move his car once they were open for business.

"Oh, yes. That's Dr Brown's." Linda looked embarrassed.

"But you said that only Gauri was in?"

"Yes. Dr Brown left his car here last night." Linda was busying herself and not looking at Callie. "He does that sometimes."

"Why would he do that? He lives in Fairlight, he can hardly walk home from here. Can he?"

"I wouldn't know," Linda said tersely and turned away before Callie could question her further.

Callie took her work basket through to the doctors' office where Gauri was just finishing her own paperwork and packing everything away. She looked up and smiled as Callie entered the room.

"Good morning, Callie," Gauri said brightly. "You are in early." It was said as a statement, but made Callie feel guilty that she didn't come in early more often.

"Hi, Gauri. Yes, I needed to catch up." Callie indicated her overflowing work basket. "Did you know that Gerry Brown leaves his car here sometimes?"

"Wednesday and Saturday nights," Gauri answered her.

"Every Wednesday and Saturday?"

"Yes, indeed. Every Wednesday and Saturday night."

Callie was having difficulty interpreting the look she was getting from Gauri.

"What does he do on those days? And doesn't his wife mind him not going home?"

"I do not have the answers to your questions, Callie. Perhaps it is Dr Brown you should be asking?" and with that, Gauri left. Callie was bemused. Everyone seemed to know something about Gerry Brown that she didn't, and they seemed unusually tight-lipped about it, as if they disapproved.

Looking at the pile of work in front of her, Callie decided she would have to think about it later, perhaps even ask Gerry himself, although she suspected he wouldn't tell her the truth if it was something shameful or embarrassing. Perhaps she should invest in some chocolate biscuits and tackle Linda again over a cup of coffee to see what she could prise out of her. That usually worked. With a shake of her head, Callie got on with her pile of test results and letters.

* * *

Callie's plan to pop over to the supermarket had been delayed by a call from Helen Austen, the social worker, letting Callie know that Mark Caxton's mother had called and telling her that the police were searching their house. Helen was angry because Mark's mother was as vulnerable as he was and in a terrible state. An agoraphobic alcoholic, it was extremely distressing for her to have the police invade the only space in which she felt she was safe. Helen believed the police were fishing and had no real evidence against Mark, but her reason for calling Callie was that she was worried that the pressure was getting to him and that he might do something stupid like confess, or go out and commit arson again. After all the hard work Helen and his psychologist, Adrian Lambourne, had put in to help Mark, and with such success, it would be a crying shame if the police pushed him into re-offending.

"What do you want me to do?" Callie asked her, warily. Sensing that her two roles were about to collide, again, and much as she was angered by Miller's interference in her role with her patient, she had no wish to either obstruct his investigation or get beaten up by anyone.

"Can I bring him in to see you this afternoon? See what you think?" Helen asked.

"Erm…" Callie scrolled through her evening list, which was completely full as usual. She knew that Helen was essentially covering her back. If Mark confessed or re-offended, a doctor's view that he had been put under undue pressure would be invaluable. It would also seriously irritate the police, if it was possible for her to irritate them more than she had the day before.

"What about Adrian Lambourne? Wouldn't he be better placed to see Mark? His opinion would carry more weight, surely?"

"I tried him. He can't see Mark until next week and I am worried that might be too late."

Callie conceded defeat. Helen was right, her first duty was to her patient. "Okay. Could you get him here before evening surgery?" she asked Helen. "I'll fit him in first." The supermarket would have to wait, better that than see him at the end and risk being alone with him. She wasn't that stupid.

* * *

The baby clinic was just finishing and the last screaming infant had been tucked up in a nice warm push chair when Callie heard from Helen that Mark had been arrested. It seemed that the police had found a box containing old match books similar to the ones used to start the fire, and Helen was on her way to the station to be Mark's appropriate adult alongside his solicitor. Callie immediately felt guilty about the wave of relief that washed over her. Now she would have time to nip to the supermarket and fill her car up with petrol before evening surgery. She was also undeniably happy not to have to interfere with the police handling of the investigation.

It wasn't until later, sitting in her consulting room, finishing off the last of her chicken and salad roll that the guilt overtook her, and, with a quick look at her watch to reassure herself that there was still time before she was due to see her first patient, Callie reached for the phone. She hoped that Detective Inspector Miller would have either finished or, if he was being particularly obstructive, have left Mark and Helen kicking their heels and had not even started the interview. She would bet on the latter. Either way, she was put straight through to his office and he answered.

The conversation, in which Callie had hoped she could express her concerns for Mark's welfare, find out how the investigation was going and offer her help and support to both the police and her patient, didn't quite go the way she had planned.

Miller seemed deeply suspicious of her motives in asking about Mark.

"Why do you need to know how he is?" he responded to her enquiry about Mark's mental state.

"Because I'm his doctor," she replied and was met with stony silence. "Look, I know he over-reacted earlier but–"

"Dr Hughes," Miller interrupted her. "Your patient is fine and I have an investigation to conduct. Whilst I appreciate your concern, he has an appropriate adult here, and probably a more appropriate one than yourself."

Callie silently smarted at that, even though she knew Miller was probably right.

"I am sure I don't need to remind you that you also have a role as a police employee. Have you been asked to come in to check his fitness for interview?" he continued.

"Er, no." Callie was surprised to be asked. "Why? Do you think he might not be fit for interview? Perhaps it might be a good idea if–"

"No." Miller quickly interrupted her. "You are not needed, he's fine, and perhaps it would be better if you admitted that you have a conflict of interests and remove yourself from any further involvement in this case."

He hung up, leaving Callie seething with anger.

"Rude, arrogant, stupid–" Callie struggled for a word to describe Miller, "man," was the best she could do, before slamming the phone down and realising that Linda had come in after a perfunctory knock and was looking at her in surprise.

"I take it someone's upset you?" Linda asked.

"Was it that obvious?" Callie replied, embarrassed.

"Only to me and everyone in the waiting room."

"Well, that's all right then." Callie managed to smile despite her irritation.

"I just popped in to give you a couple of telephone messages." Linda handed over two notes and left.

Callie saw that the first one was a patient wanting advice but the second was from the police station. The custody sergeant wanted her to come and examine a prisoner who had minor injuries incurred during his arrest, and, despite Miller's insistence that Mark was fine, from the way he had jumped in and told her so vehemently that her patient was okay, Callie had a pretty good idea who that prisoner would turn out to be. She checked her watch: four o'clock. If she was quick, she would just have time to see him before evening surgery, and with a bit of luck, she would seriously irritate Detective Inspector Miller by doing so.

* * *

Mark's injuries were very minor, it looked as if he had taken a slight blow to his face, either from a policeman's fist or some other solid object. There was a small amount of bruising but his lip and nose had long since stopped bleeding and she only had to clean him up a bit, making sure she explained what she was doing and getting permission from him before touching his face at all. She didn't want to prompt any kind of reaction. Her main concern, and the custody sergeant's as well, was his level of anxiety. She was seeing him in the treatment room, alone, but there was a panic button nearby if she needed help, and a police constable hovering just outside the door with orders to come in if he heard anything untoward.

"Can you tell me what happened, Mark?" she asked. "How did you get these injuries?"

"I tried to stop them taking my collection."

"Collection?"

"My dad's match books. They're mine now. He gave them to me. They have no right."

"You are not allowed matches, Mark," Callie explained gently. "Not when–"

"I don't use them to light things. They were my dad's."

Callie could easily imagine Mark had tried to stop the police from taking away his precious collection, a memento of his dead father, and his injuries were consistent with a struggle to get them back. She tried to get more detail from him but he became barely coherent, one minute asking her if she could help him get his matches back, unlikely under the circumstances, and the next worrying about his mum and asking who would look after his cat. Worrying about everything and everyone except himself.

Callie considered prescribing him an anxiolytic but thought she would prefer to speak to Adrian Lambourne, his psychologist, before doing that because he was on a number of other drugs to help control his behavioural problems and she didn't want to make matters worse. Instead, she spent some time talking to Mark and trying to calm him. Unfortunately, it wasn't very long before the custody sergeant apologetically knocked on the door and asked if he was okay to interview because the detectives were waiting. Callie would have liked longer but, knowing that at least Mark had Helen and a solicitor to support him, she agreed that he was and allowed him to be taken to the interview room. She took her time writing up her notes before leaving the treatment room in the hope that she wouldn't meet Miller on her way out, but just as she was leaving the custody suite, he came flying down the stairs and almost knocked her over in his rush to grab the door before it shut behind her.

"Sorry," he said before fully taking in who she was. "Oh, um, I'm in a hurry," he explained unnecessarily and continued through the door, letting it slam behind him.

Callie was too angry, and too slow, to give him a sarcastic response but as she looked at his retreating back, she was pleased to notice his neck slowly reddening as he approached the custody desk. He must have been told she had been called in to see Mark despite his insistence that her patient was fine and she hoped that he was embarrassed about it. She would make sure she reminded him of it if he ever tried to interfere in her work again.

* * *

Back in her flat, and still furious with Miller who, she now felt, was not only arrogant and chauvinistic, but also could not be relied upon to protect the vulnerable, Callie poured herself a large glass of white wine. A very large one. She knew all the reasons why this was not a good idea. She had counselled patients on not drinking to relieve stress. She knew alcohol was empty calories and raised her risk of a variety of cancers. She knew precisely how many units of alcohol were in the glass and she knew it was more than her daily limit, according to the current government health guidance but she was going to drink it all the same.

As she began to feel the relaxing effect of the wine, she thought about Mark. And Miller. She wondered if he was responsible for Mark's injuries, but, in the spirit of fairness, decided that it was more likely to have been Jeffries. She had to admit, even to herself, that the damage had been minor and didn't really need to have been examined by a doctor, the custody sergeant was probably just covering his back because Mark was listed as vulnerable. She took another sip of wine. She didn't know if Mark was innocent or guilty and that wasn't really her concern, her job was to make sure he was fit to be detained, and as his GP she also needed to consider his physical and mental wellbeing; with that in mind, she resolved to contact Adrian Lambourne again, to make sure he was made fully aware just how fragile Mark was currently, and this time she'd back up any conversation with something in writing, just in case he fobbed her off again.

Callie was nicely relaxed now, and flicked through the television channels whilst eating an omelette and salad, looking forward to a long, hot soak in the bath before an early night. She had to concede that a glass of wine could sometimes be the answer to a stressful day, but she was never going to admit that to her patients.

Chapter 6

It had been a long and frustrating morning. It was Callie's study and administration time. However, just because she was free to make phone calls didn't mean that everyone else was also available. She had started out by calling the custody suite to check if Mark was still being held. Under PACE he could be held for twenty-four hours and that could be extended to thirty-six by a senior officer's review. As he had only been arrested the previous afternoon, she thought it was likely he was still there, which he was. On hearing he was still there and that he remained anxious and stressed, Callie decided to ring his psychologist straight away and get some advice on how to help her patient.

As she listened to the phone ring and waited for the answer phone to kick in, she made a note to visit Mark's mother and see how she was doing, and also decided to call Helen to try and find out how the interview had gone. She left a message asking Lambourne to call her back as soon as he was free and mentioning that it was about Mark and that it was urgent. Then she tried unsuccessfully to reach Helen and left a message for her too. Next on her list was Jillian Hollingsworth and she left a message on her phone as well, asking her to collect a blood test form and to get one done before her next prescription was due, stressing the importance of monitoring her thyroid function regularly.

Half an hour and a dozen abortive phone calls later, Callie had had enough. She took a look at the pile of paperwork, shoved it back in her "To do" pile, grabbed her bag and went out.

* * *

The row of council houses where Mark Caxton lived with his mother was shabby and in need of repair. The render was cracked and could have done with a coat of paint, fences were broken and had been mended with old bits of wood and wire, and a variety of old cars, broken toys and household implements decorated the front lawns. Callie looked carefully up and down the street before she walked up the path to Mark's house and pushed the doorbell, thankful that the press didn't seem to have got hold of the story of Mark's arrest just yet and noting that the yellowed net curtains next door twitched as a neighbour checked who was visiting. There was no answer and realising that she hadn't heard any chimes from the bell, she also knocked on the door.

Callie heard footsteps in the hallway but still no one answered. She knocked again.

"Mrs Caxton? It's Dr Hughes," she called through the letterbox. "Please, can I come in? I just want to see how you are."

After a few more moments of foot-shuffling, the door was finally opened, emitting a blast of stale smoke, and Callie was allowed in. She followed Mark's mother into the kitchen, which was surprisingly clean and tidy. Only a dirty glass and a half empty bottle of vodka betrayed the fact that Mrs Caxton had been drinking, until Callie took a closer look at her. She was haggard and swaying slightly as she stood, using the counter to help her stop the room from spinning. She took a deep drag of her cigarette before crushing it out in a dirty ashtray. It was by no means her first of the day, by the look of things.

"Why don't we sit down?" Callie said gently, indicating the two chairs either side of a small breakfast table.

Mrs Caxton gratefully lowered herself into one and grabbed her packet of cigarettes. As she took out another cigarette and went to use the lighter tucked inside, Callie hoped it would help her to relax enough to talk about what had happened and, sure enough, it didn't take long for Mrs Caxton to open up and tell Callie about the police search of her house and how it had affected her. How terrifying it had been, how she felt violated. This was her space, her safe place, and they had come and trampled over everything, messing it up searching. In fact, once she had started it was hard to get her to stop for long enough for Callie to ask any questions. It seemed that, as she had thought, Mark had got hurt when he tried to stop the police from first finding and then taking his precious collection of match books away as evidence.

"Stupid, bloody match books. Rubbish. That's all they were. Dennis used to bring them back from all these places he visited as a salesman, picking them up in the bars and hotels and that."

"He was a travelling salesman?" Callie queried unnecessarily, just to keep the conversation going.

"Yeah. He sold cleaning services for factories and businesses, like, you know, all over the South East. Brought a new packet back for Mark every time he stayed away. Not much of a present, not really suitable for a kid but Mark was always fascinated by them, thought his Dad was staying in all these exotic places. Littlehampton, Ipswich and that, not so exotic really."

Callie silently agreed.

"'course, not many places give away matches these days, what with the smoking ban."

Callie was grateful that she blew smoke out the side of her mouth rather than directly at her.

"Mark adored his dad. Became obsessed with those stupid match books, the only thing he had left of him when he was gone."

"How did he die?" Callie asked.

"Heart attack whilst he was driving home. He called and said he'd had some chest pain and I told him to go to the hospital but he wanted to get back for Mark's tenth birthday, stupid bugger." She took another drag and ignored the ash that fell onto her lap.

"And Mark used these match books when he set fires?"

"Yeah. It was all his fault. Giving a kid matches. Asking for trouble. After Mark got done for arson the third time, they told me I had to get rid of them, so I threw them out, honest, but Mark must have taken them out of the bin and hidden them."

"And he carried on using them?"

"No, he used boxes of matches after. I didn't know he still had the ruddy books or I'd have got rid."

"But he could have gone back to using the books?"

Mrs Caxton thought about that for so long that Callie thought she might not have heard her, but just as she was about to ask again, she answered.

"I suppose he must've." There didn't seem to be much to add to this depressing acceptance that her son had killed a woman, and Callie decided to leave her to her cigarettes and vodka. A sad case, but there was little she could do for the woman except refer her to the drug and alcohol team, again.

* * *

As it was still technically her study morning and no one was returning her phone calls, Callie decided to go back to her flat and do a bit of research online about arson and arsonists, and shower and change to get rid of the smell of cigarette smoke that had lodged in her clothes and hair. Once online, she typed arson into a search engine and started working her way through the vast numbers of hits the search threw up. She was not surprised to find that most arsonists started their experimentation with fire when they were young, unless they were burning properties for reasons of fraud or personal gain. She read that in cases where the subject has difficulty relating to people in a one to one situation, fire could become their friend, mentor and even lover.

She knew that Mark's first conviction came when he was ten. Shortly after his father died, he had set fire to a neighbour's garden shed. There followed assorted rubbish bins, sheds and outhouses set alight around the neighbourhood, which must have made Mark and his mother unpopular with the locals. By the time he was fourteen he had escalated to torching cars because he liked the explosion when the fuel tank went up. Initially he had set fire to them where they were parked but after an incident when the car fire had got out of control and spread to a nearby house, he had changed to taking the cars away and setting them alight in remote locations.

Callie wondered about the match books. If he had stopped using them, why start again now? Callie could only think that it was because he had escalated to a more serious crime which in itself posed another question: if Mark was indeed the arsonist, why had he started killing? And why a woman? Unfortunately, Callie had already thought of one scenario that might explain it. Perhaps something had happened in his relationship with his mother, and, unable to hurt her, he had found a substitute. It was even possible that she had abused him. Much as that was a repugnant thought, it could be the cause of his dislike of being touched. Callie hoped she was wrong, but it did make a sort of sense, if burning a woman to death could ever be said to make sense. She shook her head in frustration. She couldn't honestly believe it. He was such a gentle lad and the murder had been truly brutal but, if it wasn't Mark, who else could it be?

She decided to concentrate on the match books, as they were unusual and the one physical link to Mark. Callie knew that forensics might be able to identify the burnt remains of the one used in this case, even when it seemed impossibly blackened and damaged. If they were able to, they might also be able to show whether or not it could be one from Mark's collection, that is, an old one and from a place his father might have visited. That would show an almost direct connection to Mark and the police would have enough to charge him with at least arson and probably murder as a result. The provenance of the match book was crucial both to the likelihood of Mark being charged, but also to Callie's belief that he wouldn't have done it.

Thinking about where someone would get one these days, Callie googled match books and discovered that they were remarkably easy to buy. Apparently phillumeny, the hobby of collecting match-related items including boxes, labels, covers and books, was very popular. She could buy them branded to promote her company or bar, or order personalised ones for her wedding. And if she wanted to buy a whole collection of old ones, eBay had them grouped together according to vintage or country. There were even collections with saucy covers being advertised for sale. Perhaps it wasn't going to be as easy to show a direct link to Mark as she had thought. Anyone could have got hold of them and if that was all the evidence the police had, they would have to let him go.

* * *

Callie had just finished evening surgery when she heard from Helen that Mark had been released. She also told Callie that he was in such a state that he was having an anxiety attack and wouldn't leave the house. With a sigh, Callie agreed to visit him. She would have preferred not to do it so soon after he had been released and to give him more time to settle, but the weekend rota started at six and she wasn't on call, so she felt it would be better to go and see how bad he was rather than leave the initial assessment to a doctor who didn't know him. She could then leave a note with the out of hours service that Mark might need further help over the weekend.

Before leaving the surgery, she tried calling Adrian Lambourne again, as he was the psychologist who had been working with Mark with such success and she wanted to see if he could give her any pointers on the best way of helping their patient. She had already left Lambourne several messages without getting any reply, and was surprised, given how late it was, when she managed to get through to him this time.

"Oh, hello, Adrian, it's Callie Hughes, Mark Caxton's GP. I wondered if you could spare a moment to discuss his case with me?"

"Ah yes, Dr Hughes. Yes, um, it's a bit difficult."

Misunderstanding his reluctance to speak to her, Callie assumed it was because she was calling too late in the day.

"It won't take long, but if it's a bad time, just say when would be better."

"No, no, it's not a bad time, as such, it's more that I have to consider client confidentiality."

Callie was taken aback by this response.

"I'm Mark's doctor," she clarified, "so confidentiality isn't an issue."

"It's more complicated than that, though, isn't it? Because of who you work for, I mean."

"I'm not sure what you are referring to," she countered, but she was beginning to get an idea. "Do you mean because of my work as a police doctor?"

"Exactly."

He seemed relieved that she was the one who had actually broached the subject.

"Anything you say to me as Mark's doctor remains strictly confidential and I would not disclose it to the police unless I had Mark's permission to do so."

"I am sure you wouldn't, Dr Hughes, but I am anxious to avoid putting you in a difficult position."

"I am quite used to difficult positions, Dr Lambourne." Callie was beginning to get very irritated by his prissy attitude.

"Even so, there is always the danger of the police finding something out on their own, and suspicion falling on you as having revealed it in some way. I really wouldn't want you to be accused of breaching confidentiality."

"I certainly won't breach any confidentiality, and I am sure the police would support me if there was any misunderstanding, so I don't see it as a problem, Dr Lambourne."

"But it could very easily become a problem, Dr Hughes."

"Is that a threat?" Callie was incredulous.

"No, no, of course not. However, I really think it would be in my client's best interest if I do not speak to you, and indeed, I shall be recommending that he change doctors. Goodbye." He hung up on her.

Callie took a deep breath. Whilst she knew that her joint roles could potentially put her in difficult situations, and that was without the added complication of her acting as Mark's appropriate adult, it had never been a problem before and his assertion that he was doing it to protect her as much as Mark, made her blood boil. The fact that Miller had made the same suggestion about a conflict of interest the day before, only made it worse.

* * *

It was with a feeling of déjà vu that Callie parked her car in front of the terrace of council houses where Mark lived and knocked on the door. She heard footsteps and could see someone standing in the hallway through the textured glass in the door. She knocked again.

"Mark?" she called through the letterbox. "It's Doctor Hughes. Helen asked me to visit and said she'd let you know I was coming."

There was no response, but she could hear some shuffling, and peering through the letterbox she could see a pair of feet covered in a pair of grubby, worn, sport socks. One big toe poked out from a hole.

"Mark, I know you are there, so open the door for a minute and speak to me, will you?"

The feet shuffled some more. Mark was thinking.

"I just want to help you, Mark, so let me in, will you?" Callie said gently.

"I can't," Mark told her, anxiously. "Dr Lambourne told me I wasn't to speak to you. He made me promise."

Callie sighed. Lambourne must have rung Mark straight after her conversation with him.

"Is your mum there?"

"She's asleep," he said. "I don't want her bothered."

He sounded worried and Callie knew that he was probably covering for the fact that his mother had passed out drunk. Children of alcoholics learnt to lie and make excuses from an early age.

"It's okay, Mark," Callie didn't want to put him under yet more pressure. According to Helen he was close to breaking point, so she backed off. "How about another doctor, Mark? Would you let another doctor in if I arranged for someone to visit? Would that be okay?"

"Dr Lambourne said I wasn't to speak to anyone from your surgery as you work for the police and would tell them bad things about me. He's going to see me Monday, he said," Mark answered in a rush, knowing that what he was saying wasn't likely to be well-received.

Callie gritted her teeth. She was very cross, but managed to keep her voice steady, not wanting to make Mark think he was the one making her angry.

"That's good, Dr Lambourne's the best person to help you, but promise me you will call the duty doctor if you need to speak to someone before then, will you? It's a doctor from another practice on call this weekend, no one from our surgery, okay?"

"Okay," Mark responded although his voice was far from certain. Callie left him, still standing behind the door in his holey socks, panicking quietly about everything.

Callie was fuming but managed to remain professional when she rang Helen to let her know what had happened. Helen wasn't nearly so restrained in her views of Dr Lambourne.

"It's slanderous. You should sue him. He basically told a patient you and your colleagues would grass him up to the police."

"I know, Helen," Callie placated her, "but we only have Mark's word for what Dr Lambourne actually said, and he could have got it wrong."

Callie didn't really believe that. Mark had seemed quite sure of what he had been told by his psychologist.

"But it's outrageous."

"Yes, but at least he's done it out of a misguided idea of helping his client, and it certainly wouldn't be in Mark's best interest to force him to repeat what he was told in court, even if I could persuade him to appear. He'd be a wreck."

Helen had to concede the point and told Callie that she would visit Mark over the weekend to make sure he was okay and would decide whether or not she needed to call out the duty doctor.

Relieved to know someone she trusted was looking after Mark's best interests, Callie walked back up the path and made her way back to her car, watched all the way by the neighbour peering round her net curtains.

Chapter 7

Saturday turned out to be one of those crisp, sunny, spring days that are just made for a long walk by the sea. Kate didn't agree, however, telling Callie she would rather hang out at the gym, and it was late morning before Callie gave up on trying to persuade her and set off for a solo trek across the cliff tops to Fairlight Lighthouse. She had packed a sandwich, an apple and a bottle of water into a light rucksack, along with a waterproof jacket, sunglasses, extra jumper, mobile phone and money. She liked to be prepared for any eventuality.

Knowing that the path from the East Hill was still closed due to a landslip, she walked along Rocklands Lane to join the path that took her to Ecclesbourne Meadow. The path was steep in parts, both up and down along the hilly route, better than any workout on a treadmill to Callie's mind, and the views were in a completely different league. Callie wasn't sure what it said about her that she liked to look at rolling hills and rocky shores more than well-muscled men in tight vests. She just knew that she did. She couldn't help a small smile of satisfaction as she walked through the meadows and took in the views. She had passed a few other walkers on her way, but for the most part, Callie had the wonderful scenery to herself. She paused to drink it in, and then, after a few deep breaths of clean fresh, sea air, she set off again.

Walking always gave her the space and time to think through problems, sometimes helping her to find an answer, more often just allowing her to come to terms with the fact that there was no answer, and therefore, no point in worrying about the problem. She listed the lack of a partner in her life as one of the 'no point worrying problems'. She had tried taking courses and joining clubs of various sorts, including the gym, thinking that perhaps she wasn't meeting enough men, but the few men who were also joining courses or who hung round the gym to find a partner seemed either dense or desperate. The upside was that she could now speak conversational Italian, cook an authentic Indian meal and she had found astronomy and stargazing for beginners fascinating, but she had dropped out of the car maintenance course because she hated the dirt and oil under her fingernails, and she certainly wasn't getting her money's worth out of the gym.

Once again, she stopped to look at the view and have a drink of water at the top of a particularly steep set of steps that had taken her from a densely wooded valley to a long grassy stretch of the cliffs. The sea looked calm from this height but the number of white caps on the waves told her that it wouldn't be pleasant if she were on a small boat such as the few she could see out there. Sailing was another hobby she had tried, only to discover she suffered from terrible seasickness. Callie would never forget how ill she had felt. The poor man who had taken her out was unlikely to forget either. She moved on, both physically to the next stage of the walk and mentally and, as she tackled the final climb up to Fairlight coastguard station, moved onto the next problem, Mark Caxton.

Except that the problem wasn't just Mark Caxton. There was Adrian Lambourne as well. Callie would need to speak to Hugh Grantham and ask his advice about the psychologist and whether they needed to do anything about his insinuation that Callie and her colleagues might leak information to the police. The risk was that complaining would only make the situation worse. Callie reached Fairlight and the string of coastguard cottages. Feeling pleasantly tired after a good morning's walk, she sat on a bench overlooking the sea and ate her lunch.

* * *

The intricate preparations he made were part of the thrill. He had spent weeks checking streets and car parks for cameras, both public and private, and logging where they were so that he could avoid them, not just when he took the cars, but also as he drove around after he had stolen them. Making fake number plates for the cars had also proved easier than expected, the flimsy plastic replicas wouldn't fool anyone close up, but they were good enough to confuse any cameras, either CCTV or the automatic number plate recognition cameras located around the town. For the latter, he always made sure the numbers he used were cloned from cars similar or identical to the cars he stole. Hastings was well-endowed with CCTV throughout the town and he needed to make it as difficult as possible for the police to track him through the streets. He didn't want to get caught for something stupid like car theft or speeding, before he had finished, before he had killed enough to ensure that when he told them why he had done it, they would listen. That was why he had spent months in preparation, to make sure he killed enough to make an impact, and now he was ready for her, for victim number two. He had taken the car earlier, a fifteen-year old Ford, new cars being harder to steal and hot wire. He had fitted the fake plates, and put a full can of petrol in the boot with his fold-up bicycle and a can of drink. With a final check that he had the book of matches in his pocket, he smiled and set off for his rendezvous.

Chapter 8

"Another Sunday morning, another crispy critter," Jeffries said cheerfully as he suited up ready to inspect the burnt-out car and its gruesome contents.

Callie, who was just taking her suit off having pronounced the victim dead, resolutely refused to respond, but was unable to stop an angry flush spreading up her neck and betraying her feelings. Hoping that no one, and in particular neither Jeffries nor Miller would notice that he had got to her, she kept her head high and her back straight as she silently walked to her car.

She had parked a short distance along the track that led to the cliff top car park, but as she opened the driver's door to get in, she couldn't help but glance back. Even from that distance, she could see Jeffries watching her and smirking as he pulled the suit hood over his once ginger hair, so he had presumably noticed, but at least there was a chance Miller, already suited and with his back to her, taking a closer look at the car with a corpse in the passenger seat, might not have done.

A thin, grey dawn had finally arrived whilst Callie was inspecting the body and pronouncing death, so once she was sitting safely in her car to write up her notes, she took the opportunity to look around her and take in the crime scene. It was similar to the previous one a week earlier, although there were fewer trees around and none between the car park and the coastguard cottages further along the lane towards the cliffs – just a few scrubby bushes shaped by the wind. There would have been nothing to shield the view of the fire if any of the cottage windows had pointed in that direction, which they didn't. As it was, the initial alert had only come from the houses on the edge of Fairlight village after there had been an explosion, presumably when the petrol tank blew up, taking most of the visitor centre with it.

From Callie's memory of her walk just the day before, the visitor centre had been little more than a wooden shack anyway, but now it was just a pile of burnt planks and broken glass, with leaflets scattered around it. As in the first case, the burnt-out car was parked against a line of wooden posts delineating the parking area. No one would have envisaged anyone using them to stop a passenger from getting out. From Callie's brief examination of the body, the victim did not appear to have been trying to escape from the blazing car at all this time as she was sitting upright in the passenger seat with her seat belt still clasped. It was possible she had had a few drinks and was slower to react. Maybe that was a good thing, not knowing that she was about to die, not having time to be terrified. Callie certainly hoped so.

With only these minor differences from the first scene, she felt sure this was the hand of the same killer and with wooden posts or similar being used in many country carparks, the killer would have a big choice of venues for future killings. The two murders were only a week apart and Callie now had no doubt that there would be more if the police didn't catch the killer soon. She looked across the crime scene, now thronged with crime scene examiners and police, and on to the coastguard cottages beyond. To think that she was only up here yesterday, happily admiring the view, and now, well, she would never be able to think of it the same way again. This was no longer a place of peace and beauty, in her mind it would forever be associated with a horrific crime, and the smell of burnt flesh.

* * *

Once home, Callie tried to go back to sleep, but the sight and smell of the body, so awfully contorted in death, made sleep impossible. She couldn't help thinking about the poor woman and how she had died, and of the friends and family left behind to hear the dreadful news of her death. Who was doing this? What sort of a person was capable of setting people on fire? Of watching them die?

She finally gave up on sleep and took a leisurely, scented bath whilst trying to think of ways of distracting herself throughout the day in the hope that if she had fresher, happier things to think about, she would be able to sleep better that night.

She was just thinking of going to the gym for some mindless jogging on the treadmill or seeking out Kate for a comforting chat over coffee or wine when her mobile rang. Picking up her phone, she saw that it was Helen.

"Hi Helen, what's up? Is Mark okay?"

"No. Not really. He's been taken in for questioning again."

It was to be expected, Callie thought. Perhaps she ought to have warned Helen first thing this morning.

"They'll need to check his alibi for last night. There was another car fire."

"So I heard on the news. Was it another woman? They didn't have any details."

"Probably. We'll know for sure after the PM." She checked her watch. "Do you need me to go in as appropriate adult?"

"No, no. The duty social worker is doing that," Helen answered quickly, and Callie understood. She hadn't called until she was sure she had it covered.

"Probably for the best as I'm no longer his GP."

"Exactly. I knew you'd understand. I didn't want to make things more awkward than they are, but I also didn't want you hearing about it on the grapevine."

"Thank you."

Once she had put the receiver down, Callie felt like kicking something and swearing but decided to vent her frustration with a bit of cleaning instead. Armed with rubber gloves and bleach she set to on the bathroom. She knew that it was only natural for the police to want to question Mark given that it seemed likely that the same method of starting the fire had been used, but there really wasn't anything she could do to help him given Adrian Lambourne's interference. She had no right to go and see him at the police station as a police doctor unless they asked her to, and she couldn't go as Mark's own doctor because he had effectively dismissed her. After an hour scrubbing the already pristine bathroom, still unable to banish her concern for Mark and imagining him being railroaded into confessing to a crime he might or might not have committed, Callie decided to give up and go into the surgery to review his notes.

* * *

Once Callie had got over the initial, and wholly unreasonable, irritation she felt when she saw that Gerry Brown had left his car in the car park again, and her subsequent relief on finding out that it really was just his car and that he wasn't hiding anywhere in the surgery, Callie made herself a pot of Dr Grantham's personal, and very expensive, coffee and raided Linda's stash of chocolate digestives. There were definite perks to coming into the surgery when it was closed, and not just that she would get far more work done with no interruptions.

She took her drink and a couple of biscuits into the office, cleared herself some space at the main desk and opened Mark Caxton's personal electronic record. Having read through her own notes from over the years, she then went into the scanned document section which included the records of his psychology assessments and letters from Adrian Lambourne and Helen's case notes as well.

Callie made notes as she reviewed Mark's files. She hadn't really been involved in any of his court cases, so the detail in some of Helen's case notes in particular was helpful, but if she had hoped that Adrian Lambourne's records of the sessions with his patient would be revealing, she was sadly disappointed. He probably had more comprehensive records at his office but simply sent summaries to her. At least she hoped he had more comprehensive records somewhere, because what she had from him told her little, if anything, useful.

What interested Callie most were the notes that Helen had made regarding one particular incident in which the initial fire from the car had spread to a house. The old lady living there had had to be evacuated by the fire brigade, and although she was unhurt, she had lost everything.

Mark had been sent to a young offenders institution for a while after that fire, and, close as he was to his own grandmother, had apparently shown profound remorse and anxiety that he had caused the old woman to lose all her belongings and, indeed, that he had so nearly killed her.

Once released, he returned to stealing and torching cars, but he never again set fire to them in residential areas, always taking them to remote locations before setting them alight. Whilst this change of location fitted with the new crimes, it also seemed to suggest that he didn't want to hurt anyone. So why would he suddenly change? Why would he suddenly want not just to hurt them, but kill them in such a terrible way? There was nothing in his notes to suggest what might have triggered such a dramatic escalation, but Callie knew that the lack of an obvious trigger didn't mean it hadn't happened.

Going onto the internet, Callie searched the local and national news sites and discovered that the second body had been identified. There was a photograph of a smiling Carol Johnson – thirty-four, accountant, married, no children. The photo and personal details looked like they had been lifted straight from her Facebook page and Callie thought that she recognised her as a patient. A quick check of patient records confirmed it and also that the Dunsmore family were not, which was a relief, at least the women weren't being targeted because of their doctors. Callie wondered what else they might have in common, apart from being young women in their thirties, but she couldn't think of anything.

The sound of a car starting up in the car park distracted her and she looked out of the office window to see who was there. Gerry Brown was collecting his car. It was almost lunchtime so perhaps he had finally decided to go home, she thought. Seeing him reminded her of her patient with thyroid problems, Jill Hollingsworth, and that she couldn't remember seeing a blood test result for the thyroid function tests she had asked Jill to have done. She checked Jill's electronic record, there were no results recorded there, and then Callie went through the office pending baskets. Nothing there either. Knowing that there was nothing she could do on a Sunday, Callie left herself a note to remind her to follow up with a phone call the next morning and a note for Linda to check as well, and decided to call it a day. She suddenly realised that she was starving, perhaps Kate would be free for a late lunch and a drink in the Stag. It was supposed to be her day off, after all.

Chapter 9

There was a persistent wail coming from the waiting room and Callie sincerely hoped that the child making the noise wasn't waiting to see her. As a woman she had more than her fair share of families on her list, with mums thinking, quite erroneously, that she would be good with children. She was a single woman, with no children, no siblings and therefore no nephews or nieces, and it was a sad fact that most of her male colleagues were better with children, simply because they had experience dealing with their own offspring.

Taking a break from seeing patients, Callie popped up to the office to check her basket and to see if Jill's blood test result had come in overnight.

"I count my biscuits, you know," Linda said as soon as Callie walked into the room.

Deciding that honesty was the best policy, Callie smiled and held her hand up in apology.

"Sorry, I'll buy you a new packet."

"Make sure you do that," Linda said. "And before you ask, no, we haven't had any results for Jill Hollingsworth, and I phoned pathology, but they have no record of her attending for the test."

"Thanks, Linda, I'll give her a call then." Callie was puzzled. Jill had always been a very compliant patient and this behaviour wasn't like her.

"Oh, and a patient of yours was admitted to hospital Saturday." Linda checked the fax sheet in her hand for the name. "Mark Caxton. Acute anxiety attack."

That news stopped Callie in her tracks.

"What time Saturday?"

Linda checked.

"He was seen by out of hours at five thirty. An ambulance was called and the doctor stayed until he was on his way. Then there's a note that the hospital called to say he was discharged Sunday morning with a psychiatric follow-up appointment in two weeks, and the out of hours doctor called round Sunday afternoon to check on him as requested but there was nobody home." Linda handed Callie the sheet and she read it eagerly.

"Thank goodness for that." Callie felt relieved. She had been increasingly convinced that he couldn't be the murderer but that he might confess anyway. Now Miller would have to drop him as a suspect. He had an alibi. If he went to hospital by ambulance at five thirty, he would have been in the emergency department for at least two hours and more likely four on a Saturday night, and there were security cameras around, and people like nurses, receptionist, other patients who would be able to testify that he was there, and once on a ward, say ten o'clock, quite possibly sedated, he would be under the watchful eye of the night staff, who had almost certainly been tasked with checking on him at regular intervals. There was no way Mark Caxton could have sneaked out, stolen a car and killed a woman unnoticed. Miller would have to let him go. Callie hurried down to her consulting room to make the call, just in case Mark hadn't already told them that he was in hospital at the time of the latest murder.

* * *

"There is absolutely no way he could have done it."

Callie took a bite of her prawn salad on wholemeal bread. When Callie had phoned the police station, she had been told that Miller was already on his way to the surgery to see her and was doubly surprised when he appeared clutching a brown paper bag holding fresh sandwiches from a local bakery.

"We are doing our best to prove or disprove it."

Miller looked tired although he was tucking into his ham and mustard roll with obvious hunger. Callie could sympathise. He must have been working every hour since the second body was found, not just trying to find the killer, but also dealing with the press and distraught families. Food and sleep would have taken a back seat.

"We're speaking to staff and reviewing CCTV footage to see if there's any possibility of him leaving, but, I agree, it doesn't seem possible."

Much as he would have liked it to have been, Callie thought as they both continued to eat. Miller saw Mark as the obvious suspect, but she saw him as the easy suspect and life was never that easy. Even if the night nurse fell asleep, getting out of the hospital ward, not to mention back in, before he was missed would be nigh on impossible.

"Particularly as he was sedated soon after he arrived," Miller continued with his mouth full.

Callie sent up a silent prayer of thanks. They absolutely had to scratch Mark as a suspect now.

"The, um, second victim was identified by her husband initially from a necklace she always wore, but that's now been confirmed by dental records. She's a Carol Johnson, married, no children, and you are listed as her doctor," Miller said.

"That's right. Both she and her husband, although I don't think I've ever seen him."

"Anything you can tell us about her?"

"I looked her up as soon as I realised, but there's little in the records apart from birth control and well woman checks." Callie was irritated by the sigh of disappointment from Miller. "What were you hoping? That Carol might have confided salacious details of her private life with the practice nurse?"

"It would have been nice." Miller finished the roll and swept the crumbs from his suit.

"Well, sorry, but you've had a wasted trip."

"Not at all," Miller smiled and looked Callie in the eye. She could feel a flush slowly rising up her neck. Why did her body always betray her in this way? "I actually managed to eat lunch."

"Do you have any other information for me?" Callie asked curtly and was pleased to see that he had the good grace to look slightly embarrassed.

"The pathologist's initial findings are that both she and the previous victim died in the same way. Also, the fire investigator confirms the same method of fire starting."

"So, you think it's probably the same person?"

"It does seem likely."

"What about the husband?" Callie asked, knowing that family was always high on the list of suspects. "Could he have done this as a copycat of the first death?" Callie didn't want this to be the case, as it could still leave Mark in the frame for the first death.

"We never released the details of how the fire was started."

"Anyone who had access to Mark's historic cases would know that."

"Well, yes, that's true, and there seem to be plenty of people on that list," Miller conceded. "But I don't think the husband could have had access and he had a lot to lose financially. We're checking him out of course, but Mrs Johnson was the main breadwinner, she had no life insurance and they live in rented accommodation, so he won't even get the house."

"Sounds pretty conclusive, if you think money is important to him."

"Oh yes. He certainly seemed more upset about being left out of pocket than losing his wife, plus he was out with some friends until nearly 2.00 am and she was already dead by then." Miller managed to convey his dislike of Mr Johnson. "And the first victim's husband has a pretty good alibi too."

At least he was keeping an open mind and looking at other suspects, Callie thought, even whilst trying to persuade himself it was Mark.

"I don't suppose there's any evidence the two men knew each other?"

"And colluded, you mean? Not yet, but of course we are looking for any connections between the two victims and their families, and where each husband was when the other's wife was murdered, but it doesn't seem probable."

Callie agreed. She just couldn't see it. She knew that it happened in fiction, she had seen the film *Strangers on a Train*, like most people, but in real life? Would two unconnected men really agree to kill the other's wife? It was just too complex.

"Have you managed to trace any men buying cans of petrol?"

"Checking them all out now," he assured her.

"And no ideas about where the two women were before they got killed?"

"Nope." If he objected to her quizzing him about what was his job rather than hers, he didn't show it. Callie thought that he actually appreciated someone going through all the possible lines of enquiry just so that he felt sure he hadn't missed any.

"What about other leads, like CCTV?" she asked.

Miller shook his head.

"Nothing worthwhile so far."

"It can't be easy to avoid CCTV in a town like Hastings."

"Almost impossible," Miller agreed. "But we haven't found anything even vaguely interesting. So, the killer's either highly skilled or incredibly lucky.

"We're also working through the list of other arsonists in the area, and extending our parameters on that, both geographically and to include those who might be on a trajectory that could lead them to commit this sort of crime."

Callie nodded.

"And, of course, we are trying to find anyone who saw the victims the night they were killed."

"What about asking the press to help with that? Put out an appeal for anyone they met to come forward."

"We are going to, although we have to be careful. These women have families and we don't want to insinuate they were doing anything wrong by being out."

Callie was surprised that he was showing such sensitivity to the feelings of the families. Maybe he wasn't as tough and no nonsense as she had always thought him to be.

"We've decided just to ask for witnesses who may have seen them. We aren't sure they were anyway, it's just the most likely explanation. The appeal will go out later today."

"I'm glad you're thinking about the families."

"Well, not sure my superiors are," he confided. "They just don't want it to come across as though we are in any way suggesting that the victims were to blame for their own deaths. That always looks bad, apparently."

Callie could see that Miller was angry at this.

"Personally, I don't think anything should stand in the way of us finding this man before he does it again," he said.

Callie agreed, but Miller being removed from the case for upsetting his bosses wouldn't help anyone.

"Whatever the reason, the result's the right one. It's the right message to put out."

She was pleased to see him nod in agreement. He gave a long sigh and wiped his face with his hands.

"It's a tough case," she murmured.

"Pretty full on," he agreed. "It's been nice to get out of the office and have a break. Even if we have been discussing the case. It's less frenetic here. More civilised."

"Huh, you should come during baby clinic. It's not civilised then."

"Anywhere without Bob Jeffries counts as civilised," he said with a small smile, and she had to agree.

* * *

Callie had decided to visit her parents and her decision, so she told herself, had nothing to do with the fact that the route to her childhood home took her past the farm where Jill Hollingsworth lived with her husband. Callie decided to take the opportunity to stop there in person, to put her mind at rest about her patient. She had tried calling but there had been no answer and, unusually in this day and age, no facility to leave a message, so an unannounced visit was the only option.

As she pulled up outside the small farmhouse, there was no welcoming curl of smoke from the chimney and no lights on that she could see. Callie expected a working farm to be muddy and utilitarian, but even by those standards, this seemed uncared for and unclean. The windows were grimy and the woodwork paint was cracked and peeling. A dog barked in the yard but there was no other sign of life about the place and it felt cold and empty. She could see a car parked by the side of the house which suggested someone was in, so she went up to the front door and knocked. There was no response. She knocked again with the same result, but once the dog stopped barking she was sure she could hear some sound inside, the television perhaps? Or radio?

"Hello?" Callie called out to anyone who might be inside and set the dog barking again. "Jill? Are you there?"

She put her hand on the doorknob, uncertain if she should try and open the door in the hope that her voice would be heard better.

"She's out."

Callie jumped and gave a little, involuntary scream at the sudden voice behind her and turned to see a man in his thirties, dressed in dirty overalls and muddy boots and looking at her with deep suspicion.

"I'm sorry," she said to him, smiling with relief. "You startled me. Jill's out, is she?"

"That's what I said, yes. Who are you?"

"Her doctor. Dr Hughes." Callie held out her hand and the man reluctantly took it.

"Are you her husband?" She knew that Jill was married, but didn't think she had ever seen her partner. He was probably on someone else's list, or even registered at another practice. There was no rule that said married couples had to have the same doctor.

"Yes. Is something wrong?" he asked. "Did she call you?"

Callie detected genuine anxiety in his voice.

"No, no, I just wanted a word, that's all," she said reassuringly, but he didn't look like he quite believed her. "I could hear the television on, so I just thought she hadn't heard me knock." Callie gestured at the door and stood slightly to one side to allow him to open it, but he made no move to do so.

"She's staying at her mother's for a while," he explained. "I must've left the telly on when I went to check the cows." He still made no move to go into the house, or to invite her in, despite her smiling and waiting for him to do so.

"Well," Callie finally said. "Do you know when she'll be back?" He shook his head and said nothing, but looked pointedly at her car. "Could you give me her address, then?" Callie persisted. She wasn't sure why, it wasn't urgent after all, but there was something about the man's attitude that had got to her, made her want to be sure.

"I'll be seeing her tomorrow and I'll tell her you've been round."

"Perhaps I can give you a note for her then?"

Callie dug in her bag for pen and paper and scribbled a quick note to her patient, just asking her to get in touch with the surgery, nothing confidential as she didn't have an envelope to put it in and seal the message from prying eyes. She handed the note to the man, who shoved it in a pocket.

"Bye then," he said and turned away, leaving her no choice but to walk back to her car. "Thank you for calling, Doctor. I'll let Jill know," he said from the doorway, as she got into the car, friendly now that he was sure she was leaving, but he still hadn't opened the door and Callie wondered exactly what it was he didn't want her to see. She gave herself a mental shake. He probably just didn't want her to see the piles of dirty dishes as he hadn't tidied up whilst his wife was away. But as she turned the Audi round and drove away, watching the man in her rearview mirror, he still didn't go into the house but stood and watched her until she was out of sight.

* * *

Kate was sitting in their usual corner of The Stag, a pint of her favourite Shepherd Neame Spitfire in front of her as Callie went to the bar to buy herself a large glass of Pinot Grigio. The barman didn't need to be told she liked it served with one cube of ice, he had served Callie many times before. The Stag was a convenient place for the two of them to meet, close to both their homes in the Old Town. It had everything you could want from a pub: a warm welcome and an open fire, not to mention Kate's favourite beer and a display case containing an ancient mummified cat for some obscure reason.

"Sorry I'm late, I got side-tracked by a patient."

This didn't even cause Kate to raise an eyebrow she was so used

to her friend being called out.

"Did you catch the press conference?" Callie asked. "I missed the evening news."

"Ah yes, the scrummy DI Miller."

Callie rolled her eyes.

"He's not scrummy."

"Really?" Kate was unconvinced. "I'm disappointed in you, Dr Hughes, you need to be on the look out for fanciable men. Even at work." Kate drank some of her beer. "Unless, of course, they are a patient, or, in my case, a client."

"I'll have you know that he's not fanciable, Ms Ward, even if he is good-looking. For me to consider him fanciable he would have to have a nice personality as well, and he hasn't. Not to mention the fact that he is married." Her point made, Callie changed the subject back to the press conference. "What did he say, then?"

If Kate was disappointed at her friend's response, she knew better than to show it.

"Well, he was appealing for anyone who might have seen either of the two victims earlier in the evening or night they were killed to get in touch. They are trying to trace the women's movements and who they were with."

"It makes you wonder, doesn't it?" Callie said thoughtfully.

"What?"

"I mean, these were both married women, weren't they?"

"And your point is?" Kate asked.

"Well, if the police are trying to track their movements, it's unlikely they were with their husbands, otherwise the police would know where they were, wouldn't they?"

"I see where you are going with this," Kate replied. "You think they were out with their lovers."

"I wouldn't necessarily go that far," Callie said. "I just think they must have been out with someone they didn't want their husbands to know about." She paused. "Which quite possibly might mean they were seeing someone else, like a lover, or potential lover."

"Exactly."

"But it might be something entirely different."

"Like what?"

"Like, ooh, I don't know, a surprise. Planning a party for their husbands or something."

"You think these women were out with a party planner?"

"Well, it's possible, isn't it?"

Kate shook her head at her friend's innocence and drank more of her beer before responding.

"Which brings me onto a bit of gossip I heard." Kate leant closer to keep the conversation more confidential, although there was no one seated near them. "A friend told me that a friend of a friend told her that this latest victim, what was her name…?"

"Carol Johnson," Callie told her.

"That's right. Carol, used a dating website to find men."

"That's awful. She was married, for goodness' sake."

"Maybe the marriage wasn't a happy one."

"Well, clearly not, if she was looking for someone else."

"Not necessarily," Kate said. "I hate to tell you this, Callie, but sometimes marriages can be, you know, open?"

"Do you think she told them she was married?"

"Yes. That's the point, Callie, she was using an adultery website."

Callie was horrified.

"An adultery website?" she said, rather more loudly than expected and Kate shushed her. They both looked round to see if anyone had heard her exclamation, but fortunately no one seemed to be giving them funny looks.

"I cannot believe such a thing exists," Callie continued quietly. "I mean, that there would be people openly looking for affairs like that."

"I can assure you, they do exist." Kate got out her phone and started searching on the internet. "Look."

She handed her phone to Callie, who stared at the screen, open-mouthed in amazement.

Chapter 10

"I'm going to say something really sexist now," Callie warned Kate as they walked back to Callie's flat, climbing the steep twitten, one of many narrow, unlit passages and flights of steps between houses that could be found all over Hastings Old Town. "I can see that there might be enough men wanting to have affairs to keep a website like that going, but women? It's just unbelievable."

They reached the top and turned into the lane that zig-zagged to the top of the hill.

"Well, it wouldn't work if there were only men registered, would it?" Kate responded, slightly out of breath despite all her time in the gym. "Or rather, that's a different sort of website altogether."

"Have you ever tried internet dating?" Callie asked her friend.

"God, yes." Kate paused for a moment to catch her breath. "Complete disaster. Why? Were you thinking of giving it a go?"

"Well, yes." She searched in her bag for her keys and opened the door. "I have thought about it, but never actually had the nerve. What happened to you?"

"I learnt a very valuable lesson." Kate followed Callie up the stairs. "Never give anyone any real details about yourself until you are absolutely sure they aren't some kind of crazy stalker. Good job I'm a lawyer, because it took all sorts of legal threats and an injunction to scare him off."

Callie stared at her in amazement.

"I'll remove that from the list of things I can do if I get desperate, then," Callie said as she filled the kettle with water from her filter jug, before asking: "Coffee or wine?"

Kate looked at her as if she were mad.

"Wine of course. Coffee at this time of night would keep me awake."

The advantage of an open plan living room and kitchen was that they could easily continue their conversation as Callie opened the bottle.

"To be fair, I know lots of people who have managed to find what they were looking for and not had any problems, so I'm not a good example. You just have to be a little more careful than I was."

"What exactly happened?" Callie asked once they were settled.

"We exchanged emails on the dating site, and agreed to meet in a wine bar, and I had a perfectly nice evening with him. He made me laugh, seemed a nice guy, and we agreed to meet again so I gave him my mobile number. Then I met Pete, do you remember Pete?"

"The plumber?"

"That's the one. Came to fix a leak and stayed for six weeks."

"That was soon after I met you, but he seemed a nice man."

"He was indeed" – Kate smiled wistfully at the memory – "so I cancelled the second date with the internet guy. Of course, he had my mobile number and kept calling and texting, refusing to go away, even when I ignored him."

"I remember you telling me you were changing your number because some man was harassing you. I hadn't realised you met him on the internet. Didn't he track you down at work as well?"

"That's right. During the evening I'd told him a bit about myself, you know, about being a solicitor working in criminal law, having an office in the main town. I didn't give him my life history, but he had enough to track me down again after I changed my phone number. Turned up at the court to try and speak to me, but I refused to see him and they threw him out. Stupid of him really, there's bound to be security at a court, but he honestly thought I'd change my mind I suppose. Couldn't believe I wouldn't fall at his feet. It got a bit awkward but fortunately the threat of legal action against him was enough to scare him away."

Callie brought her laptop over to where they were sitting.

"In some ways it was lucky you found out what he was like so early. Imagine if you had tried to end it after you had been going out a while."

Kate nodded.

"I know, lucky break. Of course, you don't just find nutters like that on the internet. I've dealt with stalking cases a couple of times, and neither of them were from internet dating."

"Right. Let's take a look at this website, then, what was it called?"

"SusSEXtra.co.uk," Kate answered, spelling it out. "It's a conflation, you know, a word made up of others, in this case Sussex, SEX, helpfully in capitals just to make sure you know what it's all about, and extra, I presume for extramarital."

Callie looked horrified.

"I know, I know, but I didn't name it, did I?" Kate took the laptop from Callie and typed the name in.

The first page asked if they were a woman looking for a man or a man looking for a woman, for a first name and email address. Kate paused.

"Why are we doing this?" Kate asked.

"If you'd rather not–"

"It's not that, but are we going on to the site simply to see what it's like out of curiosity? Or to see if we can find either or both of the victims registered? Only, if we want to see if we can find the two ladies, we are going to have to register as a man, or as bi or wanting a threesome."

Callie looked appalled.

"You think they were into that sort of thing?"

"I don't know, and that's the problem. We don't know what they would be interested in and therefore we can't put in a profile likely to bring them up as a match."

Callie looked as if she was rapidly changing her mind about everything.

"But if we did put in a fairly basic profile, do you think we would be able to find them?"

"It's unlikely, in my view. Apart from anything else, they probably wouldn't use their real names."

Callie thought for a while.

"I just want to have a bit more of an idea about the site and if it could be where the killer meets his victims," she said finally. "And I have to admit to a certain amount of curiosity."

"Me too," Kate said with a smile as she clicked and typed. "Let's say we are a woman looking for a man then. First name?" She looked at Callie. "And don't say Callie."

"Mary?" Callie suggested.

"Nice name, but not really, you know, sexy. How about, Vicky short for Victoria's Secret." Kate didn't wait for Callie's approval but added the name Vicky.

"Ah, now we have to put in an email address."

She clicked open a new tab and quickly registered a new email account for Vicky S.

"Have you done this before?" Callie asked. "Only you seem rather experienced."

"I told you, I learnt from my first foray into internet dating. Now if I do it, I don't just use a fake name, I have a

91

fake email and a throw away phone, a suitably unrecognisable photo and I make sure I never tell them anything true about me."

Callie thought about this as Kate continued setting up her new persona.

"What if you meet somebody you like though? And want to start a real relationship. There has to be a time when you tell them the truth."

"Of course," Kate said glibly. "Once you've thoroughly vetted them."

"Well, don't they object to the fact that you aren't who you said you were?"

"Dunno, never got that far." Kate typed Callie's new email address in. "And anyway, you have to remember they may not be who they say they are, either. Password. How about '2ladies'? Like in *Cabaret*? Think you'll remember it or do you want to write it down?"

Callie wrote the password down on a notepad.

"Right. Next question. A little about me…" Kate read from the screen. "For example, if we were alone for the night, how we would try to make it sexy and inviting. What do you think we should write, Vicky?" she said to Callie, who was looking bemused. "On second thoughts, I think you need to leave this to me."

Callie had no argument with that, she was still struggling to take it all in. She looked at what Kate was writing and decided to drink her wine instead.

"Right, photo. We can use one we download from the internet or we can dress you up and take one."

"I don't know, I mean I don't think anyone I know would be on this website but it would be really embarrassing if they were and they, you know, recognised me." The thought of a colleague, or even worse, a patient, seeing her picture was enough to make her blood run cold.

"Relax, Callie." Kate laughed. "The advantage of using your own picture, suitably blurred or photoshopped to ensure your own mother wouldn't pick you out in a line-up, is that photos taken from the internet are so obviously fake, it's got to the point that some models are threatening to sue people who use their photos on these sites."

"It's really that common?"

"Yes. It's called catfishing but most people don't fall for it and along with not posting any picture at all it just tends to suggest you have something to hide, and you get ignored."

Callie didn't seem convinced but Kate filled up her wine glass and sorted out a revealing top and having rejected all Callie's understated jewellery, insisted Callie wore her own dangly earrings and matching necklace. Then she did Callie's makeup more heavily than she would ever do herself and fluffed her hair up. Kate rifled through Callie's jewellery box again and picked out her grandmother's wedding ring and went to slip it on the fourth finger of Callie's left hand but she pulled away.

"What are you doing?"

"You are supposed to be married, so you need a wedding ring."

"No, no, you can't do that. It's bad luck." Callie snatched the ring from her and threw it back in the box.

"I didn't know you were superstitious!"

"I'm not." Callie paused. "Except about this. Wearing a wedding ring when you are not married means you will never get married."

Kate was amazed that her normally rational friend was so superstitious.

"How are you supposed to try it on for size?"

"I suppose, that would be okay, provided you were engaged."

"Well, anyway, if you are right that means I won't ever get married then, because I've done it hundreds of times, whenever I needed a bit of space."

But Callie wasn't going to be persuaded.

"I know it's stupid, but indulge me. I'll put my left hand out of sight."

She put one hand behind her back and Kate decided to let it go.

"Okay, now pout like you are taking a selfie."

Callie obediently pouted and Kate took a photo on her phone.

"There you go, no one would ever think it was you."

She showed Callie, who had to acknowledge that she was right. Her normal image was understated, smart, controlled, professional and the picture Kate had taken was of a far more free spirit, sexy and rather wanton. Callie was surprised and, she had to admit, slightly excited to see this alter ego.

"Never knew you had it in you, did you?" Kate teased as she uploaded the picture and Callie poured them both another glass of wine.

"Now, what's next, ah yes, your preferences."

Callie sat down and looked at the new page that Kate had opened.

"Definitely a non-smoker, and he needs to be taller than me."

"I'll put six foot then, because they all exaggerate their height." Kate took a sip of her wine. "Build: let's say toned. Back to you. Marital status: married. Favourite position?"

"For what?" Callie asked and then giggled as she realised what Kate meant. "Really? I haven't even met the guy yet?" She looked at the list. "What on earth is cowgirl?"

"Oh, for goodness' sake, woman!" Kate took over again, as she completed her list of Vicky's preferences. "And finally, what gets you going?"

They both looked at the list.

"Wow," Kate said.

"Are they even legal?" Callie asked, astounded.

"Most of them," Kate replied. "Between consenting adults, anyway, but not all of them. I suggest we keep it legal." She ticked a couple of the tamer suggestions and submitted them before Callie could object.

Payment and phone number were not required at this stage, only once Vicky decided to contact anyone who was matched to her or who responded to her post, so Kate clicked finish and raised her glass.

"Here's to Vicky."

They clinked glasses.

"What's next?" Callie asked.

"You just wait for some suggested matches picked out by the computer or, I suspect, chosen by a particularly malevolent administrator, or for a man who has been sent your details in the same way to respond. I suggest you get a pay-as-you-go mobile ready."

"I'm not going to actually contact any of them," Callie said, horrified. "One of them could be a serial killer."

"Good point."

The thought made them both feel suddenly sober.

"That's why I need to tell the police about Carol being on here. I mean even if they can't find him through this, they need to warn people."

"That could be difficult, from a legal perspective. I mean they don't know the killer meets women through the website, the only evidence we have is that one of the women reportedly used it."

"I can't just not tell them. It might be their only way of tracking him down."

"I know, but–" Kate said dubiously. "I suppose I ought to do it really, it was my friend who told me about it. I just don't want it brought up every time I go in there to see a client. I mean, if I tell those Neanderthals that I've been looking at websites like this, I'll never hear the end of it. I can't do it, Callie, I'll never be taken seriously again."

They both thought for a moment.

"Presumably they gave out a number for people to call with information, we could ring it anonymously, couldn't we?" Callie suggested.

"They get thousands of calls after a press conference," Kate responded. "It would be easy for one call to get missed, but you're right, it's better than not telling them at all."

They both thought about it some more, knowing that it wasn't an ideal solution and feeling guilty.

"I'm sorry but I think it's best if we tell them direct." Callie was suddenly decisive. "I don't mind doing it." She thought for a moment. "I know, there's this sergeant I know from custody but I saw him in the incident room, I think he was setting it up. Oh, what's his name?" Callie asked herself, then it suddenly came to her. "Nugent."

"I know him." Kate responded with excitement. "Nigel Nugent but they all call him Nerdy Nigel. He's a sweety, you could certainly ask to speak to him. He'd pass the message on and might not even involve you at all."

"Okay. I'll go and speak to Nerdy Nigel tomorrow as it's my morning off."

"Thank you." Kate hugged her, very aware that she had chickened out, and Callie was braver and doing the right thing for her friend, and the women of Hastings.

Chapter 11

The office Callie had been taken to by Nigel was little more than a stationery cupboard, but it offered the privacy she felt she needed to explain about Carol Johnson's use of an internet dating site. She had hoped that he would be as shocked as her that it seemed to be aimed at people already in relationship, but he wasn't.

"I have heard of them," he said, clearing his throat in embarrassment. "There are quite a few offering no strings sexual encounters and swinging and such like, at least, I believe there are."

At least he seemed to be taking it seriously, Callie consoled herself, although she quickly changed her mind when he said she would have to tell DI Miller.

"Can't you?" she pleaded.

"He's going to ask me how I heard and want to speak to you anyway, so it's best to get it over with." Nigel stood and turned to open the door for her and she squeezed past him into the corridor. She would have liked to tell him to make sure that she spoke to Miller alone or at the very least not have Sergeant Jeffries present, but Nigel was already heading off down the corridor at speed and she had to hurry to keep up with him.

He opened the door of the incident room and ushered her in. Callie reluctantly came into the room behind him and tried not to show her dismay, and, indeed, horror as she realised the whole team were there, in the middle of morning briefing. A sea of tired faces turned to look at her with undisguised interest, including Miller, who was standing at the front of the room by the whiteboard. As she felt a blush of embarrassment developing, Callie looked around and, unfortunately, saw Sergeant Jeffries, clutching a mug of tea and a bacon roll. Did the man ever stop eating?

Miller raised an eyebrow at Nigel's interruption before nodding to the middle-aged man in a cardigan who was standing next to him to continue his report. As everyone turned back to the front, Callie could feel the redness spread up her neck until she could feel the heat radiating from her cheeks as she hoped against hope that she wouldn't have to talk about the website in front of everyone. She tried to concentrate as the man who was, she presumed, the civilian who collated all the reports as they came in, listed a swathe of negatives in a monotone: no sign of the car being stolen earlier in the evening on CCTV, no one from the door to doors having seen or heard anything, until the explosion, of course, and no car heard leaving the scene after that.

He went on to report on the predictably massive response to the press briefing and the call for information on where the two women had been on the nights they were murdered, but none of the callers were looking likely to have any useful information. According to the people who had rung in, Carol might have been in The Hastings Arms, but it could have been on another night; the two women were definitely together in Brighton, the day after the first was murdered, one caller was sure; and Sarah, the first victim was apparently at school with a very weird boy fifteen years ago and he probably killed her.

"We checked him out" – the collator seemed more animated at this point – "but it turns out he joined the police and was custody sergeant in Brighton the night of her murder, as witnessed by large numbers of colleagues and criminals, some of whom did agree that he was weird, however."

There was a ripple of laughter as he continued to tell Miller and the room that some calls were still being followed up, but not one credible sighting of either woman had come to light. Callie was silently praying that Miller would end the briefing and she could speak to him in his office but he nodded at a female officer who Callie recognised as PC Jayne Hales, whom she had worked with several times in the past, and she came up to the front.

"The drug screen result is through on victim one." She paused and Callie could sense a quickening of interest. "It's positive for GHB, mixed with quite a high level of alcohol."

Callie knew that GHB, or Gamma Hydroxybutyrate as it was more properly known, lasted in the blood for two to four hours and in the urine for up to twelve hours. It was known as the date rape drug because when victims were tested for it the next day, it was usually negative, but in this case, the victim had died and metabolism of the drug had been halted in time for the test to still be positive.

"So, he could meet them for a drink and then slip them the drug that way," a youngish constable commented.

Jayne nodded.

"That would explain why they went with him."

"It also explains why they don't do more to try and escape the car when he pours petrol in," Miller added. "Between the drugs, the alcohol and parking up against the post so they can't open their doors, these women don't stand a chance of getting away."

"Let's just hope they were out of it enough not to know what was happening," Jeffries added sombrely.

While Callie acknowledged that it was a horrific way to die, she was strangely comforted to know that at least the second victim might not have known much about it, and she could tell others in the room were thinking the same.

"Nigel?" Miller called him to the front and Callie felt a spasm of fear, it would be her turn in a minute she knew and she was vaguely grateful that Nigel didn't go to the front of the room, but stayed where he was to give the report, although, in some ways, that was worse because everyone had turned in their seats and were now looking at her.

Nigel cleared his throat and launched into his update.

"As with the first case, the mobile phone was too damaged by the fire for us to get anything useful from the SIM card. I've started the process to get the call log and data from the phone company for the second victim's mobile, but we haven't got that from the first, yet."

"It always takes time, Nigel," Miller was trying to sound upbeat. "Anything on their computers?"

Nigel shook his head.

"Not at first look, but I've sent them off to technical, see if anything's been hidden or erased, guv."

"Good. Now, last but not least." Miller looked at Callie expectantly.

Everyone turned their attention to Callie and she took a deep breath to steady herself.

"I'm sorry, I didn't mean to interrupt your meeting," Callie could have kicked herself as soon as the words were out of her mouth. It wasn't like she had just barged in, Nigel had brought her, although he hadn't explained that a briefing was taking place and everyone was there, but apologising just made her look weak. "Perhaps we could have a word in private?"

Everyone looked at Miller and were disappointed when, after a moment's thought, a moment that seemed an eternity to Callie, he nodded. She let her breath out with a sigh, not having realised that she had been holding it until that minute.

"Right, everyone, let's get on with this," Miller said and people were suddenly galvanised into action. "I want all spare hands checking CCTV or back round all the pubs and clubs, this guy must have slipped up and appeared somewhere, someone must have seen him load a drunk or drugged woman into a car. Nigel, chase for phone and laptop info, will you? We need to know where these women met him."

As people moved back to their desks to get on with their tasks, he turned and gestured for Callie to follow him to an area a bit away from the action, where there was a small amount of free space. Not as private as she would have liked, and, she noted with dismay, Jeffries followed them. They were only a matter of steps away from the rest of the team, and whilst this was definitely better than having to give a report to them all, she was sure that they were all feigning a lack of interest and were really listening to every word.

"Um, I wondered if you had checked out dating websites?" she said tentatively, her voice not coming out quite as strong as she would have liked. "As the place where he might be meeting his victims."

Miller looked disappointed, but at least that meant he had wanted her to succeed, she thought. Jeffries snorted in derision.

"What do you reckon he puts in the advert, then? Partner wanted for short term relationship, GSOH and a love of self-immolation required?" Jeffries asked and someone sniggered.

"Smokers preferred." Another voice chipped in proving to Callie that they had indeed all been listening.

"For late night barbecues in the country."

Callie was livid, she hadn't come here to be publicly ridiculed. This was exactly what she had been hoping to avoid by going to see Nigel, perhaps she would have been better off speaking to Jayne Hales, at least she was giving Callie a look of sympathy. Miller raised his hand and everyone fell silent.

"Only, you see, the second victim, Carol Johnson, was apparently a user of one," she persevered angrily.

She could feel the mood change, she wasn't just interfering, she had information.

"How do you know that?" Miller asked.

"One of her friends told a friend of mine, who told me."

"Gossip, then," Jeffries said in a tone that spoke volumes.

"Gossip that might be true and might help you find the killer." Callie was trying to stay calm. She knew her information was weak and she would have far rather spoken quietly to Miller on his own, or even better, just told Nigel, but he had brought her into the incident room, like a lamb to the slaughter, and she could feel her cheeks burning with a mixture of anger and embarrassment.

"There are hundreds of those websites, thousands even, it's a massive job," Jeffries said.

"We could start by looking at local ones." Jayne Hales was trying to be more encouraging but then turned away to answer her phone.

"We can narrow it down more than that," Callie said. "It was a local website specialising in affairs, called, um" – she steeled herself – "SusSEXtra, according to this friend of a friend."

A smirk appeared on Jeffries' face and he looked as though he was about to make another suggestive comment when Jayne Hales called out.

"Guv!" She was waving a scrap of paper on which she had been taking notes as she quietly spoke on the phone and she had everyone's attention. "Fingerprint on a coke can found in a hedgerow near the visitor centre matches Mark Caxton."

"Yes!" Jeffries raised a clenched fist and grabbed his jacket. Miller was already on his way out as Jeffries hurried after him, both passing Callie who was still standing just inside the door, without comment.

Everyone in the room was busy congratulating each other and making preparations for Mark to be brought back in by their boss. He was going to be questioned again, and maybe this time, they had got enough evidence to press charges.

Nigel looked at Callie, obviously embarrassed by how she had been treated.

"I promise you I'll follow up on your information, Dr Hughes."

"And I'll make sure of it," Jayne added.

"Thank you," Callie said with as much dignity as she could muster, and left.

* * *

Callie went straight round to Kate's office, still flushed but with anger rather than embarrassment by the time she arrived.

"He just pushed past me, with that odious little man running along behind him, and went out to arrest Mark Caxton again. He is absolutely fixated on the boy being the culprit and just isn't interested in anyone else. I mean, he was in hospital, for goodness' sake. How could he have done it?"

"To be fair," Kate responded, playing devil's advocate, "with a solid piece of evidence linking a suspect to a murder scene, Miller has no choice but to pick him up. Imagine if he didn't and another woman was killed? He'd be pilloried in the press and probably spend the rest of his career directing traffic."

Callie sighed. Kate was right.

"Why on earth did you march in and tell him about it, anyway? I thought we agreed you would tell Nerdy Nigel on the quiet."

"I did, and he insisted I tell Miller, but didn't warn me that he was in the middle of a briefing at the time." Callie put her head in her hands. "Oh, Kate, it was just awful."

Kate rubbed her friend's back sympathetically, just as Callie's mobile started ringing. Callie fished her phone out of her handbag, checking to see who the caller was before answering.

"Hi Linda," she said and then listened. "Yes, okay." Callie checked her watch. "What's this about, do you know? … What? A complaint? Who from? … Really? Right. Of course. I'll be there in about an hour."

"A complaint?" Kate queried, concerned for her friend.

"It's a long story about a patient of mine who hasn't been responding to requests to attend or have a blood test. Anyway, I popped round yesterday but she wasn't there so I left a note with her husband. Apparently, that amounts to harassment and they've made a complaint, so Hugh wants to see me. I was only trying to help."

"Hugh will see that, Callie, I'm sure."

Callie had her head in her hands again and Kate gently patted her back.

"This is not a good day," Callie said lifting her head, finally.

"No, I can see that," Kate agreed.

"I seem to be having a problem with men. First Miller and Jeffries, and now Mr Hollingsworth complaining to Hugh, and all because of that stupid, stupid Gerry Brown."

Kate stiffened.

"What's Gerry Brown got to do with it?"

Callie picked up at Kate's harsh tone and looked at her friend.

"He's our locum, and gave Jill's husband a prescription when he should have insisted that Jill came in. Why?"

Kate bit her lip.

"You know I was telling you about my stalker?"

Callie nodded.

"Well, he was a doctor called Gerry Brown. Do you think there could be two?"

"Tallish with thick, almost wiry brown hair – bearded?"

"You just described him to a T."

They sat in silence for a moment.

"I think that officially confirms to me that he is a, a–" Callie struggled.

"Twat, I think is the word you are searching for," Kate said, "or possibly tosser."

"I take it you don't want me to send him your best wishes?" Callie replied with a mischievous smile, and Kate laughed.

"No. But you can knee him in the groin for me if you want."

* * *

Callie quite quickly managed to persuade Hugh Grantham that she had done nothing wrong in visiting her patient unannounced, indeed she had been going above and beyond her duty.

He advised that she should stick strictly to protocol from then on, which meant that Jill should not be prescribed any further tablets until her condition was reviewed and that when she requested a prescription, Linda should respond to that effect.

"Worst case scenario is that they'll change doctors," Hugh said to her, but Callie worried that it might actually mean that Jill stopped treatment, and would become as chronically ill as she had been when she first saw her. Tired, depressed, overweight, losing her hair, she had been so much better once the treatment had taken effect and she had stabilised; she lost loads of weight and had come into the surgery positively bouncing with energy. Callie couldn't understand why she had stopped attending or having blood tests.

"We can't get too involved, Callie," Hugh advised. "It's her life, and we have done everything expected of us."

That was all very well, but he couldn't stop Callie thinking that something was wrong for Jill to behave like this, but a packed clinic soon took all her attention and Jill was forgotten.

Chapter 12

"They didn't even find the empty can in the car park where the car was set on fire."

Helen Austen was confiding to Callie the next day over a cup of peppermint tea in her extraordinarily untidy office.

Helen had been present when Miller and Jeffries interviewed Mark in the presence of his legal representative. Mark had been instructed to exercise his right to silence and only to say 'no comment' to every question he was asked. This time, he had managed to do that.

"Where did they find the drink can?" Callie asked Helen.

"By the overflow car park, about twenty yards up the lane."

"Not far away then."

"No," Helen conceded reluctantly before continuing. "I am sure it could have got there at anytime, but the visitor centre manager convinced them that he clears any rubbish lying around the car parks twice a week, Monday and Friday, so he insisted it had to have been left there some time between Friday afternoon and Sunday morning when the crime scene people found it."

"What did Mark say to explain it?" Callie asked. "Apart from no comment, I mean?"

"I wasn't privy to his discussions with his lawyer, of course, but when we were sitting in the interview room waiting for the detectives, Mark just kept saying he hadn't been to Fairlight in years and he didn't know how his fingerprints were found on any rubbish there."

"It doesn't look good, though, does it? Even if he was in hospital at the time." Callie believed in Mark's innocence, but even she could see that.

"No, no it doesn't, and I know that. But do you really think this is the sort of thing Mark would get up to?" A telephone seemed to be ringing somewhere but a glance at the telephone base module showed the handset to be missing. Helen searched under some of the paper strewn across her desk and finally found the handset just as it stopped ringing. She put it back down on the desk where it would quickly be covered in papers again.

"No, of course not." Callie hesitated. "I'm not sure he has the mental capacity to plan it, apart from anything."

"Absolutely!" Helen said. "Of course, the police theory is that he's working with someone else. It conveniently covers all the gaping holes in their case if there is some kind of mastermind telling Mark what to do."

Helen was dismissive but as Callie thought about it, she could see a certain logic to the theory. It could also help explain the second murder taking place when Mark was supposedly in hospital. It really did seem too complex to say that he managed to get out of the hospital without anyone noticing, steal a car, meet a woman and persuade her to go with him, kill her and get back to the hospital, all without being seen. But a partner would explain a lot. A partner who dropped a can at the scene to incriminate Mark.

"Do they have any idea who this partner might be?"

"None at all." Helen looked thoughtful. "One of Mark's problems is that he doesn't make friends easily. He's quite isolated."

"He has a girlfriend, though, doesn't he?"

"Yes," Helen agreed dubiously. "But I think it's fair to say she's quite isolated as well, because of her" – Helen waved her hands around a bit – "um, well she's a funny little thing. Terribly shy."

"But if he can manage to maintain a relationship with one person, he might just possibly be able to have a partner."

"Yes, but I still don't see it, why start killing women old enough to be his mother?" There was an awkward silence as they both realised that Mark might well have a reason to hate women of a similar age to his mother; after all, she was hardly a good example of motherhood.

"Yes, well, I still don't believe he has anything to do with this," Helen finished and despite the mounting evidence, Callie had to concede that she didn't believe it either.

* * *

He knew he hadn't planned this one as carefully as the others, but he just couldn't resist. He normally had to reel them in with promises and sex texts, endless flirting and pandering to their egos, but this one, this whore, needed no encouragement. She was desperate to meet for sex without strings, claiming a higher sex drive than her partner could cope with. She seemed remarkably unworried about who met her 'needs', treating sex as her right without any thought for her poor, cuckolded husband.

It had been so easy to persuade her to get into his car, stolen of course, and to take a drive to a secluded spot for sex. She had even suggested that he could take her to a dogging site, where she might get lucky and have multiple partners. There was no chance he would do that, of course, he didn't want any voyeurs witnessing what he had planned for her. There was no doubt in his mind that she deserved to die, but the price of not planning properly was that things went wrong.

Because she had been so happy to comply, he hadn't used GHB. He had thought it would be nice for her to know what was happening to her, why he was doing it even, but she had roared with anger when he threw the petrol over her and quickly realised that she couldn't get out of the passenger door. By the time he had hurriedly thrown the lit book of matches into the car, she was already climbing across to his side. Despite her hair and clothes catching fire, she had continued her escape, getting the driver's door open.

He had considered getting close and kicking it shut again but she was too fast and already out of the car and falling onto the ground as he rushed across from his place of safety, so he kicked her head instead. It made a satisfactory noise as his foot crunched against her face and her head jerked back. He kicked her so hard, he wondered if he'd broken her neck. It had certainly stopped her escape and he moved away watching with satisfaction as she continued to burn where she lay, her body moving jerkily as the muscles and tendons constricted in the heat.

Later, when he stopped to examine his shoe, he could see a lump of burnt flesh attached to the leather. Amusing as it was, mistakes like that could be fatal. He knew that only bleach would be able to get rid of the DNA evidence, after he had cleaned the charred skin off the shoes, but bleach would ruin the leather, so he would have to get rid of them somewhere they would never be found. He vowed that next time he would take more care, make sure the chosen whore wasn't in any condition to try and escape. Make sure nothing went wrong. After all, he didn't want to get caught, not yet, not ever if possible, but certainly not yet. There were so many more harlots and Jezebels out there. So many left to kill.

Chapter 13

"Not a Sunday this time," Callie commented as a suited-up Miller and Jeffries joined her in the brightly lit crime scene tent. Miller grunted acknowledgement of her remark, but said nothing else. The rain, gently drumming on the roof, was one of the reasons for the tent. Colin Brewer, crime scene manager as before, was anxious to protect any evidence from being damaged or washed away, and Miller wanted to keep the increasingly intrusive press at a distance from the more open area that the killer had used for this, his third murder. Callie half expected to hear the sound of a helicopter hovering overhead, filming the activity for the early morning news.

The car was parked as before, with the passenger door against the perimeter fencepost of the car park, and the driver's door open but this time with the body lying beside the car instead of inside. The tent was only just big enough to cover both car and corpse.

"She got out." Jeffries indicated the victim, who was lying in the foetal position on the ground by the blackened, skeletal remains of the car, and he crouched down to get a closer look. "It looks like she just curled up and died," he added thoughtfully.

"That's the effects of the heat causing her tissues to contract," Callie explained quickly.

Chris Butterworth strode over to the open door of the tent and leaned in to speak to them. Despite the protective suit and mask, it was clear that he was angry, very angry indeed.

"Looks to be the same method once again. Have you picked up that little shit yet?"

Miller straightened up and looked Butterworth in the eye.

"Yes. Hence our problem. He was safely tucked up in a cell all night."

That stopped Butterworth dead, as he tried to assimilate this information. He seemed shocked by the news.

"But" – he shook his head as if to clear it – "Caxton must be the one doing this. It's his MO." He looked from Miller to Jeffries, who shook his head sympathetically.

Callie was less supportive.

"I take it you will be letting him go now, or will you be checking the CCTV in the custody suite to see if he managed to sneak out of his cell?" She just couldn't help herself and was pleased to see a look of irritation flash across Miller's face.

"Been on any good websites recently, Dr Hughes?" Jeffries retaliated. "Found yourself a boyfriend yet?"

Callie was livid but not quick enough to come up with a response. It would probably be well into next week before she thought of a decent one.

"Have you finished here, Doctor?" Miller asked, pointedly bringing the conversation to a close.

"Yes. I've pronounced life extinct. Not that you really needed me to tell you she was dead," Callie responded and left the tent, pulling off her gloves as she hurried through the light rain towards the officer manning the exit from the taped-off crime scene. She signed out with a worse than usual scrawl, too agitated to write legibly as she thought about what she had heard and started piecing it all together. She quickly undressed and ditched her protective clothing in the bag provided, doing her best to keep dry as she did so, and was relieved to reach her car only slightly dampened, by the weather, at least.

She switched the engine on and put the heater on full blast to warm up and dry herself out. She sat in the driver's seat, looking out at the drizzle and thinking about what she had heard, all the while wishing that she had had the foresight to make a flask of tea before leaving the warmth of her home. If Mark was in custody, there was absolutely no way he could have committed this crime, and therefore, perhaps he hadn't committed the last one either, or even the first. So how did a drink can with his fingerprints on it turn up at the second locus? And who knew his method of starting fires well enough to have copied it?

It could have been a coincidence, she reasoned, even if Mark said he hadn't been to Fairlight, perhaps he had left an empty can in a mate's car and it had fallen out up there. It was also possible that he had been there and was lying about it, frightened to admit he had visited the site, even innocently, on that night or some other. It really wasn't beyond the realms of possibility that the manager of the visitor centre had missed the can when collecting the rubbish.

The second piece of evidence was that the killer used the same method of fire starting as Mark had in the past, but that might just be down to having read about his previous convictions, or Mark himself might have talked about the way he did it and been overheard. In which case, it was likely that Mark knew the killer.

On their own, neither fact meant that Mark was being framed, but together they were suspicious, if not conclusive.

Callie looked through the fine rain at the lights on the far side of the car park. The forensic tent glowed eerily in the half-light but the blue-clad figures seemed slightly faded as they searched the immediate area around the tent now that dawn was beginning to break. She wondered if they would find any further evidence linking Mark to this scene, because if they did, they would know for sure that it wasn't a coincidence, they would know that someone was deliberately trying to set him up. Someone who knew his history and with access to his fingerprints, on used cans at least, but who didn't know he was in custody last night.

A blue-suited man came out of the tent and looked across to where she was parked. She recognised the build and posture as Miller, and she wondered if the same thoughts were going through his head.

* * *

Unable to either go back to sleep or face breakfast after her horrific start to the day, Callie decided on a walk to work. She ambled through the streets of Hastings, making her way to the surgery by a very circuitous route in the hope that it would clear her head, and possibly even enable her to eat something before morning surgery. The rain had stopped, leaving a dampness in the air that Callie knew would make her hair frizzy, but, for once, she didn't care. In the greater scheme of things, she had to admit that bad hair was hardly a major problem, besides she had put some portable hair straighteners in her bag so she could repair the damage once she was at work.

Despite walking for more than forty minutes, she still arrived before eight and let herself into the surgery, armed with a packet of biscuits she had bought on the way to replace those that she had previously taken from Linda's secret store. Tea and chocolate biscuits would have to do for breakfast.

As she let herself in through the back door, she saw that Gerry Brown's car was once more in the car park. Wednesday and Saturday nights he left it there. That's what Gauri had told her. She stopped in the hallway as she thought about that. Gerry Brown used internet dating

114

sites. Gerry Brown was a known stalker. Gerry Brown had access to her files on Mark. Gerry Brown left his car at work on Wednesday and Saturday nights. The murders were committed on Wednesday and Saturday nights, well, one on a Wednesday and two on a Saturday.

There was a sudden noise of the alarm going off and Callie realised that she had been too busy thinking about Gerry as a suspect to key in the code in time. She did it quickly and hurried upstairs to call the alarm company and let them know it wasn't burglars, and to give more thought to her theory that Gerry was a killer. Did it really hold water or was it just that she didn't like the man? And if he was the killer, how could he have got hold of Mark's fingerprints, or rather, a drink can with his fingerprints on it?

She hadn't been in the office long before Linda arrived and informed her that Gerry Brown had called in sick. The news added weight to Callie's earlier thoughts about whether he was linked to the killings and it occurred to her that he might even be off sick because he had accidentally got burnt. Once the thought was there, it wouldn't go away until Linda thrust a list under her nose.

"So, which of his patients are you going to see?"

* * *

"Are you sure about this, Callie?" Kate asked as she logged into the SusSEXtra website in her office later.

"I know it sounds a bit silly, but I just want to be sure it isn't him and he's off sick because he got burnt or something."

"Look, I have no reason to defend the man, but from stalker to serial killer is a bit of a leap."

"But not impossible?"

"No." Kate hesitated. "Do you think you should tell the police about this?"

"After what happened last time? No." Callie shook her head vehemently. "I don't want them to think I am even more loopy than they already do."

"Hmm, are you more concerned about the handsome inspector thinking you are mad than whatever his sidekick thinks, by any chance?"

"Of course not." Callie knew that she didn't sound completely convincing and she also knew that Kate would have spotted it. "It's a good thing Gerry was off sick because I wouldn't have been able to stop myself from staring at him, wondering if it could be him."

Kate snorted with amusement at her deliberate change of direction.

"Watch it, he'd probably think you fancy him. You might end up with him stalking you."

"I certainly hope not. He is so not my type."

"You surprise me," Kate responded as she navigated to the web page. "Is it the beard?"

"No, I'm happy with beards, but strangely, I just don't find serial killers attractive."

Kate laughed as she put in the password and went to Callie's page.

"Right. You have had twenty-three responses. Not bad, not bad at all."

They looked at the messages.

"No one called Gerry Brown and none of the pictures could be him unless he's changed a lot."

"No, but he could have used a false name and picture, I have heard that people sometimes do that," Callie countered, with a knowing look at Kate.

"Point taken."

They began to read the details the responders had entered for themselves.

"Why, oh why, would anyone seriously call themselves The Stud?" Callie asked.

"Maybe it's ironic?" Kate replied as she opened the first response and they read the message.

"Why would he want to know if I can burp on demand?"

"That's clearly his thing. Look here." Kate pointed. "Girls who belch get him going, he even asks what fizzy drinks you like best."

"He doesn't want time wasters, just the real thing. Dear Lord, what is the world coming to?"

"You don't share his eructation fetish then?" Kate couldn't help but laugh.

"Eeuw!" Callie said a moment later. "Fancy actually writing something like that down!"

"Actually, writing down your fantasies can be incredibly erotic," Kate responded. "You should try it some time."

"Writing them down is one thing, letting someone else read them is another matter entirely."

Slowly they worked their way through all the messages, with Callie making notes, and found two responders that could possibly match Gerry Brown if the photo was discounted, one of which did actually mention that he was bearded, although the photo attached was clean shaven, and could, at a stretch have been a younger version of Gerry Brown.

"He actually sounds quite nice," Callie said.

"You are only saying that because he's one of the few not talking dirty."

"That's very true." Callie looked at the list she had written down and thought for a moment, then sighed.

"Do you think I'm a prude, Kate?"

"Erm, why do you ask?"

"You do! Admit it, you do think I'm a prude."

"Well, it's more that you have limits, and perhaps your limits are set at a lower level than mine."

"I prefer to think of them as standards."

"Okay, well then your standards are higher than most, Callie. Or, at least, higher than mine," Kate continued, anxiously trying not to offend her friend.

"And certainly higher than these people."

"I think most of us have higher, or rather different, standards to these people."

"But do you think I should, I don't know, loosen up a little?" Callie asked.

Kate was reluctant to say yes, although it was something she had often wanted to say to Callie.

"Everyone has different ways of living their lives and behaviours that they feel comfortable with and no one should ever make fun of them for that, or try and push them to do something that makes them feel uncomfortable. You know me, I'm a live and let live sort of person. I don't feel I am in a position to either criticise or advise," she said.

Callie thought about that for a while.

"I just worry that I might be missing out on the fun sometimes."

"Maybe, but if you don't actually find whatever it is fun to do, you're not missing out on it, if you get my meaning."

"I do," Callie readily agreed. "It's like, you know I hate roller coasters, but everyone tells me how exciting they are so sometimes I force myself onto them just to see if I've made a mistake, and then I find out, all over again, that all I am missing is terror and sickness and I promise myself that I will never do it again under any circumstances."

"Until the next time you doubt yourself."

Callie nodded her agreement.

"That's right. But there is a difference between not going on a roller coaster and being over-cautious with other aspects of your life; being too frightened to live a full life."

Kate couldn't disagree. Callie sighed and looked at the two possibles on her list.

"So, what do I do next?"

"Are you sure about this, Callie?" Kate asked anxiously.

"I'm not going to meet them, just try and get to know them a bit better and see if I can spot if one of them is

Gerry, or giving out other serial killer vibes. Have you got an unregistered pay-as-you-go phone I could use?"

Kate rummaged in her desk drawer and pulled one out. "The number is on it."

Callie turned the phone over and saw that Kate had stuck a bit of paper with the number onto the back of the phone.

"You are going to have to pay to contact them. That's how these websites work. It's free up to the point where you want to exchange contact details."

Callie looked anxious.

"I don't really want my credit card details logged here, or SusSEXtra appearing on my statements. It's not exactly subtle, is it?"

"In my experience, there are two ways you can do this," Kate told her. "We can set up a PayPal account for Vicky S and use your credit card to put money into the account, as if you had bought something from her over the internet, making it slightly more than you need for the website so it isn't too obvious. Vicky can pay you back later. Or if you are still concerned about that we can put in an extra layer of anonymity, by setting up an intermediate false account that you pay money into which then pays Vicky and she then pays SusSEXtra, if we use different amounts each time and put other bits of money in and out of the accounts to make them seem real, it will look Kosher, superficially at least."

Callie looked at Kate in astonishment.

"You've done this before."

"Yes," Kate acknowledged. "Like I say, I learnt after that incident with Gerry. Of course, the police or whatever would be able to track it all down, but no one else is likely to be able to connect you financially with Vicky S."

"Right, let's do it. Just the first level of anonymity will do. I don't plan to make a habit of it." Callie handed the laptop to Kate.

"Don't knock it till you've tried it," Kate said and started setting up the accounts for Callie and Vicky.

Once she had done that and Callie had transferred some money into her account and then across to Vicky, she paused to reflect on what she was about to do.

"Sure?" Kate questioned her.

Callie nodded, suddenly decisive, and quickly, before she had a chance to change her mind, she paid SusSEXtra. Response boxes appeared for her to contact the men who had responded to her original post. She typed in a suitably oblique response to the first man, saying that she liked the look of him and giving him the number of Kate's special purpose mobile, suggesting they text each other, signed off as Vicky S and hit enter.

"In for a penny…" she said as she did exactly the same to the second man on her list, and then a few others for good measure.

"Promise me you won't do anything stupid?" Kate said.

"I think it's probably too late to tell me that," Callie said and managed a weak smile.

"I meant when they contact you, just don't agree to meet up or tell them anything that could identify you."

"Don't worry. I'm the over-cautious one, remember?"

"I do, but you have to remember it too."

Neither of them was smiling.

Chapter 14

Later that night, as Callie waited to see if she would get a response to her expressions of interest on the website, she passed the time by searching for information about the use of fire to kill people, and specifically, to kill women. Once again she was stunned simply by the amount of information available on what she had considered to be an unusual way of killing.

According to her research, by far the most common use of arson was to destroy buildings for insurance purposes. Sadly, people sometimes died in these fires because they were there at the wrong time, or because they were firefighters.

More interestingly, fire could also be used to cover up a murder – to destroy DNA or other evidence – which was plausible as a reason in the current killings, it had certainly caused problems for the police. Continuing her search, there was a considerable amount of immensely sad information about bride burning and honour killings that were a form of domestic violence practised in Pakistan, India and Bangladesh, and which had certainly occurred amongst those communities in England as well, but none of the victims was of Asian ethnicity, so this seemed an unlikely explanation of the current murders.

She read discourses on the Koran that stated that death by burning was considered by some to be a martyr's death, with an equal number saying that it was expressly forbidden. News websites also talked of Buddhists who had been known to douse themselves in petrol and set themselves on fire as a form of protest. Older versions of The Old Testament were cited as saying that the sentence for adultery was death and on at least two occasions as death by burning when combined with exacerbating circumstances such as prostitution. So, the murderer could be some sort of religious fanatic, but it was hard to know which particular religion and it seemed it all depended on your interpretation of the various texts on which the beliefs were founded.

Carrying on with her research, Callie then read about Tristan and Iseult, in which some versions have King Mark sentencing the lovers to death at the stake. Burning at the stake was apparently mentioned as a punishment for sexual immorality in old Irish literature, possibly because it had taken inspiration from the Old Testament. She found that many societies have used death by burning as an execution method, usually for treason, heresy or witchcraft but sometimes also for adultery or other sexual transgressions. It was usual for the condemned to be bound to a wooden stake, sometimes alone and sometimes in groups. She also found a chilling reference that burning alive for murder in England was abolished in 1656, but that burning for adultery and heresy remained a legitimate form of punishment, for a while longer, at least.

She stopped at that point because it was getting all too horrible. There were even videos of people being burnt to death if she wanted to see them, but she didn't want to – she didn't want to see them at all. She had seen the results in real life three times now and that was more than enough.

She looked through her notes. The first two victims seemed almost certainly to have been committing adultery, the cars were parked up against wooden stakes to stop them escaping, and they were then burnt to death.

To Callie's mind, the case was pretty much made, even if she didn't have all the evidence. The murderer was killing these women for committing adultery, using his own variation of the medieval punishment of burning them at the stake.

Callie jumped as Kate's throwaway phone pinged, letting her know she had received a text from one of the men she had given the number to on the website.

Her hands shook slightly as she opened the message.

Hey Vicky, thx 4 msg. U look hot. Txt me wot UR doing. Lee xx

Callie was tempted to text back straight away, and ask how old he really was but controlled herself and texted back:

Just playing on internet. Waiting for you to contact me. What RU doing?

She was quite proud of herself for sounding quite flirty, but would Gerry Brown really use textspeak like this, she wondered.

The phone pinged again.

Watching porn like U we shd meet do it 4 real. Im nkd, what RU waring? smthg sexy?

There followed some descriptions of what Lee was currently doing and would like to do to or with Vicky. Callie shuddered. There was no way she could continue this conversation, so she turned the phone off.

"Can't believe Gerry would ever use such bad punctuation or spelling anyway," she told herself before going to bed. At least Lee had taken her mind off the horrific images of women being burnt at the stake. She just hoped they didn't come back to haunt her in the night.

Chapter 15

Callie was incredibly nervous as she approached the police station because she suspected that the only reaction she would get would be laughter. In the damp morning air, she had to admit that it did sound ludicrous. What sort of madman would kill women to punish them for committing adultery? And resurrect a medieval punishment for it, at that? But try as she might, she couldn't come up with an alternative motive that fit the murders as well as this one did, and she was determined to tell Miller, and anyone else who would listen, even if they discounted it out of hand and laughed at her. She could never forgive herself if she didn't tell them and she turned out to be right.

She had been anxious ever since she had decided on this course of action at about four in the morning, having woken after a nightmare. Her rational mind told her it was just indigestion, but as she had tossed and turned she had finally come to the conclusion that she had to tell the police her theory if she was ever going to be able to sleep again, and having made that decision, she promptly fell asleep.

She was in a rush because she wanted to make good her resolution to tell the police about her theory and she needed to do it before morning surgery as there was a practice meeting at lunchtime. She also needed to do it before she had second thoughts.

As she parked her car and headed towards the modern office block that housed the main police station, she wished she had a stock of beta blockers she could raid. She had used them before for practical exams and stressful situations as a student to try and help her maintain her cool professional image and stop her getting flustered or flushed, but she didn't have any left, so she would just have to breathe deeply and hope that Jayne Hales or Nigel were the only ones in at this early hour, or that if Miller was there, Jeffries was not.

Despite her role as a forensic physician, Callie wasn't allowed to roam the building freely and had to be escorted, so she waited in the reception area and was surprised when Miller himself came down to fetch her and take her up to the incident room, and even more surprised when he led her into his office, rather than speaking to her in front of everyone else. She had been dismayed to see the room so full at that early hour, but there was no sign of Jeffries, thank goodness.

As he held the door for her to enter the office and she passed close to him, she could smell a subtle mix of sandalwood and shaving foam for a few moments before she moved into the office where the smells were more redolent of stale food and bodies.

"Sorry about the mess," Miller said as he cleared some files off a chair and invited her to sit down. "Can I get you anything? Tea? Coffee?"

"No, thank you." She sat down and was just formulating what to say in her mind when the door crashed opened again and Jeffries came into the room carrying a chair which he managed to bang against several items of furniture, as well as Callie's leg.

"Oops, sorry, Doc. The room's a bit small," he said as she rubbed her leg, gratified to see that Miller looked annoyed, but not annoyed enough to ask Jeffries to leave.

"So." Miller looked at her. He seemed genuinely interested in what she had come in to say and, like her, slightly anxious about what his sergeant might say in response. She cleared her throat and with an apprehensive look at Jeffries, explained why she was there.

"I know that my simply telling you the gossip that the second victim had used a dating website was not enough, but I have been thinking about the women who have been targeted, and, I know you haven't identified the last one yet, have you?" She looked for confirmation from Miller.

"Not yet."

"But it seems likely that at least the first two women were married and on a night out with a lover." Both Miller and Jeffries nodded.

"And it's possible the third one was married as well. We obviously don't know that yet." She hesitated. This was the moment of no return. Her last chance to stay quiet about her theory and leave with her dignity intact, albeit with a guilty conscience. "I have been thinking about motive." Jeffries looked as if he was about to interrupt, but Callie held up her hand to stop him. "Bear with me, Sergeant, I won't take long to get to the point."

He subsided and allowed her to continue.

"I have been looking at the use of fire as a murder weapon around the world, and discounting arson for monetary gain or to cover up a murder that has already taken place, death by burning is most commonly used as a punishment. A punishment for heresy, treason or adultery."

She let that sink in for a moment and was pleased to note that Miller was giving it some serious thought.

"Come off it, Doc…"

She might have known Jeffries wasn't going to be persuaded.

"…that's an Asian thing, isn't it? None of these women are—"

"That's very interesting." Miller interrupted his sergeant before he could say something politically incorrect.

Callie glared at Jeffries before continuing.

"It isn't only Asian cultures that have used it as a punishment. We used to burn women at the stake for adultery in this country, and the car park posts could be interpreted as symbolic stakes."

Jeffries snorted with derision.

"Blimey, if someone is out there killing people as a punishment for committing adultery, why aren't they killing men rather than women? After all, there's a lot more men fucking around out there than women. Trust me, I know."

Before Callie had time to respond, to tell him, and Miller, that it has traditionally always been the woman that pays, there was a knock at the door and Jayne Hales came in, with a glance of apology at Callie, although she wasn't sure if Jayne was apologising for interrupting her again or for how she had been treated the day before.

"Got an ID on the latest victim, Guv," she said, and both Miller and Jeffries jumped to their feet and headed for the door.

Callie stood as well, she had said what she wanted to say and if they chose to ignore it, then more fool them, she thought as she followed them out of the office.

"Thank you, Doctor," Miller said to her as she headed for the incident room door. "That's a very interesting theory." But he was already turning to Jayne and listening to her as she gave him the information she had gathered.

"Teresa Hardwick, aged twenty-seven, freelance hairdresser," she said as Callie opened the door to leave.

"Married, no children. Husband didn't report her missing straight away because she often stayed out overnight, apparently. He said it was for her work, but I'm not sure why a hairdresser would need to work overnight."

Callie smiled to herself. So, another married woman, lying about where she was and what she was doing. She knew she was right about the motive for these murders, but it wasn't any great consolation if Miller wasn't going to take it seriously.

* * *

"Yes, Linda, I do understand, but given the problems we have recruiting locums who are on the approved list, we have no choice but to do everything we can to keep him."

Hugh Grantham was digging his heels in about Gerry Brown in face of growing complaints, not just from his medical colleagues and the practice nurses, but from the administrative staff as well. Apparently, over his illness, and with no signs of burns as far as a disappointed Callie could see, he had been rude to one of the receptionists this time, and she had been so upset she had left work early, leaving her colleagues having to cover at short notice.

"It's not easy to find good reception staff either."

"Of course not, I admit that Dr Brown needs to brush up his social skills and I will remind him to be polite to practice staff at all times." Hugh looked round the room. He knew the weight of opinion was against him. "But he is a competent GP" – he held up his hand as Callie looked as if she was about to interrupt – "not good, but competent, and I shouldn't need to remind you that if he leaves, we will all need to pull together and cover his work load."

There was a sulky silence. Everyone knew he was right and no one wanted any extra work when they were struggling to cope with what they already had.

"Perhaps it would be a good idea if we were to at least look at the alternatives out there." Gauri was again being practical and pragmatic. Agreement to look at the alternatives might appease some people even though they knew there were no alternatives and it had taken them several months to find Gerry.

"And to have a plan for if he decides to leave us," Callie chipped in. "I don't get the impression he likes it here very much, and we all know there are plenty of other locum jobs going."

Hugh nodded and looked round at his colleagues in the senior team which consisted of the four full-time partners, Callie as a long-term salaried GP, Linda the practice manager and Sally, the senior practice nurse.

"Of course." He turned to Linda. "Can I ask you to ring the agencies again and see if there is anyone available?" Linda made a note of the action allocated to her. "And I will speak to Dr Brown about not upsetting the staff, and I will also draw up an emergency rota and circulate for comment."

He checked that there was no other business, the complaint about Dr Brown having been the final item on the agenda, and left, signalling a mass exodus of others from the meeting, leaving just Callie, Gauri and Linda behind.

"The man has the social skills of a gnat," Linda complained. "I'm not sure Mo will come back after what he said to her."

"What did he say?" Callie asked.

"He suggested that there was no point in him telling patients to lose weight when she clearly ignored the advice."

"Ouch!" Callie said. There was no denying that Mo was morbidly obese, but she was a good worker and the patients loved her.

"Do we know anything about his personal life?" Callie asked, trying not to sound too interested.

"He put married as his status on his personal details form," Linda said with a slight sneer, "but I'm not sure how much that means."

"How do you mean?"

"Rumour has it he has a bit on the side. Stays with her every Wednesday and Saturday. That's why his car's always left here on those nights."

"You wonder what his wife makes of it."

"He probably tells her he's working. Staying in the hospital on call or something. I knew a surgeon who did that."

Callie tried not to look as if she knew exactly who Linda was talking about.

"I have no time for gossiping." Gauri stood up. "There are some visits I must do."

Gauri left and Callie felt a little guilty. Everyone knew that Linda loved to gossip, and Callie encouraged her, so long as it never crossed the line into breaching confidentiality. Her view was that it sometimes paid to know who was sleeping with whom, if only to stop yourself from putting your foot in it.

"His girlfriend must live in the Old Town then, if he leaves his car here," Callie remarked to Linda, fishing for further details. "Do you know who she is?"

"No, I have asked around but got absolutely nowhere, and short of following the man, there's not much more I can do to find out." Linda sighed with genuine regret, and Callie felt much the same. If there was one definite person he was having an affair with, and seeing regularly, it would potentially rule him out as the killer.

* * *

Callie looked at the picture of Teresa Hardwick, victim number three, that Jayne had printed off from her Facebook page. The photo was clearly a selfie, her chin was tipped up to prevent a double chin, eyebrows slightly raised to make her eyes look larger and the obligatory pout looked forced. The result was unnatural and Callie wondered what possessed people to post pictures like this online.

She handed the photo back.

"Is Steve, the DI, okay with you talking to me?"

They were in a small café just down the road from the surgery, that Callie sometimes used for lunch when she wasn't able to get home because of pressures of work or because her mother was there. It was after the lunchtime rush, so she and Jayne Hales had the place to themselves apart from the lady behind the counter who also served as a waitress.

"Of course. Don't worry, I'm not about to jeopardise my career going behind his back. I'm sure he would talk to you himself but he's a bit busy at the moment."

Callie could imagine he was. With three murders almost certainly committed by the same person or persons, journalists were pouring into the town and the pressure on him to find the serial killer before anyone else died was intense.

"He wanted you to know that he wasn't dismissing your theory that this is some kind of punishment for adultery but he's not sure how to investigate that, although he's got me checking to see if anyone connected with Mark's past had a particularly bad divorce and cross checking to see if they have any current contact with him using the TIE process. Unfortunately, that's still quite a few and I'm only a quarter of the way through the very long list of policemen, firemen, social workers, judges and so on from his past. And that list includes Sergeant Jeffries, by the way." A fact which seemed to please Jayne Hales.

Callie knew that TIE stood for trace, interview and eliminate, and she could sympathise with the frustration Jayne was feeling. Too often medicine was like the TIE process – doing investigations to rule out diagnoses one at a time until you hit on the right one.

"Although," Jayne continued regretfully, "Bob's wife divorced him for his adultery not hers, and he knew Mark was in custody, so if he really was the killer trying to frame

Mark, he would have known not to leave his fingerprints at the most recent scene."

"Another soda can?" Callie asked and Jayne nodded. Callie was surprised to hear that news, it definitely looked like someone was trying to frame Mark, unsuccessfully, and she filed that particular piece of information away.

"Oh, congratulations on your promotion to sergeant, by the way." She changed the subject. "And your move out of uniform."

"Thanks. Unfortunately, the secondment to CID is only temporary, but I'm hoping that I do well enough on this investigation to make it permanent some time in the future. Although, I don't think Bob Jeffries would be very happy if I did."

Callie nodded sympathetically. Bob Jeffries probably didn't think Plain Jayne, as she was sometimes called, mostly behind her back, could possibly be a good addition to the team because she wasn't a) pretty or b) a man.

"I'm surprised you have time to come and see me." Callie still wasn't quite sure why Jayne had contacted her and suggested this meeting.

"The boss knows it's not easy for you to come and see him in the incident room." Jayne gave her a sympathetic look. "What, with Bob and his attitude, but he does value your opinions, says you are sometimes spot on, and also, that if you think we aren't taking you seriously you might go off and investigate on your own."

Callie cleared her throat guiltily, took a bite of her hummus and salad sandwich and tried not to look pleased, but she didn't feel quite able to admit to Jayne that she had already done a bit of investigating.

"What about the internet dating site?" she asked instead.

"Not being very cooperative at the moment. As you can imagine, they really don't want any sort of rumour starting that a serial killer is working his way through their clientele."

"Then they should cooperate. If I'm wrong, they can prove it; if I'm right, swift action is their only hope. No chance of forcing their hand with a warrant, I don't suppose?"

Jayne shook her head.

"Insufficient grounds, apparently."

"I take it the identification has been confirmed?" Callie asked.

"Yes. The body is definitely Teresa Hardwick." Jayne sighed. "Not sure how she would feel about the way her husband described her though."

Callie raised an eyebrow questioningly and waited as Jayne finished her mouthful of bacon and egg roll and glanced round to make sure no one could hear what she was about to say. But even the serving lady had disappeared out to the back room where they could hear her washing up the dishes piled there earlier.

"Mr Hardwick knew his wife looked elsewhere to supplement the sex she had at home. He used words to describe her like 'very physical and active', 'high sex drive' and even admitted that he had suggested she should seek treatment for sex addiction."

"So, she's another who might have used the website."

"I know. It's frustrating isn't it?"

* * *

As she hurried back to the surgery after her lunch, Callie gave more thought to the meeting and how useful her burgeoning friendship with Jayne could be. Useful for Steve Miller because she could give him her ideas and any medical input and explanations he needed, useful for Jayne because she had a hotline to her boss's ear and it could further her career, and useful for Callie because she had a way of getting news of how the investigation was going and a way of helping where she could, without getting herself into danger and without having to meet up with Sergeant Jeffries and hear his sexist or inappropriate comments. It had indeed been a clever move of Steve's to send his ambitious new sergeant to her. Callie was surprised to find that she felt just a little disappointed that it also meant that she had no need to contact him directly anymore.

Chapter 16

"They've only gone and questioned Mark again," Helen was telling Callie on the telephone.

"What?" Callie was astounded. "But they know he couldn't have done it. He was in custody, for goodness' sake."

"At least this time they questioned him at his house rather than the station. Honestly, I think the boy's going to have a complete breakdown."

"Do you know why they questioned him?" Callie was cautious about letting Helen know she already knew about the fingerprints, in case she felt she ought to have warned the social worker, and Mark.

"Apparently they found another can with his prints on."

"I can see why they wanted to talk to him then, I mean, the killer has to be someone Mark knows well enough that they can get hold of his discarded cans to leave at the scene."

"Quite, but they could have done it more gently and not make him feel he's stupid or lying when he says he doesn't know who it is." Helen hesitated. "Look, I suggested he come and see you, and he wasn't averse to the idea."

"I thought he was going to change doctors?" Callie queried.

"I think I convinced him that you weren't really anything to do with the police thinking he was a suspect. Besides, he wouldn't have a clue how to do that, poor lamb, so you're still his GP."

"Has he been to see his psychologist again?" Callie couldn't even trust herself to mention Adrian Lambourne's name after his insinuations.

"He was supposed to see him last week, but the doctor kept Mark waiting so long that he walked out. Please, Callie, he needs all the support he can get. At least give him a call, just so he knows you don't hold anything against him, if nothing else."

"Okay, I'll do that tonight, and I'll offer him an appointment tomorrow morning as it's my turn to do a Saturday. But it depends on him agreeing to see me, and on the police not picking him up again," she added.

"I wouldn't put it past them," Helen agreed.

Once Callie had hung up, she took a deep breath. What on earth was Miller thinking? Why was he still hounding Mark? He couldn't possibly still think that he had anything to do with it. Callie wondered if she should mention to Lambourne her worries that the boy might have been abused at some point, but decided that now probably wasn't the time to tackle that particular hang-up. It could wait until he'd recovered from all the police attention.

She was so angry, she had to wait a while to calm down before ringing Mark and leaving a message on the answer machine saying she would hold an appointment at the end of morning surgery for him the next day. It would have been better to have spoken to him, but he was probably too anxious to answer the phone, and who could blame him? She just hoped he listened to her message and felt able to come and see her tomorrow, or she would have to find time to visit him at home again.

* * *

It was a Friday evening and the pubs in the main town were surprisingly packed with people celebrating the end of another working week and the prospect of two days of rest. Even with the persistent rain, groups had spilled out of the bars, huddling under the limited cover, smoking, shouting and laughing. Most of them were already so drunk that Callie suspected they wouldn't remember much of the night at all, unless friends helpfully reminded them with photos of their most embarrassing antics.

She was interested that women were still socialising, seemingly unworried that there was a serial killer around, something they were unlikely to forget given that a number of journalists were making the rounds and asking people if they felt frightened. But even they were growing tired of the endless stream of people saying that yes they were frightened but no they weren't about to change their habits and stay home – that would be, like, letting him win, wouldn't it? Callie wondered if the pubs would be as busy tomorrow night, or would these diehard, fun-loving women take the risk even on a Saturday?

Kate was just locking up her office, juggling keys and umbrella, as Callie arrived to meet her. They too were going for a drink but they would stay together, and then they were going home. Early. Perhaps Callie misjudged the giggling women in the bars around her, perhaps they had also made plans to stick together and make sure they all got home safely and were tucked up in bed nice and early.

"Ugh." Kate looked round and the scenes around them. "Let's hurry over to the civilisation of the Old Town, quick."

"I thought you liked the bars round here?" Callie queried. "You said they were a happy hunting ground, as I remember."

"Well, yes," Kate said, unabashed, "it rather depends on what you are hunting though, and right now I want relaxation, good beer and intelligent conversation. None of which are likely to be found in a sports bar."

Callie had to agree, the noise level in most of the places was such that you couldn't hear yourself speak, let alone what anyone else was saying. Not being a beer drinker, she couldn't comment on their standards, of course, but she had found that most places stocked a decent enough Pinot Grigio these days.

Once they were settled in the warmth of The Stag, drinks and crisps in front of them, they both certainly felt more relaxed.

"Well?" Kate asked, almost beside herself with curiosity, "have you heard from any of them?"

Callie fished Kate's cheap mobile phone out of her bag.

"Four, so far." Callie told her and Kate leant closer to see as they scrolled through the various instant messages that Callie had been sent from the responders from SusSEXtra.

"Ooh, he's a charmer." Kate was reading the short conversation she had had with Lee, and the many, many further messages he had sent trying to persuade her to meet him. Kate was being sarcastic. At least, Callie hoped she was being sarcastic.

"And a dick pic from this one! What a surprise."

Callie grabbed the phone back.

"This one sounds nicer." Callie showed her a message she had had from someone who called himself Lance and took a little while to understand why Kate was sniggering.

"Honestly, I do wish people would just use their real names," she said crossly.

"What? Like Calliope?" Kate responded.

"No! Look, I would never use that name, but Callie, or whatever, something normal, all these names with innuendos are just so, puerile."

They sifted through the various messages.

"Which one was this Lance then?" Kate asked.

"He was the one who said he had a beard although his picture was clean shaven."

"I think you should try and draw him out a bit then. See if it could be Gerry."

Callie sighed.

"I'm not sure this will work."

"Why is that?"

"Well, I don't know how I could tell if it was him. I mean, it was fairly clear that Lee wasn't Gerry. He was virtually illiterate."

"Pretty imaginative though," Kate said with a smile.

"Behave!" Callie threw a cushion at her.

"No, seriously, though. I do know what you mean, Callie. And even if we do recognise him, it isn't evidence that he is the killer, is it?"

"I'd be pretty convinced."

"But would Miller be?"

"Maybe we would do better to pretend to be a bloke and see if we could find the victims, that way we'd have some hard evidence to take to Miller."

"Right. I suggest you try and draw Lance out, see if he says anything that makes you think he might be Gerry. And I'll register as a man and see if I can find any of the victims. Okay?"

"Okay." They chinked glasses. "We have a plan."

"Not necessarily a good plan," Kate qualified. "But still a plan."

Chapter 17

Saturday morning surgeries usually ended at twelve thirty and Mark was late for his appointment. Very late. Callie was just getting ready to go home having decided he wasn't going to come at all, when the receptionist rang through to say that he had arrived, hinting that Callie should refuse to see him. Callie wouldn't. He was anxious enough without her adding to his problems, so she turned her computer back on and went out to the waiting room to collect him, bumping into the practice nurse who had finished her clinic as she did so. The practice nurse took one look at Mark still waiting to be seen and nipped out of the surgery door before Callie could ask her to stay and help.

The receptionist was looking disapproving as well and Callie, knowing the woman was probably keen to get back to her family, offered to let her go home.

"I'll make sure everything's closed up, don't worry."

The receptionist didn't look in the least bit worried as she grabbed her coat and hurried out. If Callie was mad enough to see patients on her own after the surgery should have closed, then it was her own look out.

Callie smiled at Mark as she let him back into her clinic room and gave him a little time to get settled, hoping he would speak when he was ready. She hoped she hadn't made a mistake seeing him in an empty surgery. She had a panic button but it only rang at reception and there was no one there to come running if she needed help. She had to admit he didn't look aggressive, he just looked tired and worried, with blue smudges under his eyes. He was wearing torn jeans and a grubby, misshapen T-shirt revealing his full arm tattoos. He must have been cold walking around without even a jumper, Callie thought.

"How are you feeling?" she asked when she realised they would be there all day if she waited for him to speak.

He shrugged and examined his cuticles.

"It's been a difficult couple of weeks, hasn't it?" she encouraged him.

He nodded.

"But the police know that the fires weren't anything to do with you, don't they?" she persisted. Mark still didn't answer, just plucked at imaginary bits of fluff on his trousers.

"Are you managing to sleep at all?"

He plucked harder at his jeans.

"I didn't do nothing," he suddenly blurted out, and once he started there was no stopping him. "They keep on and on about who knew about my past, where I've been, and that. It's doing my fucking head in. On and on, they go. What do I drink, where did I drink it. I can't think anymore. I just can't fucking think!" He banged the desk as he finished and then looked guilty.

"Sorry," he said, straightening the pen holder that had fallen over.

"That's all right. I can imagine how frustrating it all must be."

He nodded.

"They ask the same stuff, over and over, and, like, I don't know the answer. I can't remember and I can't even remember what I said before."

"That's OK. That's normal. None of us remembers everything, not when we have no reason to think it's important at the time."

"I wish I could. But, like, the more they ask, the more I dunno, I mean, I feel like maybe I should, like, make it up, get them off my back–"

"No!" Callie interrupted quickly, then continued in a more even, reassuring tone. "That wouldn't be a good idea." She paused, she didn't want to say anything that might alarm him further, like he could get in trouble if he lied. "It could stop them finding whoever is doing this, and that's the most important thing. They will leave you alone once they have this guy."

Mark looked at her, unsure.

"They don't fucking believe me, but I just, like, don't remember stuff. Sorry."

Callie was surprised that he was apologising for swearing and it reinforced her opinion that despite the clothes, the terrible home life and the tattoos, Mark was a good lad at heart.

"I can talk to them, if you like, Mark. Make sure they understand?"

Mark nodded.

"Thanks," he mumbled.

"Now." Callie was back to being briskly business like. "How are you coping? Have you had any more panic attacks?"

Mark shook his head.

"I hear there were some problems with Dr Lambourne running late for your last appointment. Have you made another one?"

Mark nodded.

"He sent one in the post, but I don't see the point. He don't do no good. The man's a prick, and I didn't believe what he said about you."

Mark looked out from under his floppy fringe, checking that Callie believed him.

"I am sure he was doing what he thought was for the best." Callie was determined to remain professional and not let Mark know just how much she agreed with him. "And I think it would be a good idea if you continued to see him, see if he can help. After all, Helen seemed to think he was doing some good before. Okay?"

"'kay," Mark said.

"I don't want to change your pills if you are not having any more attacks and you are going back to see Dr Lambourne."

Mark nodded.

"I'm alright really, Doc. Now I know they aren't going to lock me up again."

"Good, that's settled then. Now, don't forget, you can call if you need to see me or the duty doctor, anytime." Callie showed him out and watched him walk down the street, jeans hung so low she could see the make of his underwear. Once he was out of sight, she heaved a sigh of relief, knowing that seeing Mark in an empty surgery could have so easily gone horribly wrong.

As she pulled out of the car park, and drove down the High Street towards home, Callie saw Gerry Brown signalling to turn into the street and presumably, park his car in the surgery space. Callie was tempted to stop and run back and confront him, to ask him what he did every Saturday night, but an impatient toot from the car behind reminded her that she was blocking the road and she drove on, thinking about the fact that today was a Saturday, and wondering if there would be another murder that night.

She was almost home when her phone rang. She pulled into the side of the road and was relieved to see it was the police station. One of her regulars had been picked up and needed attention. Dani was probably in his thirties and was originally from an Eastern European country, but no one was quite sure which, any more than they knew how long he had been in Britain. He said he came to find work, but whether he had ever found any was unclear. He had lived on the streets of Hastings, begging, and drinking, for many years now and was regularly picked up for being drunk and disorderly. He was considered a nuisance more than a threat but, despite offers, he resisted all attempts to help him dry out or to re-house him, claiming he needed his freedom, not a roof.

Today, he had apparently relieved himself in George Street, in full view of a number of tourists, and unfortunately splashing a basket of lavender bags on display outside a craft shop as he did so. Once arrested, he fell asleep in the van taking him to the police station and they had difficulty rousing him, hence the call to Callie. Having checked that Dani really was just drunk and had no signs of injury or illness warranting transfer to hospital, Callie left him to sleep it off and persuaded the desk sergeant to take her through the locked door to CID where she made her own way up to the incident room. She had been unsure whether speaking to Miller about Mark would actually do any good, but being called in to see Dani had made the decision to try easier.

The incident room was quieter than she expected. She hoped that meant that everyone was out following up leads, warning any women who hadn't got the message yet and doing their best to find the killer. The only person she knew in the room was Nigel, who looked up from his computer and quickly shut down the page he had been looking at but not before Callie had seen the distinctive logo of SusSEXtra.

"How's it going?" she asked him. "Have you managed to find any of our victims on there?"

Nigel cleared his throat and looked round the almost empty room guiltily. No one was paying them any attention.

"We've confirmed that the second victim was registered on the site, Dr Hughes, like you told us, but, um..."

Callie had a slight panic, what if he had found her on there and recognised her?

"That was because her name came up as a possible match to my want list and she had used her own picture and her middle name," he continued. "But I haven't managed to be matched with any of the others so far, as far as I know." He looked round guiltily.

"You've gone on as a client?" Callie was surprised and quickly went through the list of people she had contacted from there. The last thing she wanted was for her alter ego Vicky to be having covert conversations with a policeman.

"Um, yes, well, the website owners haven't yet responded to our request for a client list, so in the meantime..."

"And did you find anyone else interesting on there?"

But Miller came into the room before he could reply.

"Dr Hughes?" he looked surprised to see her and she was saddened to see how tired he looked. His sleeves were rolled up and he had loosened his tie to undo the top button, and his hair looked as though he had been running his hands through it. The strain of this investigation was definitely beginning to take its toll.

"I was seeing a prisoner and I just thought whilst I was here, well, um, could I have a word?"

He ushered her into his office and cleared a chair for her.

"What can I do for you?" he asked.

"I promised Mark Caxton I would speak to you."

He couldn't disguise a flash of irritation.

"Please, tell me you haven't been seeing him alone."

"He is my patient and we have a very good system for summoning help in the surgery." She didn't add that it only worked if there were staff there to be summoned.

"He has told you he is no longer a suspect, hasn't he?"

"Yes, of course. And he knows that you just keep asking questions because you think he must know the killer or have had some contact with him."

Miller relaxed.

"Good."

"But he is still finding it quite stressful having to answer all your questions. He feels you don't believe him when he says he can't remember."

Miller sighed and rubbed his face.

"I know. It's not that I don't believe him, it's just incredibly frustrating that he can't seem to tell us what he was doing only a few days ago."

"The more pressure you put on him to remember things, the less he can. He gets into a panic and his mind goes blank. Look, if you want to talk to him again, why don't you get Helen or me to be with him. Just so that he feels like there's someone there to support him."

"Of course. Yes, I'll do that. Where it's possible, that is."

"I realise that it won't always be practical," she conceded, "but please, don't let Sergeant Jeffries anywhere near him."

He nodded his understanding and stood to show her out, but hesitated when she didn't immediately stand herself.

"I was just wondering how things were going?" she asked and he hesitated for a moment, before deciding to answer.

"We're trying to get a warrant to get the records of the company that runs the website, but with only one confirmed victim on there, well, who knows if we will get it?"

"Won't the company co-operate without a warrant? Surely they don't want to be the reason another woman gets murdered?"

"I spoke to the owner, a Ms Hepton-Lacey, but she felt her hands were tied. Her lawyers had advised her that without a warrant she could be sued by anyone who felt she had breached their right to privacy by letting us see their details."

Callie could see the problem.

"Could you not issue a warning? That you think he meets his victims online, at least, even if you can't name the specific website?"

"Apparently not. We don't want to frighten the public, or damage anyone's business, do we? We might end up getting sued ourselves."

Miller was unable to keep the bitterness from his voice.

"That's just ridiculous," she retorted angrily. "The public are pretty scared anyway and if a woman dies tonight and the police have not done everything possible to stop it, I would imagine you might be in trouble anyway."

Miller threw his hands up.

"You don't need to tell me."

"Who do I need to tell, then? Because, believe me, I am quite happy to give the Chief Constable a piece of my mind if that's what it takes."

Looking at the righteous indignation on her face, Miller could quite believe she would too, and he couldn't help but smile.

"What?" she asked, angry that he didn't seem to be taking her seriously.

"God, but she's beautiful when she's angry, isn't she, boss?"

Both Miller and Callie turned guiltily at the sarcastic voice from the door interrupting them and then scowled when they saw Jeffries standing there.

"But don't let me stop you, Doc," Jeffries continued, coming into the office. "I'd pay to see you give the Chief Constable a piece of your mind, especially as the CPS just turned down the request for a warrant to get SusSEXtra's client list."

* * *

"The women of Hastings are locking their doors and staying in tonight, frightened to go out, knowing that a vicious killer is stalking the streets, picking them off, one by one." The reporter finished as the camera panned round at the near empty streets in the town centre.

Callie pushed her plate of prawn stir fry away from her in disgust. It wasn't that it tasted awful, it was the endless ghoulish speculation about the possibility of another death that seemed to be on every television channel that was putting her off her food. Would there be another Saturday night murder? She sincerely hoped not but she knew she wouldn't sleep tonight, expecting to be called at dawn to pronounce another woman dead. At least the female population were staying in if the report was true, although Callie wouldn't put it past the reporters to have just shifted everyone out of sight for effect.

Callie switched channels as the special feature news programme cut back to the studio. She didn't want to watch the picture parade of victims she had come to know too well, and the endless sanctimonious platitudes about them: good wife, perfect mother, best friend ever, I'll never find anyone like her again. She had heard it all before, the women had become saints overnight, no one willing to speak ill of the dead. Everyone who had ever met any of the victims, or who thought they might have, queuing up for the fifteen seconds of fame, weeping and wailing in an effort to convince the world of how traumatised they were. Callie chastised herself for being so cynical and channel-surfed hoping to find something different, something interesting enough to distract her from her tense wait for the telephone to ring, but she couldn't find anything and switched the television off in disgust.

She would have liked to chat to Kate, even over the phone, but Kate was out at a dinner party given by one of her many friends. Kate was funny and gregarious and found herself in almost constant demand at dinner parties to balance any single men who had been invited. Callie found herself invited by friends as well, but usually because they were trying to pair her off with some completely awful relative they were desperate to see settle down, so she rarely accepted.

Callie checked her watch. Nine o'clock and the killer was probably meeting his victim, buying her drinks, GHB at the ready, planning how to get her into the pre-stolen car he would have waiting outside. A thought occurred to her: if he was busy with his fourth victim, even with texts and instant messaging on his phone, he wouldn't be able to manage a conversation whilst he was chatting up another victim. She hurriedly fetched her laptop and signed in to the SusSEXtra website, sending messages to all those who had messaged her and then sent instant messages from her phone to any that she had conversed with, including the unlovely Lee, and waited to see which of them got back to her.

By ten-thirty she had chatted with ten men, mainly using WhatsApp as this seemed to be the messaging service most favoured by the majority. She was surprised that the list of men responding included Lee, who seemed completely unabashed by her previous put downs. Like a puppy he was up and bouncing, full of energy, wanting to meet, and do a lot of other things which he described in great detail, but which Callie quickly deleted. She kept on her flirty sexting with each of the men long enough to convince herself that it was unlikely that they were also holding a conversation with a woman who was with them. Not a woman they were trying to chat up, anyway. They could, of course, be with a long-term partner and were just ignoring them and concentrating on their phones, as seemed to be the norm nowadays, even when out for a drink or dinner. Callie drew up a list of all the men who had contacted her and crossed off the ten names she had managed to get responses from in the last hour. Only another twenty-two suspects then.

* * *

He sat, furiously playing with his glass. How dare she be late. The bitch. How dare she stand him up like this? He checked his phone again, at least he had developed his relationship with Vicky whilst he waited, but that was scant consolation for a wasted night. He stood up to leave the packed pub. It seemed full of people who were there because it wasn't a town centre pub and they thought they would be safer. Such stupidity. He had never used a venue in the town centre because of the ubiquity of CCTV. He checked his watch again. He had given the whore enough time, she clearly wasn't coming. He ignored the comments from the couple who had been waiting for his table as they slid into his seat the moment he left it. Perhaps it was a good thing the bitch hadn't turned up: sitting alone and blocking a table, they would have been able to remember him if she had eventually arrived. He made a note to himself. If the place was packed, do not occupy a table until the date had arrived, even if that meant there were none free. They could always find a space outside.

He had to think about what to do with the car. He could leave it somewhere, open, hoping that it would be stolen, but what if it wasn't? It would have his DNA all over it without the cleansing effect of fire. If he held onto the car, hid it in his garage for the next time he needed it, that was a risk as well. What if anyone saw it there? Or him driving it back? How could he explain away a stolen car with fake plates? It was too direct a link to the murders. No, he had to get rid of the car, stick to the plan, burn it like the others. Only this time, the car would be empty.

Chapter 18

Callie woke with a start and looked at her watch in surprise. It was nine o'clock on a Sunday morning and she could hear church bells as well as the usual raucous screech of the seagulls. She reached across and quickly checked her phone. Perhaps she'd slept through the ring, or the battery had died overnight, but no, the screen burst into life and showed she hadn't missed anything. There had been no early morning call to pronounce life extinct.

As she picked out her clothes for the day she thought through the implications of her unbroken sleep. There had been no call. Therefore, there had been no killing. Unless they just hadn't found the body yet. The killer might have chosen somewhere so remote that it would take a while before the body was found.

She picked up the pile of clothing and hurried back into the living room, grabbing the remote from the coffee table and switching the television on. She wasn't sure why she was checking as there wouldn't be anything on the news if they hadn't found the car or a body yet, would there?

She watched the headlines as she made a pot of English breakfast tea, using loose leaves and warming the pot carefully in her regular Sunday morning ritual. She might even walk down to the seafront for a leisurely coffee and a read of the Sunday papers. Except that the papers would be full of the murders.

On the television news channel, there was a lengthy discussion taking place on whether the killing spree had stopped. The debate consisted of more speculation than fact, and Callie was just pouring herself a second cup of tea when there was some breaking news and the anchor woman cut to a reporter rushing breathlessly into a country car park. Callie sat forward and gripped her bone china mug so tightly there was a danger it would break.

Having got the wreckage of a burnt-out car into frame behind him, the reporter continued his story. Callie looked closely and could make out the blackened remnants of what appeared to be a small hatchback and tried to work out where the car park was, but she didn't think it was anywhere she knew.

"Another Saturday night and another burnt-out car, Laura, and as the fire brigade and police responded early this morning, they feared there had been another murder. Thankfully, when they got here, they found out that this time, there wasn't a body inside."

Callie hadn't realised she had been holding her breath until then, but let it out in a huge sigh of relief, and put her tea down. She imagined Miller must have reacted in a similar way when he was told that there wasn't another burnt corpse of a woman inside the car.

"Are the police connecting this to the previous incidents?" Laura the anchorwoman was asking her colleague.

Callie could see Colin the crime scene manager in the background, well away from the car and indicating to a constable that he should move people back. The moment he realised he was on camera, Colin ducked out of sight and a police constable appeared from off camera rolling out crime scene tape, forcing the reporter and camera man to move further away from the car. As they moved back,

Callie saw Chris Butterworth, the fire investigator, standing, hands on hips, and looking around the area intently. Then the camera moved and focussed on the reporter again.

"The car park venue, in an isolated area of the countryside, would suggest that this is the work of the same man, Laura, but the police are keeping an open mind at this stage."

Somehow, Callie doubted that any police officers had spoken to the reporter, let alone told him that they were keeping an open mind and she suspected that the only reason he knew there was no body in the car was the lack of a mortuary van, or herself, at the scene. And remote car parks were often where cars were dumped and torched. The killer wasn't the only arsonist to use them.

"Thanks, Giles," Laura said to the reporter before turning back to the studio camera, her face serious and focussed. "We will, of course, keep you updated on developments in Hastings as they occur," she said, before finally allowing herself a little smile. "And now over to Casey for the weather."

Callie switched the television off and wondered about why the killer hadn't added to his victims. The car could be coincidental, of course, just left by a bunch of joy riders this time. If so, it wouldn't take Colin and Chris long to uncover the discrepancies. Callie rubbed a hand across her forehead, she just hoped Mark wasn't involved. He torched cars for pleasure and to relieve stress, and he had undoubtedly been under stress recently. The more she thought about it, the more it seemed possible that if this car wasn't the work of the killer, then Mark might be the culprit and she knew he would find himself under a whole lot more pressure pretty quickly if that was the case, and even if it wasn't. Although she wasn't on call as a GP this weekend, perhaps a pre-emptive visit was in order.

* * *

Callie knocked at the door of Mark's home and waited. She could hear him inside and called out.

"Mark, it's me. Dr Hughes. Can you open the door please?"

There was a bit more shuffling from inside and then the door opened and Mark peered out. He looked relieved to see she was alone and opened the door wider to let her in.

He showed her into the untidy sitting room and she sat, or rather perched on the worn and stained sofa after he had cleared her a space.

Mark sat on an armchair and began the in-depth study of his cuticles again.

"I wondered if you had heard the news this morning?" she asked tentatively.

He shook his head, but looked up for a moment, interested.

"Was there another one? Another woman burnt, like?"

"No, well, there was another car fire, but there wasn't anyone in the car this time."

Mark nodded.

"That's okay then." He went back to picking at his fingers.

Callie was more than a little anxious about her next question.

"Um, I don't want you to take this the wrong way," she started and leant forward with what she hoped was a reassuring smile as he looked at her at last. "I don't suppose it was you this time?"

For a moment he didn't understand what she was saying but then his eyes widened as it finally registered.

"What!" he shouted. "You think I done this?"

"No, no. Not necessarily." She tried to reassure him. "I don't think that but I just need to be sure so that I can head the police off–"

"The police, no!" He was really agitated now and, too late, Callie realised that her visit was having the opposite effect to the one she had hoped for. "Dr Lambourne was right. You're trying to stitch me up!"

He jumped up and Callie forced herself to sit still, hoping that this would help cool the situation down.

"Calm down, Mark. I came here to help you. The police are going to have to question you, they are probably already on their way, but if we can–" But he wasn't listening and ran out of the room and out of the house, slamming the door behind him.

With a sigh, Callie got up and headed for the front door to leave, berating herself for having made matters worse rather than better. She heard some shouting and as she opened the door came face to face with Miller and Jeffries, who seemed to be holding a struggling Mark in a bear hug.

"Dr Hughes!" Miller looked surprised to see her.

Callie nodded to him but went straight to her patient and went to touch him gently on the arm before remembering that this might trigger a more violent reaction and hastily dropping her hand.

"I didn't call them, Mark, but I did know they would want to question you. That's why I came to speak to you. To help you." Her words seemed to have a calming effect on the boy and he stopped struggling, whilst he tried to think about what she was saying.

"Why don't we go inside and get this cleared up?" She turned to Miller. "He didn't even know there had been another car fire," she explained. "He got frightened when he heard, that's why he was running away."

Miller decided to follow Callie's quiet reassuring lead.

"We just want to ask where you were so that we can rule you out, Mark." He gestured to Jeffries to let the boy go, and, reluctantly, he did.

"Like Dr Hughes said, why don't we go inside?"

* * *

Miller and Jeffries quickly established that Mark had been with his girlfriend staying at her nan's overnight and that he had only just got back to his home when Callie arrived. Jeffries went outside to get the alibi confirmed and Miller continued to question Mark, with Callie there as his appropriate adult.

"You know what we talked about? That we found a can at each scene?" Miller asked Mark gently.

Mark shrugged.

"A brand of drink that we know you like."

"Lots of people drink it. Gives you energy," Mark said, anxious to make sure Miller wasn't trying to put the blame back on him.

"Of course. But your prints were on the cans at the previous sites, and we will find out soon enough if that's the case with a can we discovered near the car this morning."

Callie registered this new fact. The killer obviously didn't know that Mark had been eliminated as a suspect if he left it there to implicate him.

"But I didn't put the cans there." Mark was beginning to get agitated and Miller hastened to calm him.

"We know that, but whoever is planting them is trying to get you into trouble. Do you understand what I am saying, Mark?"

Mark nodded.

"Do you have any idea why anyone would want to do that?"

Mark shook his head.

"It seems mad," he said, clearly not having any idea why anyone who wasn't mad would do this to him.

Miller reached into his pocket and pulled out a piece of paper. He unfolded it and showed Mark what was on it. It had three pictures on it.

"Do you recognise these?" Miller asked Mark gently.

Mark nodded.

"They're match book covers," he leaned forward. "Nice ones." He looked closely and then nodded to Callie. "They're pretty, aren't they?"

"Yes," Callie agreed.

"I've got that one, and that one." He pointed to two of the pictures, and then the third. "But not that one." He looked at Miller. "Will I get them back?"

"I don't know, Mark, probably not," the detective said, actually thinking that there was absolutely no chance of him getting them back.

Mark looked saddened as he realised his collection had finally gone.

Miller pointed back at the paper.

"These are the match books used in the three murders. The lab has managed to bring up enough detail with infrared photography to identify them."

Mark looked at the pictures and shook his head in dismay.

"I never used nice ones," he told them. "I used the boring ones and the ones I had more than one of. I would never have used ones as nice as these. That's mental, that is. And I never had that last one. I've never seen one like that, I would've kept it if I had."

Miller changed tack.

"When you set cars alight before, did you leave drink cans at the site, as, you know, a sort of calling card?"

Mark looked at Miller as if he was now the madman in their midst.

"No!"

Miller just looked at him.

"I mean, I might have left one, you know, by mistake, but I wouldn't do it deliberate, like. I didn't want to get caught."

"So," Miller persisted, "where do you think he gets these cans with your prints on?"

"I don't know," Mark seemed genuinely perplexed. "I mean, I drink them all the time, but I always bin them, I don't litter." Once again confirming to Callie that at heart he was a good boy.

Jeffries came back into the room and nodded to Miller. The alibi was solid. Mark couldn't have torched the car.

* * *

As they walked out to their cars, leaving Mark to himself for the rest of his Sunday, Callie turned to Miller.

"Why were you asking about the cans when he set fires previously? Is it because you think someone has got hold of them from those events and is leaving them at the current sites?"

"Are you suggesting a copper nicked them from the evidence store and planted them at the scene?" Jeffries came back aggressively.

"No, but–" Callie retorted angrily but Miller stopped her before it escalated into a full-scale row between the two of them.

"Even if he had left them in the past, which he says he didn't, these cans couldn't be from then, because they are the new design and the batch numbers on the cans narrow them down to a recent purchase."

Jeffries and Callie both glared at each other, neither willing to apologise.

"Can you narrow it down to where they were bought?" Callie asked Miller.

"Only to a local cash and carry who supplied them to about forty different shops in the area."

"Pretty much every corner shop in Hastings," Jeffries added grumpily, and Callie could relate to his unhappiness this time. They had obviously tried hard to find the source.

"If it's not something Mark used to do when he set fires, then the killer has simply invented a new calling card and he must be someone close to Mark, because he seems to be able to get drink cans with his prints on them without any trouble," Miller continued. "We need to check who has access to his rubbish bags both here and at places he frequents like the youth centre."

"What about the match books? As Mark said, they aren't common or garden ones. Can you trace who bought them?" Callie added.

"It's hard because of the number of collectors out there. Jayne was checking them out, but we will need to escalate that search, check if anyone even remotely connected to Mark has bought any on any of the online sites or from a dealer."

"Don't tell me, and cross check with the lists of people who know the MO, have access to the rubbish and are divorced?" Jeffries looked dismayed at the thought of yet more lists. "That could take a sodding lifetime."

Miller nodded and added with a slightly malicious smile, "Modern policing, Bob. It's all about endless boring data searches."

Callie was pleased that they were checking names against so many criteria, searching for connections. Surely one name would come to the fore soon? The trouble was, as Sergeant Jeffries had pointed out with the unnecessary expletive, it could take a very long time, a very long time indeed.

"The killer must realise by now that you no longer suspect Mark, so why continue to leave the cans?" It seemed peculiarly vindictive to Callie.

"That's a good question," Miller responded.

"Just to fuck with us," Jeffries added.

"And to let us know he's still out there; that he hasn't stopped."

Callie couldn't suppress a slight shiver down her spine at Miller's words and the thought that more women could, and probably would, die before they caught this man. She gave herself a mental shake. There was nothing she could do about that.

"Right," she said, "I'm off to enjoy the rest of my Sunday in relative peace, I hope. Goodbye." She walked back to where she had parked her car, leaving them both; Jeffries still looking daggers at her retreating back, and

Miller looking at her with an altogether different expression on his face.

Chapter 19

Having spent what was left of her Sunday cathartically cleaning her home in an effort to get the murders out of her mind, Callie had made a decision, about the murders, at least. She needed to find out if Gerry was involved, if only to put her mind at rest. She couldn't very well voice her suspicions to the police because she had no real grounds for them. She could imagine Miller's reaction if she told him that she suspected Gerry to be a serial killer because he was a creep or that he was not a very good doctor, let alone because he parked his car at the surgery every Wednesday and Saturday nights. No, she had to find out if there was any basis to her suspicion first.

It seemed pretty hopeless trying to prove or disprove Gerry Brown's involvement through the website. Especially since she couldn't even rule out the ones who had responded on Saturday as no murder had taken place. How could she ever know if any of the men she had been talking to were him? Unless she agreed to meet them and there was no way she was going that far. It had been whilst cleaning her little-used oven, that she had decided to stop trying to talk to him through the website and to take the radical step of speaking to him in person. She wasn't going to ask him outright if he was a serial killer, of course, but just get to know him better and see if she could find any other indications that he was the murderer. Something concrete she could take to Miller without him laughing at her.

Once she got to the surgery on Monday morning, Callie checked Gerry's morning list and worked out when he would be finishing. There was no point trying to speak to him before he started surgery as he wouldn't want to begin late any more than she would, but if she could catch him once he had finished and before he rushed off to wherever it was he disappeared to between clinics, she might just get to speak to him. Of course, that meant she would have to take a break from her own patients as her surgery was longer, but if she could just try and get a bit ahead and then nip up at the relevant time for a cup of coffee, it could work.

Her plan started well, her first three patients were all on time and only had one problem each for her to deal with: a blood pressure check, a medication review and a patient needing referral, but then the fourth patient came in armed with a list and Callie's heart sank. There was no way she was going to get through a list of problems in the allotted ten minutes. And she didn't, so she missed Gerry. He had disappeared for his lunch break long before she made it up to the office.

"Why did you want to see Gerry?" Linda asked when Callie checked if he was still there.

"Oh, you know, I just thought I'd try and get to know him better."

Linda raised an eyebrow, clearly not buying that explanation.

"It's this thing about leaving his car here twice a week, my curiosity is getting the better of me and I really want to know why he does it. So, I thought I'd try asking him, in a roundabout way, of course."

Linda laughed. Curiosity was something she could understand.

"I don't suppose you know, do you?" Callie asked, hoping Linda had managed to find out, but she shook her head, disappointed not to be able to shed any light on the reason. "I mean, you'd think his wife would object."

"Ah, well. I might not know why he leaves his car here, but I have found out that he and his wife have split up and that's why he's doing locum work. Well, one of the reasons, anyway."

"The other being?"

"The cause of his marital split." Linda leaned in confidentially and checked no one else was listening before whispering, "He had an affair with a patient."

Callie was genuinely shocked. That was an absolute no-no for doctors.

"That explains a lot," Callie told Linda. "He's probably still seeing the woman, too."

"Not sure about that," Linda said. "According to the practice manager at his old surgery, the affair only came to light when the patient complained to the surgery that she had chucked him but he wouldn't leave her alone."

That fitted in well with how he had reacted when Kate had tried to break free. He was not one to take rejection lightly.

"And then his wife threw him out, unsurprisingly," Linda continued. "She's some high-powered internet millionaire, with a very good legal team, not to mention something that she can hold over him and threaten to get him struck off for if he didn't do as she wanted. So, he lost his wife, his girlfriend and his home – everything in one fell swoop. He's probably ended up having to pay her alimony as well."

Linda seemed to take great delight from this, and Callie did too if she was honest – it was nice to hear of someone getting their comeuppance like that, but had it tipped him over the edge? Turned him into a killer? It seemed a possibility that she couldn't discount.

"And I'll tell you the final irony." Linda had really got into her stride and Callie certainly wasn't about to stop this useful flow of gossip. "His ex-wife made her money out of one of those dating websites, and not just a find-your-perfect-match sort of one, but a no-strings-attached one that actively encourages married people to use it for affairs. It's got a name that says it all, now what was it?" Linda thought for a second, struggling to remember.

"SusSEXtra?" Callie asked helpfully.

"Yes, that's it!" Linda agreed. "How on earth did you know what it was called?" she added, suddenly suspicious.

"Oh, it cropped up in another conversation." Callie tried to sound innocent, but she wasn't sure she had convinced Linda, who looked as if she was about to question her more closely.

"Anyway, must get on." Callie grabbed her basket of paperwork and hurried into the doctors' office.

* * *

Once sure she was alone in the office, Callie logged onto a computer and opened up a web browser. She needed to find out more about SusSEXtra, or SSE as some of the users seemed to call it, probably because they got fewer funny looks if they mentioned it in public. Others referred to it as SSex but she didn't feel as comfortable with that abbreviation. Companies House gave her the information on the chief executive officer and board that she needed. The person in charge and owner of the company was listed as a Ms Amelia Hepton-Lacey, and, if she was indeed Gerry's ex, Callie wasn't in the least surprised that she hadn't changed her name to Brown when she married him. Hepton-Lacey sounded very classy, although it was hard to be sure if Amelia was actually posh, she might have changed her name by deed poll for all Callie knew. Companies House also gave Callie the registered address for the company and from there Callie had little difficulty getting a contact number. Grabbing her list of visits, she hurried out.

* * *

Callie sat at her dining table holding her phone, with the note of the SuSEXtra company contact number and an untouched sandwich in front of her. For once she was not distracted by the spectacular view out of her window.

She took a deep breath and dialled.

"Hello, SSE, can I help you?" a woman's voice answered after only two rings.

"Oh, hello. Could I speak to Amelia Hepton-Lacey, please?" Callie replied.

"I'm afraid she's not in the office at the moment. Can I take a message?"

For a moment Callie was floored. She hadn't really thought through what she was going to say next.

"Um, my name is Dr Hughes and I'm with the police," she finally said, crossing her fingers. It wasn't actually a lie, she was, after all, a police FME, but there was no way her role covered what she was currently doing. "Can I ask who I'm talking to?"

"Jenny Harris. I'm the office manager. Who did you say you were?" Jenny countered.

"Dr Callie Hughes. I work as a consultant with the police, I can give you a number to contact to check my credentials if you would like?" Callie hoped Jenny wouldn't want to do that, because she wasn't quite sure who she could ask to do that for her.

"No, that's okay, Dr Hughes, I can see you listed on the police website."

"Of course," Callie had to stop herself from sounding surprised. She had had no idea that she was listed on the Hastings Police website. Jenny was clearly very efficient if she had found this out so quickly. That was probably bad news for Callie, but she pressed on regardless. "As you know, we are looking into the possibility that the murdered women were accessed through the website. It's obviously vital that we are sure if this is a real possibility or if it's a dead end, so to speak, and I wonder if you could help me?"

"It's terrible, isn't it? To think of what happened to them?" Jenny seemed genuinely distressed.

"Which is why it's so important we know how he is contacting these women. Of course, it may not be through your website, but we absolutely have to eliminate it."

"Of course, and I'm honestly happy to do what I can," Jenny said helpfully. "But Ms Hepton-Lacey has left clear instructions that we are not to divulge the names or details of any of our clients to the police without a warrant. We could be liable if we did." She sounded quite upset at not being able to help more.

"I quite understand and I wouldn't want to put you in a difficult position," Callie agreed, and decided to push that little bit more as the woman at the end of the phone seemed to want to help, if she could. "But I am sure that since you knew of our interest, you will have done a bit of digging and checked the victims' names against your client list, wouldn't you?"

"Well, the client list is usually a lot of silly made up names, but the payment details are more accurate," Jenny admitted, so she clearly had been checking out the victims. "And I can quite understand how important it is for you to know, and I'd really like to help," Jenny left that hanging slightly in the air as a hint to Callie that she was willing to co-operate.

"So, would it be possible for me to say the names one at a time, and if that person is a client you cough or something?" Callie suggested.

"How about I cough if they aren't?" Jenny countered.

"Okay, Sarah Dunsmore." Callie waited, there was no cough. "Carol Johnson." As expected, there was no cough after Carol's name. "Teresa Hardwick." Callie held her breath – this was the crunch moment. No cough again. Callie waited, in case, but the silence lengthened and there was no doubt in her mind.

"All three were clients?" Callie just wanted to be certain.

"You might like to think that, but I couldn't possibly comment," Jenny paraphrased the well-known quote from House of Cards. Callie thanked her profusely for her help before ending the call.

She sat there, with the phone in her hand, knowing that she should call Miller, but at the same time looking for reasons not to make the call. In the end, she couldn't think of any, well, none that really stood up to scrutiny, so she dialled his number and was slightly relieved to get an answerphone message.

"Hi, this is Callie," she said quickly, as she hated speaking to machines, always coming across as incoherent. "I have had confirmation that all three women used the, um, the SSE website" – somehow she really couldn't come out with its full name – "and also wanted to talk to you about the website owner's husband. Can you give me a call back?"

She ended the call and looked at her sandwich. She really wasn't feeling very hungry. She checked her watch and realised she was going to have to get a move on if she was going to do her visits and get back to the surgery on time. She grabbed her bag and, after a moment's hesitation, picked up the sandwich, popping it into a plastic bag as she hurried out of the door.

Chapter 20

Callie was surprised that Miller hadn't called back by the time she had finished evening surgery, but not half as surprised as she was to see him sitting in the waiting room when she came out with her basket of notes and papers.

"Dr Hughes?" he said as he stood, formal and professional as always in front of the public, even though that was only the receptionist and a couple of stragglers who were watching them with great interest. "I wondered if you had time for a word?"

"Um, of course, do you want to come in?" She indicated her consulting room, but he didn't move towards it.

"I thought perhaps we could go out, if you don't mind. I could do with something to eat."

He looked at her basket and Callie realised that the uneaten sandwich was still there, clearly visible, proof that she hadn't had lunch either. Again.

"Of course, that would be good, actually. I'll just sort these and I'll be with you in five minutes, is that okay?"

Callie hurried up to the office and dealt with her paperwork in record time, chucked the sandwich in the bin and nipped into the ladies to make sure her hair wasn't a mess, before going back down to the entrance where Miller was waiting for her.

"Ready," she said, slightly breathlessly, and went through the door that Miller was holding open for her, ignoring the raised eyebrows of the receptionist who was watching her intently, making sure she remembered every detail of the encounter to share with Linda, no doubt.

* * *

Miller hardly said a word as they walked down the High Street, only giving Callie monosyllabic answers to her questions about how he was and how the investigation was going. It was only a short walk to Porters, where he ushered her in and sat her at a corner table before going to the bar to order a glass of Pinot Grigio for Callie and a beer for himself. Callie was getting quite nervous about his unusual recalcitrance by the time he returned with the drinks.

"So," he finally said once they were both settled. "Tell me how you know all three victims used the SSE website?"

"Well, I spoke to someone who works there and got her to confirm it."

Callie was glad he was referring to it as SSE, as she really didn't want the other customers getting the wrong idea about the two of them if they happened to overhear the conversation.

"And is this person willing to make a statement to that effect?"

Callie cleared her throat and fiddled with the stem of her glass. Despite his rigid control, she could tell he was angry.

"Um, no, she can't because she is under express orders from her boss not to."

"And what, exactly, do you expect me to do with this piece of unattributable information?"

"I don't know," she snapped back. "I had thought you would be grateful that you were at least on the right track as you tried to get a warrant to see the client details. I might even have thought that this anonymous information might help you get that warrant."

He paused for a moment, to collect his thoughts and let her cool down.

"Which it did, thank you. But–"

"It did?" she interrupted, a smile lighting up her face. "That's brilliant." For once she really felt that she had been useful. So often, in both her jobs, she felt that she was just putting a sticking plaster over a major wound. She very rarely felt that she had made a real difference.

"Yes, but, as I was saying, Dr Hughes, Callie, you can't go around interfering like that. It may have helped this time, but what if it had gone wrong?"

"How could it? All I did was persuade the office manager to cough if I mentioned the name of someone who wasn't a client, and she didn't cough." Callie was cross that he didn't seem pleased with this breakthrough. She felt she deserved some praise for helping.

"And how did you get her to agree to do that? How did you manage to persuade her that you weren't a journalist looking for some dirt on the company?"

Callie had a nasty suspicion that he knew very well what she had done.

"I said I was from the police, which, strictly speaking is true, and she checked on the website and saw my name and was happy with that."

"You impersonated a police officer."

"No, I never said I was a police officer. I said I was with the police. I am very well aware of the difference, and when she checked my name with the website, she would have seen my job title. And yes, I was surprised she agreed, as I could have been anyone; even, as you said, a journalist pretending to be me."

"Believe me, any self-respecting reporter would have rejected such a weak plan. I mean, it was hardly likely to work, was it?"

"Well, it did, because I think she really wanted to help. She knew the information might save a woman's life."

He said nothing, just glowered at her.

"And I really didn't impersonate a police officer." Callie was childishly cross that he wasn't impressed.

"What you did was as good as impersonation. You can't expect members of the public to differentiate between someone who works with the police and a genuine policeman." He was unable to contain his anger any longer and banged the table as he spoke, causing a few other customers to look up and the barmaid to start wondering if she was going to have a problem with the couple arguing in the corner.

"I was quite clear. I said I was a consultant with the police, and my title is doctor, not constable or detective whatever," Callie said quietly, despite her anger. She was angry, in part because he was being so ungrateful, but also because a little bit of her knew that he was right and that she was in the wrong.

"But that was what she thought you were – a police officer – and that is what she would say if she gave evidence. And what if your source told her boss and there was a complaint? You could have ended up losing your job with the police or worse, get disbarred or whatever it is happens to doctors."

Thankfully, he was keeping his voice down as well.

"Struck off," she corrected him.

"Struck off then."

There was an uneasy silence for a few moments, and the people around them returned to their conversations.

"I know you are right," she conceded. "I did take a chance, and it could have gone horribly wrong, but it didn't. I don't think it would have been grounds for anything more than a rap on the knuckles from the General Medical Council, and yes, I might have lost my job with the police, but that wouldn't be the end of the world, not when compared to what it delivered. It gave you that little bit of help you needed to get the investigation moving in the right direction, didn't it?"

She was so desperate for reassurance, her hand reaching out to him, and he couldn't bring himself to resist. He rested his own hand lightly on hers and she felt a frisson of electricity pass between them. Looking at his face she was sure he felt it too.

"Yes, I know, I just don't want—" he said gruffly but couldn't finish the sentence, all anger gone now. Callie looked round and realised that a middle-aged couple who were sitting nearest to them were watching avidly and smiling at this apparent reconciliation. She pulled her hand away, quickly.

"Thank you," she said quietly. "I know, and I promise I won't do anything like that again."

They both sat back in their chairs and concentrated on their drinks, trying to forget the moment that had passed between them, and at the same time, not wanting to forget.

"So," he said, clearing his throat so that he sounded less husky. "There was something else you mentioned in your message. Something about the website owner's husband?"

"Oh yes," Callie had forgotten all about that and had to think for a moment or two to make sure she could tell the story in a coherent manner. "This is more of what our mutual friend Sergeant Jeffries would call gossip."

Miller raised an eyebrow.

"Go on," he encouraged her. "Gossip has its uses, even if it can't be used as evidence."

She told him Linda's story about Gerry Brown.

"And, I happen to know one of the people he dated from the website, or a website, anyway." She suddenly realised that Kate hadn't said exactly where she had contacted Gerry, but it couldn't have been SSE, could it? Because then they wouldn't have needed to set Callie up as a client, would they?

"Anyway," she repeated whilst she collected her thoughts. "He refused to accept that she didn't want to see him again, and basically stalked her, even arriving at her work place demanding to see her, until she threatened to take legal action against him, which could have led to him getting struck off. She didn't know about his transgressions with a patient of course, but it's just–" she paused again and realised that he was showing considerable interest in what she was saying "– I just think he could be a person of interest, that's all."

"Would he have access to information on Mark?" he asked.

"I don't think so," she admitted. "I didn't get Mark's full notes from Helen until a few days ago so he could only have accessed my own notes, which didn't have any details of his methods of starting fires."

"That's a shame," Miller said. "I don't suppose he could have got hold of the drink cans either?"

"I don't see how he could," she admitted. "His consulting room is on the first floor, so even if Mark did throw away a can in the waiting room when he came to see me, he would have had no way of knowing that, and Mark hasn't been to see me enough times for him to have got however many you've collected. Three or four, isn't it?"

He nodded and she sighed, aware of how flimsy her case against Gerry was, but thankful that Miller hadn't laughed outright at her information.

"It's just that if you are listing men who have connections to SSE, have had acrimonious divorces, and who perhaps have abnormal attitudes to women, he's got to be on it."

"Quite." He smiled. "Unfortunately, I think we'll find that's true of most of the men that use the website." He looked up at the menu board. "Have you decided what you want to eat?"

Callie looked at the board as Miller stood ready to go to the bar and order their food.

"The sea bass, I think." She quickly checked the rest of the board. "Yes, definitely the sea bass."

Miller pointed at her still almost full glass but she shook her head.

"No, this is fine, thanks."

Callie checked her phone whilst Miller ordered their food and got another beer for himself, and thought about what people on their own did before the invention of smart phones. It seemed that no one was allowed to just sit anymore, they had to make sure no one thought for one moment that they weren't busy, connected and communicating with friends or work at all times, in case they were thought of as some kind of sad loner. Fortunately, Miller returned quickly so she didn't have to think about it too long.

"When will you be able to get the client details from SSE?" she asked once he had sat down again.

"Already have. Nigel's going through the list as we speak." He took a swig of beer. "They had everything ready for us as soon as we served the warrant, so I think you are right, they really were happy to co-operate, or, as my cynical sergeant said, they wanted to make sure no one could accuse them of not cooperating fully in case they got sued for that."

"He has a point. They will need to cover themselves as much as possible if they want to continue in business."

"I got the impression that Amelia Hepton-Lacey has already decided that SSE won't survive this. She was busy planning to close the site down and re-open under a different name, different branding."

"It would be too much to suppose the new website would have a different ethos, would it?"

"I rather think it would." He smiled, but then his phone buzzed and he pulled it to check who was calling. Clearly it wasn't from someone he could ignore, because with a rueful smile and a wave of apology, he took the call and hurried out into the street where the background noise would be less.

Callie went back to examining her own phone, but, again, not for long as Miller soon hurried back to her.

"Sorry, I have to go, something's come up." He grabbed his jacket from the back of his chair, before pausing. "Will you be okay?"

"Of course," she lied, "but you need to eat."

"I'll pick up some fish and chips on my way back to the station."

A waitress arrived at that moment with their cutlery and condiments.

"I don't suppose you know anyone who might want to eat my steak and ale pie, do you," he said to Callie. "I've already paid and it would be a shame to waste it."

"I'll call Kate," Callie said with a smile. "She only lives round the corner and I'm sure she'd be delighted to join me."

She reached for her bag. "Let me give you the money." But by the time she had pulled out her purse, he was already on his way out of the door and the waitress was giving her a sympathetic smile.

Callie smiled back at her and the diners at the surrounding tables who clearly thought that she had been stood up after an argument, which she had in a way, but she could hardly tell them that it was work that had come between them, calling him away. At least it probably was, she thought as she realized that she knew little of his private life except that he was married. For all she knew, he could have hordes of children too, but somehow, she thought not. She reached for her phone to ring Kate; at least she was going to make someone happy tonight.

* * *

"Mmm hmm. Nothing tastes better than a free dinner," Kate said as she wiped her lips with her napkin. "Particularly when it's steak pie."

She scraped the last of the pie onto her fork.

"Just lucky you were able to get here before it was served."

Callie had sat for several minutes suffering the sympathetic looks from fellow customers and servers alike before Kate had breezed into the restaurant and saved the day. She had seriously considered walking out, and would have done if Kate hadn't said she would drop everything and rescue her friend, but she hated the thought of leaving the food to go to waste, and where would she go? Home, alone and hungry? No, better to wait for Kate.

"I can move pretty quickly when I need to," Kate said. "Nothing worse than a cold and congealed pie."

"Yes," Callie replied, although they both knew that she would never willingly eat a steak pie, whether hot or cold. Callie indicated Kate's nearly empty glass of red wine. "Wine or coffee?"

"Wine please, and a portion of cheese and biscuits would be good."

With a shake of her head, Callie went to the bar to order wine, cheese and a decaff for herself. Kate need never know.

When she returned to her seat, Callie pulled out the mobile phone Kate had lent her and that she had been using when texting the men from the SSE website and pushed it across the table to her friend.

"Thanks for lending me this, but I won't be needing it anymore."

"Why?" Kate asked as she spread lashings of butter onto a cream cracker and added a generous chunk of stilton, completely ignoring Callie's look of disapproval.

"The police are on it now. They got their warrant and Nigel is going through all the SSE clients as we speak." She paused, and suddenly looked panicked. "Oh my goodness!"

"What?"

"He'll find me, my details will be on there."

"Relax, we put in fake ones for you, remember?"

"Yes, but once he realises they are fake, he'll check the profile, won't he?"

"And won't be able to recognise you. No one would."

"But what if he does? What should I do?"

"Look, Callie. Calm down. He'll be concentrating on the men anyway, once he's identified the three victims. What Miller will want to know is who has contacted all three of them – and then they'll be busy arresting anyone who has, I should imagine. They are not going to be looking at all the other women on there."

"You're right." She took a deep breath. "I know you're right. I'd just be happier if we took my profile down, just in case."

"That's fine, I'll do that for you, I promise. Tonight. Although Lee and Lance will be heartbroken."

Callie was relieved. Kate had convinced her that all would be well.

"I really don't care how disappointed they are."

"You did swap to WhatsApp after the initial contact, didn't you?"

"Yes."

"So, all you have to do is delete the conversations and their contact details and ask them to do the same, then no one will ever be the wiser. Except–"

Kate paused as she finished the cheese and biscuits and sipped her red wine as Callie looked at her expectantly.

"I mean, Nigel will definitely play by the book but I can imagine that Sergeant Jeffries bloke going through all the profiles and contacting any women that he thought he might get lucky with–" Kate ducked as Callie threw a napkin at her and managed to at least smile as Kate guffawed at her own wind-up.

"That is my worst nightmare," Callie told her once Kate managed to stop laughing. "Promise me you'll take my profile down tonight or I won't sleep a wink."

Kate finished her wine and grinned.

"Don't worry. Of course I will take it down. Why don't you come back to mine and we can do it now?"

Callie followed her friend out, relieved that her adventure on the web site was finally going to be over.

Chapter 21

The sun was shining and the air had a clear, clean feel after the overnight rain and as Callie walked to work, across the clifftop park and then quickly heading down the narrow steps that led to All Saints Street, she was feeling positively light hearted. She had slept unusually well, safe in the knowledge that her profile had been taken down from the SSE website and that she almost certainly wouldn't have to confess to Nigel, or Miller, that she had posed as a client.

Whilst she knew she had done nothing wrong in doing so, she also knew it would be embarrassing if they ever heard about it, and, in particular, if Sergeant Jeffries ever heard about it. She knew that he would never, ever, let her forget it. She still had a slight worry that they would trace her through the client list, but Kate had reassured her that the police would be concentrating on tracing the men using the site, not the women and Callie hoped that Jeffries hadn't got it into his head to check out the ladies, including those who had removed their details. It would be just like him to do something like that, hoping to find willing and available women for himself rather than searching from a work point of view, but even that small, niggling anxiety wasn't enough to dent her good humour.

She was sure that the police would quickly discover who the murderer was now that they had all the contact details. After all, there couldn't be too many men in common between the three victims, could there?

Callie's mobile rang and she stopped walking to search for her phone in the depths of her bag, heart beating slightly faster when she saw that the call was from Miller.

"Dr Hughes speaking," she answered, mentally kicking herself for sounding so formal and unfriendly.

"Hi, Callie," Miller said and Callie could immediately detect some embarrassment in his voice. She started to slowly move down the hill again, putting her slight breathlessness down to the speed she had been walking rather than because she was speaking to Miller.

"I wanted to apologise for last night and to, um, let you know that Mark was arrested again this morning."

"What?" Callie stopped dead, her good humour fading fast.

"Nothing to do with the murders. Apparently, he torched a disused barn last night," Miller told her. "He confessed, said he needed to stop the roar in his head."

Callie took a deep breath.

"I told you this would happen if you kept pushing him. I told you he couldn't take the pressure."

"I know, I know and, for what it's worth, I'm sorry."

Callie believed him, and knew that it wasn't his fault, he hadn't, in all reality, had any choice.

"Is he at the station now?"

"Yes," Miller confirmed. "I told them not to interview him until either you or Helen were there and I went down to see him, just to check and he seemed okay, calmer than I've ever seen him before, in fact."

"That's the effect it has on him. Setting fires releases all his stress."

"Maybe I should give it a try."

Miller sounded tired and Callie knew he must be under an awful lot of pressure with three women dead and the press, his bosses and the public all demanding he find the culprit. She would have liked to say something comforting, if only she could think of anything that might help.

"Was anyone hurt?" she asked instead.

"No, no, the barn was in the middle of nowhere. No chance of him hurting anyone, and it was pretty much derelict, so I think the farmer's actually quite pleased with the idea he might get some insurance money out of it."

"I told you he wouldn't deliberately hurt anyone." Callie couldn't help adding what amounted to an 'I told you so'.

"I know."

Callie checked her watch.

"Look, I've got morning surgery, so I can't make it to the station until lunchtime and much as you say Mark is pretty chilled at the moment, it might be better to see if Helen can come in before then. Can you ask her?"

"That's fine, I thought you would be busy. I was just letting you know as much as anything else. It's not my case, but I'll ask them to call Helen, okay?"

"Thanks, and sorry."

Callie would have liked to ask him about the contact list from the website and if they had found any names in common. Had Lee, or Lance or Gerry contacted the women? But whilst she was still trying to work out how to put the question, he said goodbye and hung up. She would have to wait to hear, unless, she thought, she managed to finish surgery quickly and fitted in a trip to the station afterwards. The plan appealed. Even if Helen had already sat in for Mark's interview, he was unlikely to have been released by lunchtime as the paperwork always seemed to take hours. She could always say she was just checking up on him – a welfare visit to one of her patients – and it would be polite to drop in on Miller whilst she was there, wouldn't it? After all he had had the courtesy to let her know Mark had been arrested, hadn't he?

Having convinced herself that this plan was in the interests of everyone and not just idle curiosity, Callie started walking again, hurrying to get to the surgery. Although she had plenty of time before her morning list was due to start, she wanted to try and catch Adrian Lambourne and find out if he had managed to see Mark before the boy had imploded. If Lambourne hadn't, despite all her requests for him to do so, she thought that she could insist he make room to see Mark as an emergency as soon as he was released. Of course, Lambourne would also be a good target for her pent-up frustrations. She was in the mood for a good argument.

* * *

Before Callie could ring Lambourne, she found another reason to get upset. A quick check of her paperwork basket revealed a request for her to forward on the electronic patient records for Jill Hollingsworth, her patient with hypothyroidism, and husband David Hollingsworth. It seemed that they had recently registered with a new surgery. The request, as always, didn't say where they were moving to, but another note in her basket told her that a surgery in a village many miles from their home had called to try and expedite the transfer of information. Callie was surprised they had applied to join such a distant service and even more surprised that they had been accepted, unless they had moved.

A quick look at her watch told her it would be a bad time to call the new surgery, as they would be starting their own morning clinics, so, instead, she decided that she might just have enough time to call Lambourne and vent some of her anger without being too late for her own patients. She hurried down to her consulting room, switched on her computer in preparation for work and reached for the phone.

"Dr Hughes here, I'd like to speak to Adrian Lambourne immediately, please," she said as his receptionist answered the phone, and was gratified when she was put straight through.

"Dr Lambourne speaking."

His persistent use of the title of doctor irritated Callie intensely as she felt it was done to deliberately mislead patients. She knew he was entitled to call himself Doctor as he had a doctorate, a PhD in some obscure aspect of psychology, but he hadn't been to medical school or taken a degree in general medicine as most people assumed. Whilst Callie knew he was still highly skilled at treating patients, it did mean he couldn't prescribe at all or treat anything other than psychological disorders. It didn't take an in-depth knowledge of psychology to know that he insisted on being called Doctor because he had some kind of chip on his shoulder about not being a medical doctor and wanted his patients to think he actually was. Now probably wasn't the time for her to tell him her feelings on this, however, but it did add to her list of reasons to be angry with him and made her persist in not calling him Dr Lambourne, if only to irritate him.

"Adrian, it's Callie here. I was just wondering if you had managed to see Mark yet? Or get him admitted any time soon?"

She knew, of course, that he hadn't, and also that she was being unfair because it was most unlikely that he could have found a bed yet, even if he had tried.

There was a moment's silence before Lambourne responded. She could almost hear him counting to ten before speaking in a well-practised and measured tone.

"He has an appointment to see me, I believe. Let me just check my records, ah, yes, tomorrow. As I am sure you know, we would love to have the resources to fit patients in and to admit them at the drop of a hat, but we don't and I am doing my best, Dr Hughes, I really am. You might not think it good enough, but it is honestly the best that I can do."

Callie took a deep breath and told herself to chill. Much as she would have liked to have a rant at him, she knew that he was right.

"I'm sorry, Adrian, I know I'm being unfair, but Mark was arrested again this morning and has been charged with arson."

"Not another murder, surely? I didn't hear anything on the radio this morning."

"No, not a murder, they know he's not responsible for those, but he did set fire to a disused barn, probably because of the stress of being treated as a suspect."

"Oh, have they definitely ruled him out of the murders, then? That's good news if so."

"Yes, yes, he's been ruled out. He was actually in a police cell when one of the murders took place so that's no longer the problem, it's more about the continued questioning that he's been subjected to."

"Oh, right, still upsetting for him, yes. Do you think he'll be released today?"

"I should think so, but there's the worry that if the pressure starts building again—"

"Quite. Look, I'll ask my receptionist to call him later and see if she can get him to come here today and I'll check and see if there are any beds available anywhere. If not, I'll get my colleague Dr Andersen to up his medication and try and get him seen by one of us daily for a while. How does that sound?"

"Thank you."

Callie was genuinely surprised he would offer to do that much. Dr Andersen was one of the psychiatrists who practised at the sleep clinic where she knew Lambourne regularly did sessions and she was also aware that they had an arrangement whereby Andersen would prescribe medication for Lambourne's patients when it was needed urgently rather than waiting for the patients' own GP to do it.

"That sounds more than I could reasonably have expected of you. I'm sorry to have been so rude earlier," she said.

"Not at all. I really do want to try and help the boy. After all, we were doing so well before all this. Goodbye, Dr Hughes."

* * *

Callie had rushed through her morning patients and, despite having found a note in her basket telling her that Helen had been able to drop everything and go to be with Mark for his interview, she hurried out of the office, leaving paperwork and visits for her partners. Sometimes, she thought it might be nice to be a Roman Catholic and assuage her guilt by confessing and saying a few Hail Marys for penance, but deep down she suspected that deliberately sinning in the expectation of getting forgiveness was probably against their rules anyway.

She arrived at the police station, having nipped home to collect her car, at about the time she thought most doctors would be finishing up paperwork and taking calls after their morning clinics. She fished in her bag for her notepad and phone and keyed in the number for the surgery that had requested the Hollingsworths' notes.

"Hello," she said once her call was answered. "My name is Doctor Hughes from The Bourne Surgery, Hastings. I received notification today that some patients of mine from Croft Hill Farm in Westfield have registered with you, is that correct? I have their NHS numbers if that will help?"

Callie waited patiently as she was first passed to the practice manager, who insisted on checking her identity with Linda, who she knew from the practice managers' support group, before answering cautiously in the affirmative. The Hollingsworths had indeed registered at the practice, but she wasn't happy to say more than that.

"Thank you," Callie persisted. "What I am at a loss to understand is why they have left our practice and why they have re-registered somewhere so far from where they live, not to mention quite why you would have accepted them, under the circumstances." Callie waited whilst the beleaguered manager put her on hold, presumably to discuss her questions with someone else. It was several minutes before she was taken off hold, and this time she was speaking to a Dr Simms, the GP who had accepted the couple's registration.

"It's a delicate matter, Dr Hughes," he told Callie, "and I'm hesitant lest I break confidentiality." His Scottish accent still breaking through, despite living so far south.

"I certainly wouldn't want you to do that, Dr Simms, and I have to say that I am not surprised that they have decided to move practices. It's no secret that Mr Hollingsworth made a complaint against me. I am just concerned that they have chosen to register with a surgery so far from where they live and that you would take them."

"Well, I have to say it was not without a good deal of pressure from the husband. He seemed to think that all the doctors in Hastings would have it in for him because of that complaint."

"That seems rather excessive."

"Indeed. I was half expecting him to have a history of paranoia when I got the records through. I don't suppose there's anything of that sort that I should know about?"

"He's hardly been to the surgery the whole time he's been registered with us, so if he is paranoid, it's only recently become about his doctor. Although," she added as an afterthought, "it would explain how he's been behaving recently."

"Aye, well, he was very persuasive, I'll have you know. I felt I had to take them."

"I'm sorry it's come to this, and I hope for your sake it's just a misunderstanding and he isn't a problem. I'll forward their electronic records as soon as possible."

"Thank you for that, Dr Hughes. I'm obliged."

"Oh, and Dr Simms?"

"Yes?"

"Please don't hesitate to call me if you need any clarification, particularly about Mrs Hollingsworth's hypothyroidism."

"She has myxoedema?" He sounded surprised. "Her husband assured me they were both in good health."

Callie sighed.

"I'll send you a copy of the complete records directly, Dr Simms, as well as through the proper channels, and you can see for yourself."

Callie felt increasingly disquieted as she ended the call, which was the opposite of what she had hoped. She actually had more unanswered questions now than before. What on earth was David Hollingsworth up to? Did he have difficulty accepting that his wife had a long-term condition and needed monitoring and treatment? How did Jill feel about it? So many questions and none that Dr Simms had been able to answer, but they would have to wait, for now. She got out of her car and headed into the police station.

She checked with the custody sergeant and found out that Mark had been charged and was being bailed to appear before the magistrates the following morning and would be released shortly. It was moderately quiet in the custody suite and the sergeant was happy to take her to the cells to see Mark and satisfy herself that he was okay. She explained to him that his psychologist would try and see him that day and would probably want to increase his medication as well. Mark seemed indifferent to what was going on and she tried to impress upon him the need to see Lambourne but she left by no means sure that he could be bothered to go. Setting the fire seemed to have calmed him to the point of apathy.

Back at the reception, Callie asked to speak to Miller and was escorted up to the incident room. Miller looked up as she walked in and hurried over to divert her straight into his office, clearly worried she was about to lay into him about Mark's arrest. She let him stew for a moment or two before smiling and thanking him for letting her know her patient was in custody. He looked relieved, but Jeffries, watching surreptitiously through the window, couldn't hide his disappointment, which pleased Callie.

"I was just wondering how you were getting on now that you have all the contact details from SSE? Have you found a common link?"

Callie had been expecting Miller to be enthusiastic and upbeat but instead he seemed to slump slightly.

"I wish." He paused, clearly wondering how much he should confide in her. "There are no contacts in common between all three women and no one connected with Mark as far as we can tell."

Callie felt a spasm of disappointment and anxiety.

"I thought it would be all over as soon as you had that information. That it was only a matter of time before you made an arrest."

"I know, we all did. But life just isn't that easy."

"No, you're right. It's never that easy." She thought for a moment. "Did anyone contact more than one of the women?"

"Yes, we have five men who each contacted two out of three. Nigel is checking them out."

"Good." She smiled again, but then had a sudden thought. "Does the list include people who might have contacted the women but have left the website? I mean he might be trying to cover his tracks?"

Miller looked thoughtful.

"I assume so, I mean it's a list of all the contacts they have had, but–" He got up and opened the door into the incident room. "Nigel?"

Nigel looked up from his screen.

"People who have left SSE are still on the list, aren't they?"

"Yes, guv." Nigel nodded vigorously. "There are several clients that have since left." He looked round the room. "None of them contacted more than one of the women and Jayne was calling them, to find out why they left. I'll check with her and find out how far she has got."

"Thanks, Nigel. I thought you would have had it covered."

"Of course." Callie had followed Miller to the door, so that Nigel and Jeffries could hear her. "He might have more than one profile."

"I've checked methods of payment and none of them use the same ones." Nigel assured her and Callie didn't want to go further and point out that there were ways round that, in case they asked how she knew. Perhaps she could call Nigel and put the idea into his head. He was much more open to suggestions than either Miller of Jeffries.

"What about phone records?"

"We have the details of all calls and texts for numbers registered to the women, but we have nothing connecting to any of the men on SSE, and we haven't been able to find your Dr Brown on there, either. Although we did bring him in for questioning. You might want to steer clear for a while. I think he knows someone from the surgery put his name forward."

Jeffries snorted.

"He won't do anything. He was just a dickhead."

For once, Callie agreed with him, but thought that keeping out of Gerry's way could be a good idea.

"Do you think any of the victims had more than one phone?" Callie queried. "Or perhaps just swapped out the sim cards for a pay-as-you-go one, not in their names."

"It's possible, we haven't found anything to prove it though." No wonder Miller seemed so defeated. Information that had seemed guaranteed to lead them to the killer, had turned into pretty much a dead end.

"And, um, from what I can tell, after the initial contact they would have probably messaged using something like WhatsApp and with handsets pretty much destroyed in the fires, we have no hope of getting those from the company," Nigel added morosely.

"Not unless we get GCHQ or MI5 involved," Jeffries added and Callie silently thanked Kate for making her use that and vowed that any future conversations of an intimate nature would be using the App so she could delete all the embarrassing ones.

"We are working our way through everyone on all our lists." Miller tried to sound upbeat, but failed.

"We'll still be tracing, interviewing and eliminating well into next century," Jeffries said. "What we need is a way of eliminating them quicker. Who's for a cuppa before we get back on the phones?"

Callie took the hint and left them to their ongoing calls.

Chapter 22

Gerry Brown was in the general doctors' office rushing through a stack of repeat prescriptions, barely checking them to see if they were correct before adding a scrawled signature to the bottom, when Callie came in and watched for a few seconds before he realised that he wasn't alone and turned to look at her. She swallowed her irritation at his slapdash work and smiled despite Miller's warning that he might suspect her of having given his name to the police. He would hardly have been likely to remain in the room with her if he really did think she had done that, would he?

"How's it going?" she asked vaguely. He looked up, as if only just registering that there was anyone else in the room.

"Okay."

He shrugged, seemingly unsure what she was asking, which, in truth, she was as well. She was just trying to strike a conversation, so that she could get to know him better. Now that the SSE website seemed to be a washout, she was wondering again about the locum GP and was curious about what he did on Wednesday and Saturday nights.

"I was wondering, now that you seem more settled here and are spending more time in Hastings," she began, "if you wanted me to show you round one night? Introduce you to the pubs or the jazz club? I mean, I know you don't live that far away, and have probably had nights out in the town but I thought you might not know the, um, singles scene."

She knew it sounded like a desperate pick up, but she ploughed on, nevertheless. "Maybe on a Wednesday night? The comedy club has an open mike night on a Wednesday that can be quite fun."

"Wednesday's not a good night for me," Gerry looked a bit like a rabbit caught in the headlights. "I have a standing commitment on a Wednesday."

"Oh? What's that?" She tried to sound innocent but he just glared at her and went back to his work.

"Some other night, then," Callie persisted.

"Um, maybe. Let me think about it." Gerry seemed more irritated than flattered at being asked out by Callie. "Thank you." He added as an afterthought.

"Assuming your wife doesn't mind," Callie added maliciously.

"We're separated."

"I'm sorry to hear that," Callie lied.

"I doubt it. I mean, you don't seriously expect me to believe you would make a pass at me if you thought I was still married, do you?"

"Busted." Callie smiled. "I heard on the grapevine that you were working here because you had left your wife, but I wasn't sure if you already had another girlfriend and, you know, that that was the cause of the split."

Gerry abruptly switched off his computer and stood up.

"I don't know what your game is, but I don't believe for one moment that you haven't heard all the gossip. Everyone in the office must know very well why I have ended up in this God-forsaken job." He stomped out of the room and straight down the stairs, without even bothering to take his signed prescriptions into the office.

"Touchy subject," Callie said to herself as she gathered up the paperwork and took it all through to the girls in the office to deal with.

"Dr Brown gone?" Linda asked her when she saw Callie had his work as well as her own.

"Yes, I may have upset him," Callie admitted.

"Well, that's not exactly hard these days." Linda looked round the room conspiratorially and then continued in a quieter voice. "You know his wife has really taken him to the cleaners?"

"That's hardly a surprise, under the circumstances."

"No, but he was a partner in their, you know, website thingy business and he's had to resign from that as well as give her the family home. Seems that she had a controlling interest in the company and has voted him out. Good job he's got his stellar medical career to fall back on." Linda laughed.

"Ooh, who would have thought you were so cruel, Ms Crompton."

"It seems that she's happy to make her money from adultery but not so keen on her husband doing it. That's irony for you." Linda paused and gave Callie a meaningful look. "And you should have told me that his website was the internet dating agency that's been in the news."

"I wasn't sure I was allowed to, and anyway, I didn't know for absolute certain that it was them."

Linda gave her a look of disbelief before moving on.

"They were probably both having affairs left, right and centre. Mind you, he's probably quite glad he's not on the board. He doesn't need any more scandal and I can't imagine it's going to be bringing in quite so much money now it's been linked to a killer, do you?"

One of the other staff called to the manager and she hurried away, leaving Callie to think about the implications of what Linda had said.

Gerry had lost pretty much everything when he was forced to give his wife the healthy and profitable business, not to mention the house, but the situation had changed and now that he no longer had a financial interest in the success of the business, the murders meant that it was no longer profitable. In fact, it was in ruins and so his wife had lost her money too. If that didn't shout motive, nothing did. Callie hurried back into the now empty doctors' office and grabbed a phone.

There was no answer from Miller's mobile so she rang the incident room and got through to Nigel and told him that Gerry Brown had not only been a director of SusSEXtra but had lost his place there as part of the separation settlement. She told him that revenge on his wife by destroying the business could possibly be a motive for the murders.

Nigel took careful notes of what she was saying and said that he would pass it onto Jayne who was interviewing ex-spouses, and Amelia Hepton-Lacey, also known as Mrs Gerry Brown, would be added to her list. If anyone would know how to get around the website financial systems and checks, it would be Gerry, he pointed out.

"And what you mentioned about members hiding their identity, Dr Hughes," Nigel continued. "I'm following that up myself."

Callie was relieved that her information was being acted on, and began to feel renewed hope that the killer would be caught and that it might even be soon.

Callie had barely put the phone down after her conversation with Nigel when it began to ring again.

"Hello?" she said as she answered it. "Dr Hughes speaking. Oh, Adrian, how can I help?"

She listened as Adrian Lambourne explained that he had seen Mark and started him on some relaxation therapy and also changed his medication again. His colleague at the clinic had issued him with enough of his increased strength tablets to last him a week, but he wanted Callie to do a prescription to continue them on from there. He had also booked Mark into weekly sessions so that he could be monitored more closely moving forward.

"Of course," she agreed. "I'll do it straight away. Oh, and Adrian? Thank you."

She had more than a twinge of guilt that she had been so rude to him, but was pleased that it had finally made him sit up and take notice. The outcome had been better care for her patient and that was a good result in her book.

* * *

As she walked out of the surgery door, Callie was surprised to see Jayne Hales waiting for her in the car park.

"Hey, Doc," she greeted Callie casually. "I thought you'd be finishing about now."

"Why didn't you come in and say you were here? I would have been out sooner."

"I didn't know if your patients knew about your work with us and didn't want to risk one of them taking it amiss if they saw the police hanging round their doctor."

"I shouldn't worry, most of my patients would enjoy the gossip. Anyway, it's not like you are in uniform."

"True." Jayne hesitated. "Are you rushing off on visits or do you have a minute?"

"No visits, thank goodness, I was just going to walk home. How can I help you, anyway?"

Jayne looked relieved.

"Well, maybe I could just walk with you and pick your brains as we go, if that's all right?"

"Perfectly." Callie started walking. "Hope you're fit, it's a steep climb."

"Everything's a steep climb in Hastings." Jayne laughed and followed her. "I wanted to ask about a colleague of yours."

"Gerry Brown? I spoke to Nigel about him as soon as I heard about his connection with the SSE website."

"That's right, he's passed it onto me as I am interviewing the wives and partners of anyone connected with Mark."

"Because the killer has to be someone who knows Mark and be able to get their hands on his fingerprints."

"Exactly, and the boss wants to know if they also have any marital problems or whatever, because of your theory about the motive being adultery."

Having paused to ensure Callie had followed her explanation, Jayne continued when Callie nodded that she had.

"So, I have an appointment to speak with the ex-Mrs Brown tomorrow, get her side of the story. I just thought I'd speak to you first and get the low down from your point of view."

Callie quickly ran through everything she knew as they walked.

"I really don't know any more, except that he's really not a likeable man and I'm not exactly impressed with his skills as a doctor, either."

"So," Jayne said, breathing deeply as she struggled to keep up with Callie. "I'm betting you don't need to go to the gym if you are doing this every day."

"It certainly helps," Callie agreed. They had reached the top of the hill and Callie's building.

"Do you want to come in for a cup of tea?" she asked.

"No, no. Resuscitation possibly, but I'll pass on the tea and get back to my car. I've been trying to get hold of someone without success and I thought I'd try and catch her when she gets home. Doorstep her, in fact, as she doesn't seem to want to speak to me."

"I don't envy you that job, but it's hard to know why someone would try and avoid speaking to you."

"Embarrassment, probably. I am asking about their divorces and I am learning that people don't always behave well during a divorce. I don't suppose you know anything about Dr Lambourne's divorce, do you?"

"I didn't even know he was divorced," Callie replied. "I really don't know anything about him. Apart from the fact that he is Mark's psychologist. Is that who you are having difficulty getting hold of?"

"Yes. Oh well, worth a punt." Jayne smiled and looked down the steps they had just climbed. "At least going down is easier."

She laughed and called goodbye as she set off back down the hill.

* * *

It was early evening when Callie walked into The Stag and was pleased to see that Kate was seated at a table by the window, a pint and a packet of crisps in front of her had already been partly demolished, and a glass of Pinot Grigio with one cube of ice slowly melting into the wine, stood ready and waiting for Callie.

"Excellent. Just what I need," Callie said by way of greeting and sat on the bench opposite Kate.

"Bad day?" Kate asked.

"No, not really, just long, and a bit disappointing, that's all. How about you?"

"Dreadful," Kate admitted.

"Oh, dear, what happened?"

Callie looked at her friend with sympathy as she listened to an account of having to make up excuses for a client who failed to show up in court, and spending the entire day trying unsuccessfully to get hold of him.

"In the end I gave up and went home early, even though I had achieved absolutely nothing. So, tell me about your long day. What, in particular, was disappointing about it?"

"Well, in all fairness, the disappointing bit actually happened yesterday. Apparently they are no further forward finding the killer because there are no contacts in common between the three women."

"That could be for all sorts of reasons—"

Callie held up her hand to stop Kate.

"I know, and I called Nigel last night and gave him chapter and verse about how people can cover their tracks and he is following up on that, but it's a delay I hadn't anticipated. I was so sure that they would find the killer as soon as they had the information from SSE that I deleted my account so they wouldn't find my profile."

"I told you, they won't be looking at the women," Kate said in exasperation. "At least I hope not, or they'll find me pretty quickly."

"Please, tell me you aren't meeting any of the men who contact you. Not while the killer is still out there."

"Of course not. I'm not that stupid, but as soon as he's behind bars I want to be ready. There are some really dirty men on there," she said with a smile that could be described as pretty dirty as well.

"But, by definition, if they are looking on that website they are not looking for a meaningful relationship. I mean, they are all married or think you're married."

"I know, but a bit of fun without strings whilst I wait for Mr Right will keep my sexual organs in full working order."

Callie sighed. There was no way she could think like that. She wasn't interested in a no-strings relationship, she wanted one with all the strings – engagement, marriage, children, everything.

"What about your friend and mine, Gerry Brown?" Kate asked. "Do you still think he might be the killer? I mean that he could be doing this as a sort of act of revenge against his wife and the company?"

"It doesn't really fit, but the police are checking him out as well."

"Good." Kate thought for a moment. "As well as what? Or rather who?"

"Well, I can't claim to know everything they are following up, but I do know that Jayne Hales is interviewing the wives and ex-wives of anyone connected to Mark Caxton."

"The kid who likes to burn cars, but not with people in them?" Kate queried and Callie nodded.

"I think she's more likely to get a true picture of their relationships and break-ups from the women involved rather than the men."

"Ain't that the truth," Kate said, a little too readily.

"I think it's depressing that so many people have unsuccessful marriages. Jayne was saying that most of the people involved had been divorced or separated from long-term partners and that it would be a lot quicker for her to interview the happily married ones."

"But we're talking mainly doctors, health care professionals and policemen and they are all well known to have a high divorce rate. Comes with the job." Kate thought for a moment. "Lawyers are as bad, probably because of their association with police."

"That would account for psychologists as well, I expect."

"Thinking of someone in particular?"

"Adrian Lambourne, Mark's psychologist. Jayne was asking if I knew the story there but I hadn't a clue he was divorced. It's not something you ask people you work with, is it?"

"Why do think it is?"

"Why do I think what is?"

"That some professions have higher divorce rates than others."

Callie gave it some thought.

"Long hours, stress and having to deal with death, I suppose. Makes you want to live life to the full yourself."

"I can see that's why they sleep around, but divorce?"

Callie shook her head.

"I think it's more that they don't want to put up with being unhappy or to put up with second best if they think they have ended up with a relationship they can't put right. They don't want to waste the one, short life they have."

Kate sighed her agreement that this was probably the case, and they drank in silence for a moment or two.

"Mind you, you would think a psychologist would be able to make his relationships work, wouldn't you?"

"Possibly, although—"

"Maybe it's because they are all a bit mad," Kate interrupted.

"That's simply not true," Callie chastised her friend gently. "A few, maybe, but not all."

"It makes you want to find out why though, doesn't it? See if there are any salacious details?"

"Like what?"

"Is he into dressing up in women's clothing, or is he an obsessive compulsive who organises his sock drawer by colour?"

"It's more likely that his wife just realised he's a jumped-up little twerp who has a chip on his shoulder about not being a proper doctor."

"Miaow!" They laughed together until Callie felt guilty.

"Actually, he's not that bad. He has been very helpful with Mark once I managed to get him to take notice and stop blaming me."

Kate sighed.

"One day, Callie, you are going to be able to say something truly horrible about someone who deserves it, without feeling guilty." Kate shook her head knowing that it would never really happen.

* * *

Later that night as Callie watched television, her mind wandered and she thought more about Adrian Lambourne and, in particular, Jayne's difficulty in getting hold of his wife. She wondered if Jayne had been successful in doorstepping her as she wasn't returning calls. Perhaps she was away? If so, how else could Jayne get the information she needed? Callie had an old classmate from medical school, who worked as a psychiatrist in the local NHS trust where Lambourne also spent some of his time. Perhaps he would be a good source of information. Before she had a chance to change her mind, she called his office number and left a message, asking him to give her a ring when he had a chance.

* * *

He smiled to himself as he put down his latest pay-as-you-go mobile phone. He knew the police had worked out that he met his victims through the website, and since a link with dating websites had been hinted at on the news, even though they had been careful not to mention SusSEXtra specifically, presumably mindful of a potential legal case if they did, people were bound to be more careful. It was lucky that he had a number of women already prepared and communicating with him offline. He'd even made a joke about being the killer, so they better beware. There was always one who thought if he brought it up it couldn't be him, that it could never happen to them, and he had just set up a meeting with that one for tonight. He was sure she would turn up because she was stupid. Judging by her messages she was barely able to read or write and seemed desperate for sex. Anything to make her feel loved or at least wanted, and he wanted her, he really wanted her. He just hoped he wouldn't have to waste too much time talking to her first.

Chapter 23

The rain was lashing down by the time Callie arrived at the farm track that she had been told was the easiest way to the crime scene. She knew from her previous walks across the cliffs that the track led to a farm and from there to an unofficial, and often impassable, route down to Fairlight Cove where there was a naturist beach.

Callie parked her car at the top of the track as instructed by a cold, wet and miserable-looking constable who was trying to ignore the water dripping steadily off the peak of his uniform cap, and walked the rest of the way on foot. As she picked her way along the rutted track, she passed a field that was used as a campsite in the summer but was empty now. She could see the farmhouse beyond the field, with lights ablaze. She imagined that they must have seen the flames and alerted the emergency services. Callie shivered as an ice-cold trickle of rain ran down her neck. She hadn't bothered with an umbrella as she knew she wouldn't be allowed to take it into the crime scene, so she pulled the hood of her cagoule up and tightened the cord in an attempt to stop the rain getting inside. She hoped they had at least managed to set up a dry-ish area for her to change into her coverall suit, or else she would be soaked through in no time at all.

She stumbled slightly on the uneven track and wondered if she should have brought a torch, but once she rounded the final corner there was light from the headlamps and the blue flashing lights of the fire truck and police cars that were already at the scene. She could see a lone figure in a crime scene suit standing and watching the fire crew check the burnt-out car and realised it was Miller.

He turned as she suited up, trying to keep herself as dry as possible, but finally giving up because it was a fight she just wasn't going to win.

"Sorry to get you out on a night like this."

"I'd completely forgotten that it was a Wednesday night."

"I know," Miller said. "I'd thought, with all the publicity around the killings and the dating website, no one would be so stupid—" He shook his head in frustration.

"Yes. It does make you wonder, doesn't it?"

"He must be a real charmer."

"Speaking of which, no Sergeant Jeffries?" she asked, looking round as if expecting him to pop out from behind a bush.

"Not yet," he replied, continuing briskly. "He's on his way. It's pretty much the same as the previous scenes, we just need you to confirm life extinct once the firemen say it's safe for you to do so. I'll go and talk to them." He walked off in the direction of the fire appliance.

"Hi, Dr Hughes." A voice startled her as she hadn't been aware anyone else was there. Callie turned and saw a figure in a protective suit and mask that pretty much could have been anyone.

"It's me, DS Hales. Jayne," the voice said helpfully, much to Callie's relief.

"Oh, hi. Do we know anything about this one?" Callie nodded at the still smouldering car.

"No, not yet. The fire bods won't let us get anywhere near until they've finished. I would have said I hope they hurry up, but I am so wet now that it won't make any difference how long they take."

"I know how you feel," Callie replied. "I'll be straight in a hot shower when I get back."

They stood and waited in companionable silence.

"Did you manage to get hold of Mrs Lambourne?" Callie asked after a while.

"No, she seems to have gone away on a cruise around the Med. I'll try and contact the cruise line later, once I have confirmed which one it is, see if they can get a message to her, but to be fair, it might have to wait until she gets back."

"I've contacted an old friend who might know them, just to see if there's any gossip. If I hear anything, I'll let you know."

"Cheers, Dr Hughes, that would be great."

They watched the crime scene team rig some lights up for a few moments before Jayne turned to Callie again. "We, um checked up on your Dr Brown as well, and he has a pretty good alibi."

"Oh yes?"

"You didn't hear this from me, right?"

Callie nodded, trying to appear indifferent when she was, in reality, all ears.

"Seems that as a condition of his GMC hearing he has to attend a sex addiction clinic. Group therapy every Wednesday and Saturday nights."

"But they can't go on very late?" Callie couldn't see how it was an alibi.

"Yes, but he goes home with one of the other patients afterwards and spends the night with her."

"Nice to know the therapy is working," Callie said and Jayne giggled.

"Well, the clinic know about it now, because of the questions we were asking, rather than because we actually told them…"

Callie was quite sure that wasn't true, she could imagine Sergeant Jeffries taking great pleasure in telling the psychotherapist in charge of the sex addiction clinic just how well the therapy was working.

"…and it's up to them whether or not they report him to the GMC."

"Oh, heavens," Callie hadn't thought of that. Her life wasn't going to get any easier if Gerry Brown was suspended for breaking the conditions of his continued working.

Suddenly the scene was bathed in bright light as the floodlights were switched on, making the headlights and blue flashing lights seem pale in comparison to the fierce illumination that now bathed the scene.

"Also, Nigel checked the clinic where Dr Lambourne worked and the receptionist confirmed that he doesn't allow patients to take food or drink in with them," Jayne continued. "Something to do with an incident in the past when a patient assaulted him with an item of food."

"Nothing too soft, I hope?"

"A banana, apparently."

Neither could suppress a giggle as they thought about that. Callie wished that Jayne was around at more crime scenes, because not only was she a fantastic source of information, she managed to take Callie's mind off the grisly reason for her being there.

"Look." Jayne pointed to a helmeted fireman who was beckoning them forward. "I think it's okay for you to go and check the body now."

* * *

Later, once Callie had managed to warm up and dry out at home, she sat in her fluffy towelling dressing gown and sipped a cup of hot milk. It was four in the morning but the thought of another poor woman burnt to death was enough to prevent her from sleeping. That and the smell. She had showered and washed her hair, even squeezing some fresh lemon juice into the final rinse, a trick a colleague had once shared, but the smell seemed to remain. She knew it was because microscopic particles were probably caught in the hairs of her nasal passages, but even though she had tried snorting some water up her nose, the smell persisted. So she sprayed some more perfume on her wrist and breathed it in, deeply, hoping to displace the foul-smelling particles with new, nicer ones.

Before she had left the crime scene, before dawn had even begun to break, Miller had asked her if she would be free to be with Mark so that he could ask the boy more questions and she had agreed to meet him at Mark's house at eight. Callie switched the television on to a 24-hour news programme and turned the sound down low, so that the voices were little more than murmurs. The news of the fourth murder didn't seem to have reached the press yet. With lights off, and only the flickering of the screen as background, she closed her eyes and finally drifted off to sleep.

* * *

Callie was woken by the ringing of her mobile and it took her a few moments to register what the noise was, and why she was asleep on her sofa. She grabbed the phone but had just missed the call. She could see from the display that it was seven o'clock and the call was from the friend she had contacted for gossip about Adrian Lambourne, so she rang back immediately.

"Hi Johnny? It's Callie, sorry I didn't get to the phone in time," she said.

"No problem, I left a message in case you were in the shower or something. Sorry to call so early, but I've a full day ahead. It's been such a long time since I last heard from you, much too long."

"I know, I know. I've been really busy." Callie didn't point out the obvious fact that it wasn't just down to her. He could just as easily have called. "Look, I need to ask you something."

"Of course. How can I help?"

"I was hoping you were still as much of a gossip as you always were, Johnny."

"I think that's slanderous, Dr Hughes. I'll have you know I never gossip. I simply pass on information about my colleagues in the interest of freedom of information."

Callie had forgotten how much she enjoyed talking to Johnny with his particularly bitchy style of gossip and resolved to meet up with him soon, but she would have to make sure she never gave him any personal ammunition as she would hate to be the subject of his conversations with others. She was tempted to ask if he knew about her recent disastrous affair with a consultant at the general hospital, but she was sure he would have done and didn't want to hear his take on it.

"Listen, I wondered if you had heard anything about Adrian Lambourne's divorce?"

"Please, tell me you are not interested in him, Callie? The man goes around with a face like a slapped arse."

"No, no," Callie hastily reassured him, "it was just something I'd heard that might have influenced some decision he has made recently."

"Thank goodness for that. For a moment there, I thought the world had stopped turning. I couldn't imagine a more unsuitable boyfriend for you, than our Dr Lambourne. If you are on the hunt, I could name a dozen more suitable candidates and even put in a good word for you, if you wanted?"

"No, thank you," Callie said, remembering previous men Johnny had set her up with. "I really do just want to hear about Adrian's divorce for work reasons, nothing personal."

"Well, yes, you do have to feel sorry for the man."

"Do you? Why?"

"His wife felt neglected because he worked too hard, poor lamb, so she took her revenge by sleeping around, mainly with his patients, including some of his private ones, and a smattering of his colleagues as well."

"I can see that would be upsetting."

"Upsetting? The man didn't just lose his dignity, he lost most of his income once it all came out. He must have been absolutely, fucking livid, excuse the bad language. I know you're not a fan, but I would have been beside myself with anger if anyone had done that to me."

"Right, yes, it does explain a lot."

"I mean, he's had therapy and he says he's put it behind him, moved on and everything, but I'm not sure I could. Could you?"

Callie thought about some of her past boyfriends and in particular the doctor she most recently fell for, who turned out to have forgotten to tell her about his wife. It had taken a long time to get over the fact that he had tricked her into a relationship – she who had always sworn that she would never ever go out with a married man.

"No. I couldn't," she said at last. "Look, thanks for the call, Johnny, we really must meet up for a drink sometime."

"That would be lovely, and don't let's leave it so long this time. I could bring Dan and you could bring whoever your significant other is currently. Make a night of it."

Callie made her excuses and ended the call with many promises to keep in touch, but the thought of inflicting an evening of Johnny's salacious mix of gossip and sexual innuendo on a boyfriend, even if she had one, did not appeal. That and the fact he thought an evening was a disaster unless everyone got roaring drunk, despite Callie telling him time and time again that she didn't like it. She hated the feeling of being out of control, and of course, she hated the hangover she would inevitably have the next morning. Kate, of course, would enjoy every minute of an evening with Johnny. Perhaps that was the answer. She could go with Kate, and better still, she could arrange to be called away nice and early and leave them all to it.

The information she had got from Johnny had, however, been very useful and Callie started to dial Jayne's number before noticing that it was still early. Perhaps the news of Adrian's awful divorce could wait until after she'd had breakfast, or at least a cup of tea.

* * *

Callie parked her car and hurriedly got out, checking her watch as she did so. She was only a few minutes late and could see Miller's silver saloon car already parked a little further up the street. As she locked her car, she saw, with relief, that Miller had waited for her and was only now getting out of his car.

She was pleased to see that he had come alone, the last thing they needed was for Jeffries to make some crass remark and upset anyone.

"Have you identified the latest victim?" she asked as they walked towards Mark's home.

"No. Not yet."

"Someone must have missed her by now, surely?"

Miller shrugged.

"Her husband could be away, or perhaps they have separated. We just don't know."

"She might not even have been married," Callie mused.

"I think that's rather the point of the website, isn't it?"

"Yes, but people lie online, which is also rather the point, isn't it?"

And he had to concede she was right.

"Was there a can at the latest scene?" she asked as they walked down the short path to Mark's front door.

Miller hesitated before answering.

"No. At least, not that we've found so far."

"Well, they weren't hard to find at the previous scenes, so it's likely there isn't one."

"Yes."

Callie thought about what that meant. Either this latest murder wasn't connected with the previous ones, which seemed unlikely, or the killer knew that his ruse to implicate Mark hadn't worked and was no longer bothering with the misdirection. As the presence of the cans had not been revealed to the press, it once again pointed to the killer being someone close to the investigation. Callie was about to say this to Miller, but one look at his thunderous face told her he was very much aware of the fact and she kept quiet.

They reached the front door and Miller knocked.

The door was opened almost immediately by Mark, who, despite her call to him earlier, explaining why they were coming to see him, was still looking anxious. Callie couldn't blame him. Women were being horrifically killed by someone who had intentionally tried to implicate him. He'd been repeatedly interviewed and held in a police cell, and driven to re-offend because of the stress. Clearly, the calming effect of setting fire to the farm outbuildings was wearing off.

Mark showed them into the living room, where he seemed to have made an attempt to clear up.

"Sorry, we're a bit late, Mark, I got caught just as I was leaving," Callie explained as she came into the living room.

"It's okay."

Miller cleared his throat once they were all seated comfortably.

"Right, as I have said, Mark, we know that these fires are not down to you, but they must be being started by someone you know."

"But, I keep saying, I don't know no one—"

"It's alright, Mark," Callie said as soothingly as possible, "we know you don't know who it is, but what Inspector Miller is trying to say, is that he needs to ask you questions to try and help find out who it is, because I am sure you want them caught as much as we do, right?"

Mark stopped examining his fingernails long enough to look at Callie and nod. Once she was sure Mark was settled again, Callie nodded to Miller to continue.

"So, I know we've talked about the cans found at the scene, but we really need to know how the killer got hold of those cans with your fingerprints on, okay?"

Mark nodded again, without looking up.

"Okay, so you buy them at the local shop, right?"

"Yeah," Mark agreed.

"And you take them with you when you go out?"

"Cheaper than buying drinks out."

"Okay, so you take the cans out with you and when you have finished your drink, you throw them away, where? On the ground?"

"In the bin," Mark seemed insulted. "I don't just chuck 'em on the floor."

"Of course," Miller agreed. "So, you take a can with you when you go to see Dr Hughes?" Miller indicated Callie.

"Sometimes, maybe."

"Or to the hospital?"

Mark nodded.

"Or the job centre?"

"Don't go there," Mark answered. "On account of my problems, I'm on the sick long term, like."

"Can you think of anywhere else you go regularly and take your cans of drink with you?"

Mark thought for a few moments before shaking his head.

Miller sighed in frustration.

"Nowhere at all?" Callie asked him, but he shook his head again.

"Sorry." He really did seem to want to help.

"How about when you meet up with your girlfriend?" Callie persevered.

"Nah. She gets them in for me."

"Same brand?" His reply interested Miller.

"Yeah, but she's not involved right? She wouldn't do this?"

"It's okay. It's just another possible place the person might get hold of them."

"Yeah but lots of places have the same ones, they could've come from anywhere."

"Not with your fingerprints on, Mark," Miller persisted. "The killer must be picking up your used cans from somewhere and it has to be somewhere you go regularly, either with you taking your own drinks, or with somebody else getting them in for you. Do you see?"

Mark seemed to understand.

"You take the drinks with you to medical appointments and your girlfriend has them at her house. Is there anywhere else you drink them?"

Miller paused again whilst Mark gave it some more thought.

"Well, the centre," he finally said.

"What centre?"

"The youth support centre. Where I go and see Miss Austen. They have that brand there, charge 30p for a can, only have drinks and snacks on club nights though, not, like, all the time."

"Club nights?" Miller queried.

"Yeah. Once a month they have nights when they put on like, talks there, and you can play table tennis and that. I have to go as part of my, um, therapy and they're okay, but that fireman, you know the arson man, like, he's always there recently and it's—"

"Chris Butterworth? He goes to the centre?" Miller interrupted, unable to keep the excitement from his voice, making Mark more anxious again.

"Yeah. I don't have a problem with it, like, it's just…" His voice trailed off and he hunched over, looking at the floor.

"Difficult," Callie finished for him. Miller was already on his feet, heading for the door and pulling out his mobile phone.

Chapter 24

Surprisingly, Callie was on time for morning surgery despite warning Linda that she might be a bit late because of her early morning visit to Mark Caxton, and she was amazed when she was still only running slightly late by the time she finished with her last patient. She would normally have gone upstairs to deal with any paperwork, referrals and phone calls, but she decided not to give anyone the chance to delay her, and hurried out of her consulting room, pretending not to hear the receptionist calling to her as she raced through the waiting room and out of the surgery. She wanted to get to the police station and find out what was happening.

Miller had been abrupt to the point of rudeness when warning her not to call Helen before he had a chance to act on the news that Helen Austen and Chris Butterworth both knew about how Mark set fires and had the means to collect his used drink cans. He had hurried away to arrange for them to be picked up without even saying goodbye, but she couldn't blame him. They were clearly top of his suspect list now, or rather Butterworth was – particularly as it had been him who had pointed the finger at Mark in the first place. Callie couldn't imagine that Helen was seriously a suspect, it was hard to see how she could be the murderer, but Butterworth was a different matter altogether.

* * *

By the time Callie had arrived at the police station and Jayne collected her from reception, she was pleased to hear that both Helen and Butterworth had been picked up and that Helen had even had a preliminary interview.

"She really wanted to get things cleared up as quickly as possible," Jayne explained.

"And did she?" Callie asked.

"Well, to be honest, that depends if you believe that it never occurred to her that the cans came from the centre or not."

"Do you?"

"I'm not sure, but no surprises for guessing which sergeant of our acquaintance thinks it's a load of poppycock."

"But I'll bet he didn't use the word poppycock," Callie answered with a grin.

"No," Jayne agreed.

"What about the fireman, Chris Butterworth?"

"He was livid about being picked up at work and marched out in front of the duty fire crews. I think he would have refused to come if the boss hadn't made it clear that he would be arrested if he didn't. Anyway, he has refused to be interviewed without a lawyer present so, we're just waiting for one."

"Is he divorced?" Callie asked as they reached the incident room door and Jayne hesitated before going in.

"Well, that's the strange thing, both he and Helen seem to be happily married, but one of the other social workers at the youth centre said it was assumed they were having an affair because there had to be a reason why Butterworth kept coming back to the centre after the initial time when he had been asked to come and give a talk to the kids about fire safety."

"And it couldn't have been just that he was trying to help."

"Give me a break." Jayne rolled her eyes and opened the door. "No one gives up their evening to help kids like this without some sort of ulterior motive."

Callie wasn't so sure but perhaps she wasn't as cynical as the average police officer.

As Callie entered the room, Miller looked surprised to see her, but not unhappy, she thought with relief.

"Can't keep away from us, eh, Doc?" Jeffries said.

Callie looked a little abashed.

"I, um, well, just wanted to see what happened at the centre and the lead that the cans might have come from there."

Callie knew she had no real right to information about the ongoing investigation, but the fact that she had been involved, and so had one of her patients, made her natural curiosity forgivable. At least she hoped it did.

Miller ushered her into his office and indicated for Jeffries to come with them to Callie's surprise and disappointment. She couldn't help but notice that both of them seemed pumped up and that there was a palpable sense of excitement in the room. It had to mean that they felt they were getting somewhere with the case at last and she felt an enormous relief to think that it might soon be all over.

"Do you know anything about Helen Austen's personal life? Any rumours about her maybe having an affair?" Miller asked her once she had sat down in the visitor's chair. He had perched on the edge of the desk rather than sitting in his chair and Jeffries was leaning against a filing cabinet; this obviously wasn't going to be a long discussion.

"Helen?" Callie was not surprised by this question given Jayne's revelation that the staff at the centre had all assumed she was having an affair with Butterworth and she had given it some thought. "No. As far as I am aware, she has a really good marriage to a lovely guy called, oh what is his name?" She wracked her brains. "Clive! That's it. I think he's an accountant or something."

"Children?"

"Not as far as I know. Look, are you telling me you think Helen is involved? That's ridiculous."

"Why?" Miller retorted. "Why is it ridiculous?"

"Mark's her client. She's a social worker, she helps people. She wouldn't set him up. Why are you so sure she is involved?"

"If she isn't, why didn't she tell us that they served drinks and snacks at the youth centre? And not just any drinks, but the very brand that she knew we were trying to trace? And then when we questioned her about it earlier, and about anyone who might have had access to those cans, why did she not tell us that Chris Butterworth came to those sessions? The same Chris Butterworth who implicated Mark in the first place?"

Miller leant forward as he made final his point and Callie flinched at his obvious anger and conviction that the social worker had to be guilty. True, he wasn't really angry with her, she knew, but it certainly felt like it.

"I don't know," she responded with as much dignity as she could muster after this onslaught, "but I suspect you will find that she is as much a victim in this as Mark is. She would never do anything to harm one of her clients, and if she has omitted to tell you things, then it was probably for a good reason."

"Like what?"

"Maybe because she was trying not to give anyone a reason to pull the centre's funding or she was ashamed of something she had done, like... like..." Callie scrabbled for a reason, "not doing something by the book, fiddling the expenses, or... or... cheating on her husband."

Miller sat back and Jeffries looked interested.

"You think she might be nicking stuff?"

"I don't know!" Callie said in exasperation. "I was just trying to think of a reason why she might not be candid with you under the circumstances, and that seemed like a good one, but honestly, I have no idea. Have you asked her?"

There was a knock on the door and Nigel put his head in.

"Duty solicitor's here, guv."

Nigel gave Callie a sympathetic look, it was clear he had heard every word of her exchange with Miller.

* * *

"It was just awful," Callie told Kate as she curled up on her friend's comfortable sofa and sipped Earl Grey tea. "He was just so angry."

"I can understand why though. I mean, if Helen had been less economical with the truth earlier, he might have caught up with the killer before he killed at least the latest woman. Have they found out who she was, by the way?"

"I didn't even think to ask," Callie admitted. "That's terrible, isn't it? Imagine just being known as the victim, not even having the dignity of a name."

"Doesn't bear thinking about." Kate shivered. "Poor woman. I do hope they manage to identify her and let her nearest and dearest know so that she can have a proper funeral."

"That's if she does have any nearest or dearest. I mean, just because she's on an adultery site, doesn't necessarily mean she is actually in a relationship, she might just be there because promising sex without strings might be the only way she can get anyone."

They both thought about that sad idea for a moment.

"Like I said just now," Kate finally said, "it doesn't bear thinking about."

"I don't know Helen well, but I can't see her turning a blind eye to her lover murdering women, let alone covering for him. And doesn't it rather undermine the motive if the killer is having an affair with a married woman anyway?" Kate continued.

"We don't know that they are having an affair," Callie reminded her. "That's what makes me so cross, everyone is just jumping to conclusions. Perhaps they are both behaving, sacrificing their happiness in order to be faithful to their partners."

"And maybe the fireman's wife is putting it about a bit and is having loads of fun whilst he's being a good boy and the frustration has turned him into a homicidal maniac."

"Your imagination is even more lurid than mine, Kate Ward," Callie admonished her. "I'm sure Steve Miller is doing his best to get to the bottom of it and I, for one, am just pleased to know they have a suspect in custody. Maybe I'll get a full night's sleep on Saturday."

Chapter 25

It was all over the early morning news that someone had been arrested for the "Death by Burning" murders. The news vans had moved from the picturesque scenes of the crimes and were now camped outside the utilitarian police station where they continued to speculate on very little real information. It would seem that the police had not, so far, named the suspect they had arrested. As Callie ate breakfast, she sat glued to her television, watching, like most of the population of Hastings, an interview with an expert on arson who dropped the very large hint that people fascinated by fire often joined the fire service.

Callie understood that for most people, being arrested was the same thing as being charged, but she knew there was the world of difference. Butterworth would have been arrested on suspicion of the murders, but the police had to meet the prosecution service criteria on evidence before they would allow him to be charged. Callie was interested that the press, so far, hadn't named the firefighter in question but she wondered how long it would take before they did.

* * *

Throughout the morning Callie checked a news app on her phone, and also the local newspaper online, but there was nothing new reported, just endless rehashes of the same meagre facts. Despite the obvious fact that Butterworth had not been charged, Callie could feel a palpable sense of relief in the air of the main office when she went up after morning surgery to collect her paperwork. Just knowing that the police had someone in custody had taken a weight off each and every one of them.

"Is it him, do you think?" Linda whispered, startling Callie who had not noticed her follow when she left the office. Linda had a batch of prescriptions in her hand and added them to the already overflowing pile in Callie's basket. Callie realised that Linda had probably kept them back deliberately so that she could come out and speak to her.

"I hope so," Callie replied. "They must have good reason to think so or they wouldn't have arrested him."

"Yes, but you do hear of the police arresting people wrongly, like that landlord chap in Bristol," Dr Sinha said, having openly listened to the whispered conversation. "It was only when someone else was convicted that people actually believed he was innocent."

"You are so right, Gauri. And here was I hoping that now they had arrested that firefighter, Dr Hughes here might actually apologise for having accused me of being the murderer."

Callie's heart sank as she realised Gerry Brown had also come into the office and heard their conversation, and that he had been closely followed by Dr Grantham.

"I didn't accuse you of anything, Gerry. I simply told the police some things that you really should have told them in the first place." Despite her crisp tone, Callie could feel a flush rising up her neck and knew her cheeks would be burning in a moment. How she wished her body wouldn't betray her feelings of shame and embarrassment quite so readily.

Dr Grantham put a restraining hand on Gerry's arm and cleared his throat.

"Erm, unfortunately, Dr Brown has tendered his resignation, and I have reluctantly agreed to accept it." He looked around the room and allowed his eyes to rest on Callie. "He will be leaving straightaway and has just come to collect his personal belongings and to say goodbye. I am sure we all wish him the best in his new role."

Wisely, Dr Grantham didn't mention what that role would be, but Callie could hazard a guess that it wouldn't be to do with medicine as she speculated that his rapid departure was because the GMC had suspended him pending further enquiries having found out about his antics at the sex addiction clinic. Or maybe Dr Grantham had decided he could no longer support a doctor who was not taking his rehabilitation seriously.

There was a short silence as Dr Grantham waited for someone to say something and it was Linda who found her voice first.

"I'm sure I can speak on behalf of all the reception and office staff when I say we are all very sorry that you are going, Dr Brown."

Callie knew that they wouldn't be sorry to see him go at all, just sorry about all the extra work it was going to cause, and she could sympathise with that.

"Yes," she added to Linda's short speech, keeping it similarly general and vague. "And I hope your new role is all you hope it will be."

"Like you care." Gerry wasn't going to keep things impersonal, it seemed. "How do you think it feels to know that not only are you the subject of malicious gossip at work, but that one of your colleagues has actually gone and passed on that gossip to the police?"

"I think that's a little harsh, Gerry," Dr Grantham cut in before Callie could answer. "We all have a duty to be open with the police and whilst I feel that Callie would have done better to bring the information to me as senior partner so that we could discuss it and ask you for an explanation before taking it the police, her close working relationship with them probably influenced her decision."

He gave Callie a look redolent of disappointment rather than reproof and her flush deepened, because she knew he was right.

"However, I think, under the circumstances we should now close the subject. Have you got all your things, Dr Brown?" He was clearly keen to keep the goodbyes as short as possible.

Gerry nodded, and he turned to leave the room with a look that suggested to Callie that he wasn't going to let matters rest there and she would be wise to watch her back, particularly in view of his prior stalking of Kate.

"Good, now I suggest we get on with our work and remember that our patients must always come first," Dr Grantham said firmly as he showed Gerry out of the room, and, presumably, made sure he left the premises.

"At least we won't always have his car taking up space in the carpark." Gauri was practical and unfazed by it all, as usual.

"Yes, but we will have to cover his surgeries." Callie felt tired just thinking about it.

"We ended up seeing most of the patients he saw again, to actually do something or put right what little he had done, so it won't be that much extra work."

"I'll get back onto the agency and see if they have anyone on their books." Linda hurried back to the main office.

"If they did, we wouldn't have ended up with Dr Brown," Gauri said to the closing door.

"I'm sorry," Callie said.

"What have you got to be sorry about?" Gauri seemed genuinely not to know.

"Well, it's my fault he's left," Callie explained, but Gauri waved her response away.

"It's not your fault, Callie. It's Dr Brown's. Perhaps he should have learnt to keep his trousers buttoned."

Callie sat down at the terminal next to her and started sorting her work into piles: one for repeat prescription requests, another for hospital letters, then further piles for test results and post-it notes. She started with the pile of post-it notes. The third note was from Dr Simms, the GP who had agreed to take on the Hollingsworths as patients; he had left a message asking her to give him a call.

Callie reached for one of the phones before stopping. Hugh had just entered the office having seen Dr Brown out and this call would probably be better done without an audience. Hugh would not be impressed that she was still involved with the Hollingsworths after the complaint of harassment and she was already on the naughty step over Gerry, so it would be much better if he didn't know she was in touch with their new doctor. She packed all her paperwork back into her basket and left the room with a breezy, "I have some phone calls to make and don't want to disturb you all," and hurried out, but not before Hugh had given her another look of disappointment. He clearly didn't believe for a moment that she was anxious about disturbing the others.

* * *

Once she was safely in the privacy of her own consulting room, Callie picked up the phone and called the mobile number that Dr Simms had asked her to use.

"Hello? Dr Simms?" she said when he picked up and answered in his recognisable Scottish brogue. "This is Callie Hughes returning your call."

"Ah. Thank you, Dr Hughes. Let me just take this outside."

Callie heard the sound of doors opening and closing before he continued.

"Yes, thank you for getting back to me so promptly. I received your email with the summary notes on both Mr and Mrs Hollingsworth, and having read them I realised that I needed to see the lady as some tests were overdue, as you pointed out. I would have called the woman herself, but we only seemed to have a note of the husband's phone number, a mobile, and no landline or mobile number for the wife. So, I phoned the husband and left a message asking him to get his wife to make an appointment, and got no response. I called again a couple of days later without result, and so got my practice manager to try. She left another message, saying that it was practice policy for all new patients to have a check with the practice nurse and please could he make appointments for them both."

"Did you get a response to that?" Callie asked.

"Well, you could say that, yes. This morning my practice manager got a call to say they had changed their mind as I was too far away and they were going to find a GP in Hastings, which is, of course, what I suggested they do in the first place."

"Did he say what practice they were going to?"

"No, he said he'd let us know when he found one."

"And meanwhile they are in limbo with no one looking after Mrs Hollingsworth and monitoring her thyroid and with her having no way of getting her medication."

"Exactly, which is why I thought I would let you know. I have real concerns about that poor woman."

"Me too."

"Not that I've ever met her of course."

"And it's a while since I've seen her," Callie told him. "A long while," she added thoughtfully.

Of course, Callie had many patients that she never saw from one year to the next, but that was usually because they were not sick or they were avoiding her because they didn't want to hear her advice to stop smoking, cut down the drinking or lose weight, but Jill Hollingsworth didn't fall into any of those categories. She had a chronic disease that needed medication in order for her to remain well. She had been delighted with how much better she had felt once her thyroid function levels improved. So why would she stop taking her drugs? And why was David Hollingsworth being so obstructive? What possible reason could he have for stopping his wife from being treated properly?

All the while she was trying to push down the thought that had come to her when Dr Simms had said he hadn't met Jill – what if something had happened to her? What if she was dead? It would certainly explain why she wasn't responding to letters or calls and, if David was involved, it would explain why he was going to such great lengths to keep everyone from checking up on her. Callie continued with her paperwork, finishing it as fast as she could whilst still making sure it was done correctly. It was all too easy for a doctor to lose concentration and miss something important, too easy to cause harm, or even kill a patient because of a decimal point in the wrong place or a failure to spot drugs that interact.

By the time she had finished the last repeat prescription, she had made a decision. She was going to go and visit the Hollingsworth farm and hope to find Jill there on her own, despite knowing that if she bumped into David, he would make another complaint and she wouldn't have a leg to stand on. After all, Jill wasn't even her patient anymore.

* * *

Callie drove up the long track that led to the Hollingsworth farm, carefully watching for signs that David was working in the fields as she passed in case he spotted her, but everywhere seemed deserted. She parked by the farmhouse and once again she was struck by how unloved and uncared for the place looked. It was a grey, damp day although it wasn't actually raining and somehow the weather seemed to suit these surroundings. There was no sign of David anywhere, she could hear no tractor engines or dogs barking, but that didn't mean he wasn't in the house having a late lunch.

Callie gave herself a mental shake, she couldn't stay in the car forever, apart from anything else she had to get back for evening surgery, so she got out, being careful to shut the driver's door quietly and keeping the keys in her hand in case she needed to make a quick getaway. Looking and listening as she walked, she approached the silent house and knocked on the door. Her heart was hammering and her hands felt damp with sweat. She had no idea what she would do if he answered rather than Jill. Run for it probably.

There was no answer, so Callie knocked again, a little louder, and still hearing nothing, gently tried the door. It was unlocked, and she opened it wide enough to go in and stand just inside the doorway. The door opened straight into the large farmhouse kitchen. When Callie had visited here before, she had always been struck by how warm and welcoming it was with the big range cooker pumping out heat and cooking smells, the well-used, solid wood kitchen table, pretty chintz curtains and a large, saggy armchair draped with a hand-crocheted blanket. Now, the room seemed cold and untidy, the range wasn't lit and washing up was piled high in the sink. The armchair was still there though and Jill was fast asleep in it, with the blanket wrapped around her.

"Hello?" Callie said quietly, relieved to find out that her worst fear, that Jill was dead, was unfounded. There was no response other than a little snort from Jill, so Callie went up to the chair and gave her a little shake.

"Jill? Jill? It's me, Dr Hughes."

Jill woke with a start and stared at Callie without recognition for a moment before realising who she was.

"Dr Hughes, of course, yes." She struggled out of the chair. "I must have fallen asleep," she said with a little laugh. "I'll put the kettle on. I must have forgotten you were coming."

"I was just passing, thought I'd drop in. Is that okay?"

"Oh, of course. My memory's so bad these days, I just assumed—" Jill turned back to the sink and slowly filled the kettle. Callie was disappointed that, despite the layers of clothing she seemed to have on, she could see that Jill had put back on all the weight she had lost once her thyroid function had been stabilised.

"How are you feeling, Jill?" she asked her ex-patient.

"Oh, I'm fine, just a bit tired, that's all," Jill explained as she put the kettle on the range before realising that it was cold. "Damn! I must have let it go out. Not to worry, I'll just stick the electric one on."

"Jill, stop a moment."

Jill turned to look at Callie, surprised at her stern voice.

"I don't need a cup of tea. I know you are no longer my patient, but I'm concerned—"

"What do you mean?" Jill was genuinely surprised. "No longer your patient? Have you taken us off your list?"

"No." Callie was equally taken aback. "You changed doctors. Moved to a practice the other side of Winchelsea. Did you not know?"

Jill sat back down in the armchair.

"Why would I change doctors?"

"I don't really know," Callie said. "Except that you haven't been to see me in ages, despite repeated requests to do so. Look, I'm concerned, Jill, are you taking your tablets?"

"Of course. Every day, just as you said I had to, although I don't think these new ones are as good as the old ones."

"What new ones?"

"The new make of thyroxine you've started me on." Jill levered herself out of her chair again, went over to a cupboard and took out a small brown bottle containing white pills and gave it to Callie. Callie looked at the label. It had a pharmacy label on it, slightly askew, claiming the bottle contained Levothyroxine 125 mcg and that one tablet was to be taken each day before breakfast.

"Pharmacies have to dispense medicines in calendar packs these days, Jill," Callie explained. "You know, those foil strips with fourteen tablets in? So that patients can see if they've missed a dose."

"I did wonder why they seemed to have changed," Jill replied.

Callie opened the bottle and tipped a few of the tablets out into the palm of her hand. They were round rather than lozenge shaped and there was nothing etched on the back of them as she had expected. They definitely didn't look like thyroxine tablets, and Callie tentatively rubbed one between her finger and thumb and then licked the residue off her thumb. Just as she did that, the door was flung open by a furious looking David.

"I don't know what this is, but I'm pretty sure it's not your thyroid tablet," she said to Jill with conviction as she looked him in the eye.

Chapter 26

They sat around the wooden table in the kitchen drinking cups of tea that Callie had made once she had calmed the situation down. There was still a lingering atmosphere, but at least David had stopped shouting at her once he realised that it was too late and Jill finally knew what had been going on.

"I still don't understand why you did it, David," Jill said. The anger that she had felt once she realised that her husband had been substituting her medicine with sweeteners had subsided and she had reverted to her previous lethargic state.

"Because of who you became when you took 'em." David rubbed his face and tried to explain.

"When we met, you was lovely, a bit quiet maybe, but we had a good life here and you never complained. Then the Doc here" – he gestured at Callie – "said you needed tablets 'cos your thyroid wasn't working proper, like, and you changed."

"How do you mean?"

"Suddenly you was rushing round and arguing with me all the time."

"No, I wasn't!"

Callie could see that Jill wasn't sure.

"Telling me to do this, do that, fix the windows, paint the kitchen. Nag, nag, nag. That's all you did. You weren't the same woman I married."

Jill looked at her husband in shocked silence, but he couldn't hold her gaze.

"All I wanted was a bit of peace and quiet." He stood up and turned towards the door. "I've got things to do."

"Just you wait one minute, David Hollingsworth." Jill stood up so suddenly her chair tipped over and David turned back to her in surprise. "Are you telling me that you like me tired, overweight and depressed because it means you get a quiet life, to the point that when the doctor here made me better with the thyroid pills you switched them to make me ill again?"

"Well" – David did look ashamed of himself and he struggled to find a better way of expressing it – "yes, I did. I didn't want you to be ill, though, but, I suppose, I mean, I'd've been happy if you were a bit better, more cheerful like, but I just couldn't take your constant–"

"Nagging, yes, I've got the picture."

Jill sat down again.

"Why didn't you say?"

David came back to the table and sat down again as well.

"It weren't easy, like. You was so busy doing stuff all the time. Rushing here, rushing there."

"For the first time in years, I had energy. I wanted to get things done."

"I know."

Jill gave a little laugh.

"Now you mention it, I must have been hell to live with. I never stopped, hardly slept."

David nodded.

"It weren't easy."

"But I can't live like this."

"No. I know that." David sighed.

"What do you say we give it another try?"

He nodded agreement, but looked miserable.

Callie cleared her throat and they both turned to her.

"It might just be that the dose was too high and made you a little hyperthyroid," Callie suggested. "Perhaps we could start with a lower dose? Monitor it carefully and see how things go. Make sure you don't get so, um, hyperactive?"

Jill nodded.

"That sounds a good idea." She turned to her husband. "What do you think David?"

"All right."

He still didn't seem sure.

"You'll need to re-register with me though, Jill."

"Of course."

Callie looked directly at David.

"Where you are registered is entirely up to you, but you need to know that if Jill stops coming in for her regular reviews, I'll be up here in a flash. And if I suspect you have started messing with her tablets again, I'll have no option but to involve the police."

Callie wasn't quite sure what crime he could be charged with but she was sure there would be something.

"I won't do that again, I promise."

David looked honestly ashamed of what he had been doing and Callie believed him.

"Don't you worry, Dr Hughes, now I know what he's been up to, I'll be keeping a close eye and making sure I see you regularly."

Callie was pretty sure Jill would, now she knew what had been going on.

"Right, I'll just go and get my bag so that I can do a prescription for you, and I'll leave a blood test form. You need to get that done in a couple of weeks, so we can see how you are responding. Okay?"

As Callie went to her car, she wondered how they were going to get on. Whilst she had some sympathy with David if Jill had been as bad as he was making out, had Callie found out her own husband had been deliberately keeping her in a state of hypothyroidism, she would have left him without hesitation. Provided she had the energy to leave, once she was better. Perhaps Jill would do that, or maybe, she had other plans to exact her revenge. Either way, Callie had a sneaky suspicion that Jill was never going to let David forget what he had done.

* * *

Callie's hair was still damp from the shower, and her face had a rosy glow brought on by exercise and self-righteousness as she sipped her green tea and watched Kate tuck into a slice of Bakewell tart, slathered in cream. They were in the small café area of the gym where they both had membership. Kate's hair was dry, not just because she hadn't showered, but also because she hadn't exercised either.

"Yum," Kate murmured. "Are you sure you don't want to try some?"

"No, thank you. Not after working out for an hour."

"Go on. Loosen your stays and live a little."

"It's not because I'm treating my body as a temple, I can assure you, it's just that I'm too tired to eat." Callie stretched and groaned quietly. "I should do this more often and then it wouldn't hurt so much."

"Nonsense. It would just hurt more often. Exercise isn't good for you."

"I don't understand why you keep paying for gym membership when you never use it."

"What do you mean, never use it? I'm here, aren't I?"

"Yes, but—"

"And I'm enjoying myself, eating cake and watching all these fit young men in shorts getting all hot and sweaty."

"You are awful."

"But you like me." Kate finished the catch phrase for her and ate more cake. "So, have they charged the fireman yet?"

"Not as far as I know. I heard they had found a match book similar to the ones used in the crimes, in a drawer in his desk, I think, but they haven't linked him to the website yet or identified the last victim either, if my informant is right, which I think she is."

Kate clocked the fact that Callie's information was not coming from Miller direct.

"They probably won't charge him until at least tomorrow lunchtime, if they have any sense. They'll want to do as much as they can before having to commit themselves."

"That's always supposing they have enough evidence by then." Callie wasn't sure what they could have found in the time. "Are you still in touch with anyone from the website?"

"Absolutely," Kate confirmed. "I'm meeting someone tomorrow night."

Callie looked worried.

"What?" Kate asked her. "Even if they have to let him go, it can't be the fireman I'm meeting because we have been texting whilst he's been under arrest at the nick and I can't believe they would allow him to continue to contact potential victims in between interrogations."

Callie knew she was right, but she couldn't help feeling anxious for her friend.

"At least let me be wherever you have arranged to meet. Just in case."

"I'm not a child. I've done this before and I do know how to look after myself."

"I won't interfere, I'll sit quietly in a corner and just be there if you need me. At least if I see you suddenly acting like you've been drugged, I can come to the rescue."

"What are you like? Do you not think I know how protect my own drink from someone wanting to add a date rape drug? I have done this before, you know."

"I know, I know, but humour me, will you?"

Kate sighed. She knew that Callie would indeed worry if she didn't let her be there. Callie's level of anxiety about those she cared for was part of what Kate loved about her friend.

"Oh, all right."

"Thank you."

"But if I decide to take him home, you're not coming with me."

"You wouldn't, would you? Not on a first date." Callie was horrified.

"Depends how fit he is," Kate said with a wicked smile and finished her cake.

Chapter 27

The papers the next morning were full of the story that the fourth victim had been identified as an unmarried bakery worker. It could mean that Callie was wrong with her theory about the deaths being punishment for adultery, or that the killer had made a mistake and murdered someone who didn't fit his criteria. Callie knew that the police would be using that fact in their continued questioning of Chris Butterworth, telling him he had killed an innocent woman, and she hoped that the tactic worked. No one in their right mind would think it reasonable to sentence a woman to death for adultery, but the sort of man who did think that, might be shamed into an admission if he knew he had chosen his victim wrongly.

She was desperate for this to be over; for the police – for Miller – to have got his man and for the murderer to be safely off the streets, but without some concrete evidence, it was unlikely that Miller would be able to hold Butterworth and he would be bailed later in the day. Even with Kate's breezy assurance that her date couldn't be the killer, Callie couldn't help but worry about Kate's plan for the evening. Until she was quite sure the murderer had been caught, charged and was languishing in jail somewhere, she didn't think her friend should be internet dating at all and certainly not using the SSE website. If she was honest, she had misgivings about the safety of internet dating anyway, without the added danger of a serial killer using it to find his victims.

Her hand hesitated over the phone. With Chris Butterworth in custody, it seemed likely that Miller would be frantically trying to make his case and really wouldn't have time to speak to her. On the other hand, her friend's safety was at stake.

She took a deep breath, picked up the receiver and dialled the number. She needed the reassurance that Miller had the right man and she just hoped he would be able to give it to her.

Unfortunately, as she had expected, she was unable to get hold of him, and Callie had to make do with the information she managed to prise out of Nigel. He told her that Chris Butterworth was in the process of being interviewed and that therefore she couldn't speak to Miller or Jeffries, but he hadn't been able to put her mind at rest. He would not give her any further details and certainly would not hazard an opinion about the likelihood of Butterworth being the murderer. She had, at least, persuaded Nigel to leave a note on Miller's desk asking him to ring her as soon as he was free.

She then tried Jayne, who was busy overseeing the search of Butterworth's home and office and had little time to update her. The match book similar to those used in the fires which had been found, was useful but not conclusive, Jayne confided. She had little doubt that Butterworth would be able to explain it away, particularly as it was from California and none of those in Mark's collection or used so far in the murders had been from anywhere other than England.

Callie felt no further forward and she would just have to hope that either Butterworth was charged or that Miller would be able to call her back before Kate's date that evening. She wanted to hear from him that he was sure Butterworth was the man, or she would be tempted to disrupt the date to make sure Kate was safe, even if it made her friend cross. There was no way she could let Kate put herself in danger and do nothing to stop it. What if Kate became victim number five? She would never forgive herself. If she thought there was any risk, Callie would stop the date even if it made Kate so angry about it that she never spoke to her again.

* * *

So that stupid girl had been single? Having spent an evening with her, he could understand why. The bitch! It made him angry to think that he had wasted his time with her. Her constant chatter about trivial things, soaps and so-called celebrities, in which he had no interest whatsoever, had been tedious and irritating. If he hadn't been thinking about later, to what he had planned for her, he would have been unable to keep the boredom from his face. Not that she would have noticed, being so caught up in the intimate details of her idols as reported in the magazines she read and the programmes she watched. But that didn't change the fact that she had deliberately used a website for cheats and whores.

Why would she do that if she wasn't married? Did she hate married people? Had envy turned to hate when she couldn't find a man to stay with her long enough to get married? Why would she choose to tempt and ensnare married men if not to destroy marriages? Destroy other people's happy lives? She was as guilty as the whores who cheated on their husbands and he felt no guilt for wrongly punishing her, because she still deserved it and he was sure he was right to have done it. There couldn't be many unattached people using the website, the first three women had all been married, so he needn't worry too much about getting another single lady. He was sure the date he had lined up that night was married from what she had told him, but he could always check once he met her. It would be hard to walk away when he was all prepped and ready to go, but he could do if he needed to, he was sure. He just hoped he wouldn't need to. He needed to kill again. He needed the thrill and the feeling of success, of achievement for having punished another vicious, conniving, adulterous bitch. Killing tonight would be the only way he could wipe away the feeling of having been cheated by his last victim.

Chapter 28

Callie looked round the packed bar and tried to find somewhere to sit where she could keep an eye on Kate without being too obvious. The Mojo was a well-known meeting place on the singles scene most evenings, unless it was a European football night or there was some other televised sporting event, when it got too busy.

It being a Saturday night, the singles had taken precedence over sport, the multiple televisions were muted, some had even been switched off, and music was thumping out from the sound system. The current clientele were eating their gourmet burgers off what looked like lengths of plank that seemed to be the speciality of the bar and knocking back the cocktail of the week: a vivid pink affair served in a jam jar. According to the posters stuck around the room, there would be a DJ later, to enhance their entertainment. Or not. Callie hoped that they didn't have to stay for that part of the night.

Searching round for somewhere to sit, she could see a small table in the corner, but much as she would like to tuck herself away from the main throng, she rejected it because there was no way she could keep Kate in view from there. Kate was seated at the bar, sipping an incredibly expensive Mojito, having spurned all the beers on offer when they arrived. To Callie all beers tasted pretty much the same, but then, she could be very picky with her white wines, so she couldn't really complain. Callie had decided she would not drink alcohol, partly so that she would stay alert and partly because if Kate liked her date and wanted to be left alone, Callie wanted to be able to drive herself home.

Having finally found a stool to sit on at the corner of a table where she was obviously not wanted by the current occupants, Callie sipped her lime and soda. It was far too heavy on the lime, a common mistake of bartenders in her experience, and checked her phone again, hoping for a message from Miller. There was none and there was no point trying to call him from the bar as the noise level would mean she couldn't possibly hear anything he might have to say anyway. Instead she sent him a text message, asking if he was sure the killer was Butterworth and explaining that Kate was meeting a date from SSE at the Mojo bar and that she was going to be there just to make sure she was okay.

She had been reassured to hear from Jayne Hales – the only person she could get to answer a phone in the incident room when she had called yet again before coming out – that Miller had ordered round the clock surveillance on Butterworth. Jayne had really stuck her neck out telling her that, and had taken her mobile out into a corridor outside the incident room so that she would not be overheard. It was one thing for the boss to okay her giving more general information to Callie, but this was far more sensitive and she knew it could backfire on her if anyone found out. Callie was very grateful for the information, otherwise she would have had no choice but to march Kate home and lock her in to prevent her meeting anyone. Miller clearly still thought Butterworth was their man or he would not have authorised the watch, she reasoned. He didn't have enough men on the squad to waste their time like that, and even if Butterworth managed to somehow slip past the surveillance team, she would recognise him as soon as he walked in the pub.

Callie looked up sharply and held her breath as she saw Kate being approached by a man, but it clearly wasn't her date as she said something and he moved away. It was hardly surprising that Kate was attracting men in a bar like this, particularly as she was dressed in a red chiffon blouse that left little to the imagination. Callie hoped she wasn't knocking back the Mojito at the same pace she normally drank beer, or she would be on the floor before the date showed up.

Callie checked her watch again and saw that Kate's SSE date was late. Perhaps he would stand her up and they could spend the rest of the evening in the Stag or go for a meal somewhere nice. It would certainly be a relief after the noise in the bar, not to mention the men who occasionally tried to engage her in conversation, only to be given her best 'leave me alone' stare. Callie had found, to her cost on a number of occasions, that you had to be blunt in these sorts of situations, as being polite or pleasant when saying no to a drink or to a chat, was taken as acquiescence. It seemed that a couple of drinks made most men convinced that they were irresistible. And funny.

Callie looked round the room, wondering if there was CCTV anywhere in the bar, but could only see what might be a camera by the till, presumably to keep an eye on the staff rather than the clientele.

This close to the town centre there would almost certainly be cameras in the streets outside, which made her feel safer as she knew from what she had heard in the incident room, that the killer liked to meet in places where there was no CCTV around, although there must be precious few venues left without some kind of surveillance. She panicked slightly when her view of Kate was blocked by a bunch of rowdy young men trying to get served at the bar. She shifted her position slightly, ignoring the looks from the people whose space she invaded as a result, and caught Kate's eye. Kate shrugged, and held up her hand palm out, indicating that she would give him another five minutes. Callie nodded that she understood.

At last a man came up to Kate and they started talking. He was well-dressed and incredibly good-looking. Callie wondered why he had to resort to a dating website, but then kicked herself as she remembered, of course, it was because he was already married. Kate was smiling and flirting with him and when he turned to the bar to get them both a drink, she gave Callie a theatrical wink and a thumbs up. She was clearly taken with him.

Callie was so busy concentrating on watching Kate, that when she turned back to take a sip of her drink, it took her a moment or two to realise that Adrian Lambourne had just come into the bar and appeared to be looking for someone. What on earth was he doing here? She stood up and started to walk towards him just as he looked round and saw her. A look of surprise and mild panic swept across his face and Callie wondered if it was because he wasn't sure if she was still angry with him about Mark.

"Hi Adrian, I didn't expect to see you in a place like this."

"Dr Hughes. How lovely." He had recovered quickly and managed to smile at her.

"I'm sorry, you were probably meeting someone here. Don't think you have to stay and talk to me." Callie saw that her table had already been taken by someone else and she started to look around to see if there were any other spaces.

"I, um, can't see her. I think I may have been stood up. I may as well go," he explained as he indicated towards the door. He seemed eager to leave and his embarrassment was really quite endearing, and Callie felt sorry for him.

"Oh well, we're both in the same boat then." Callie nodded towards Kate who was still engrossed in her date. "My friend seems to have pulled."

"Oh, right," Adrian looked at Kate and gave a little smile of understanding.

Callie realised that she had put him in an awkward situation as he now couldn't leave without seeming ungallant for leaving her alone, but it would be easier from her point of view to have someone to talk to, even if it was only for a few minutes until she was sure Kate was okay.

"Let me get you a drink by way of an apology for being so sharp with you over my patient. I really do understand how hard it must be to find beds for them the way things are with the NHS right now. What will you have?"

"No, no, there's no need–"

"I insist, Adrian, or else I will never believe you have forgiven me." Callie turned to the bar to try and get the bartender's attention, which wasn't going to be easy given how crowded the place was. "Who were you meeting?" she asked casually.

"Oh, just a friend of a friend. Look, I really–"

"Friends always try to set you up with the most unsuitable people, don't they?" Callie could think of several tortured evenings. "I've often wondered about using dating websites, but wrote them off as full of weirdos, not to mention murderers, but my friend seems to have found someone reasonable." She nodded towards Kate. "In fact, he's doesn't look bad at all. Have you ever given them a go?" Callie had finally managed to catch the bartender's eye, so she missed the look of fear that briefly crossed Adrian's face and he had regained his anxious but unassuming look before she turned and asked, "What was it you said you wanted?"

"Um, slimline tonic, but really–"

"Slimline tonic and a lime and soda, please," Callie said to the bartender.

As they waited for their drinks, Callie went back to the topic of dating websites.

"So, have you ever used internet dating?" she asked again.

"No," he responded. "Like you, it never appealed to me."

Something about the way he said it made her think that he was lying. Perhaps he was embarrassed about it. She realised that he had spotted her disbelief and was relieved when the barman brought the lime and soda over.

"Here," Callie interrupted him again and handed him her drink to hold whilst she pushed slightly forward and took some money from her purse. She could see Kate was laughing at something the man with her had said. She seemed happy and the man didn't look like a serial killer but Callie didn't intend to leave the bar just yet. She'd keep an eye on her friend for a while longer. Having finally managed to get the tonic and pay, Callie took Adrian's drink back to him and retrieved her own.

"Can you see anywhere we can sit?" She looked round but she couldn't see anywhere free.

"It's quieter outside," Adrian said. "It's a nice evening. Quite warm for the time of year."

Callie hesitated. He was right, it was a warm evening and it would be much nicer outside but she was unsure that she wanted to let Kate out of her sight yet.

"You'll be able to see if your friend leaves."

Adrian seemed to understand her concerns, and Callie realised that he was right. There was only the one way in and Kate would have to walk past them if she left.

"Okay." Callie followed him outside where a few tables had been placed on the wide pavement, mainly to allow smokers a chance to get their fix in relative comfort. There were a few people puffing at their cigarettes or vaping but several of the tables were empty. Adrian led the way to one that was a little apart from the others, but didn't sit down. Callie looked at the seats and saw they were a little damp and also stayed standing.

"So we don't have to breathe in any second-hand smoke," he explained.

Callie was pleased by his thoughtfulness.

"I won't stay much longer anyway. My friend seems to be getting on just fine."

Callie sipped her drink, wondering if she should have had it topped up with soda because it, once again, had far too much lime in it. She shivered slightly and pulled her coat more firmly round her.

"I'm sorry. Are you cold?" Adrian asked. "It's just a relief to get away from that terrible music."

"I'm fine," Callie insisted. "And it is a relief. Why they have to have it up so loud, I don't know. Oh dear" – Callie laughed as she took another drink – "I sound like my mother."

Adrian smiled.

"Would you like to sit down?" he asked, and she decided that yes she did want to sit down, because she was feeling a bit strange. He hastily wiped the seat with his handkerchief as she sat with a bump and wondered if she was going to faint. Everything seemed very distant. She thought she could hear her phone ringing, and she pulled the phone out of her pocket to answer but it was beyond her. She was aware of someone closer by speaking to her.

"How are you feeling, Callie?"

She wanted to answer, but couldn't get the words out.

"Here let me help you over to my car, I'll take you home."

It was a kind voice, a voice she recognised but couldn't quite place and she allowed herself to be led away from the noise and the lights. She wanted to rest, to sleep, and this kind person with his reassuring therapeutic voice was offering to take her home.

"It's not far, just over here," the voice encouraged her when she stumbled and she walked on, leaning heavily on his arm, grateful for his help.

Chapter 29

As she drifted in and out of consciousness, Callie realised that she was in the front passenger seat of a car she didn't recognise. She felt ill and her mind was fuzzy, spaced out, in fact. She vaguely registered that the car was small and that she was feeling sick. She was being thrown around as the car travelled at speed through the streets using minor roads that twisted and turned nauseatingly. She turned to get a look at who was driving, but that made her nausea worse and she closed her eyes again.

"Please slow down," she thought she said but she wasn't sure it came out clearly.

"Shush now, it will all be fine," the voice responded and she thought she recognised it. Who was it? She couldn't quite put her finger on it, but the voice was reassuring, kind and she allowed herself to drift away for a moment. She came to with a start as they made a violent right turn that flung her against the door. It came to her suddenly. The psychologist, that was it, Adrian something. She really couldn't think clearly, but she was reassured, she was with a friend and she only half listened to what he continued to tell her in his soothing voice.

"I never would have taken you, but you were bound to put two and two together eventually. Tomorrow or the next day you would realise that your friend was meeting me, realise that I had connections to Mark Caxton. You'd begin to be suspicious of me then and, given your work with the police, you'd tell them. I couldn't let you do that. You must understand."

His words made no sense to Callie at all. What on earth was he talking about? And she was so tired, maybe she should have a little sleep and then she would feel better and be able to understand what was going on. She closed her eyes again and let his words wash over her. But instead of being able to sleep, she had a sudden flash of memory. It was to do with Mark Caxton, stolen cars and fire. And then it came back to her and she was wide awake.

"Stop!" she said and started opening her door. There was something stopping her from moving and she realised that her seat belt was fastened. The car veered across the road as Adrian reached across her and the door swung wide, hitting something, a car, a road sign, Callie wasn't sure, but there was a bang and she heard a shout before the car lurched again. The door swung back and Adrian grabbed it, slamming it shut. She was still struggling to free the seat belt clasp when he hit her, hard, in the face and everything went black.

When she came to, Callie's head hurt and she couldn't think straight. She had no idea how long she had been unconscious. She lay back in her seat trying to brace herself against the lurches of the car. They were driving at great speed. She tentatively opened one eye and saw they were on a minor road with cars parked on both sides of it. If anyone came the other way, they would have no time to stop. She tried to think. She was in a car with Adrian Lambourne, who had hit her, that was why her head hurt. Adrian was the serial killer, of that she no longer had any doubt. Had he hit his previous victims? She thought not. What was it he had used to drug them? GHB, that was it.

Perhaps they had all remained drugged because they'd mixed it with alcohol. That made sense. She hadn't been drinking so she had come round unexpectedly. She tensed as the car swerved round a corner and she was thrown against the door. She couldn't help a small grunt of pain escaping as her head hit the glass.

"Don't even think about trying anything at this speed. We'll both be killed." Lambourne had heard the grunt and was aware she was conscious again.

Callie knew he was right, but she would rather take her chances in a car crash than wait for him to set the car, and her, on fire.

She wondered if Kate had noticed her missing, or if any of the others at the bar had seen her being taken. Then she wondered why he was driving so fast. Surely he wouldn't want to draw attention to himself, and the car? He kept looking in the mirror and, as she realised why, her heart soared. They were being followed, that's why he was not worried about attracting attention for speeding, he was trying to get away. She listened very carefully and thought she could hear a siren in the distance, so help couldn't be far behind.

She took a closer look at where they were, the regular rows of houses and parked cars had given way to hedgerows. They were out in the countryside, but she wasn't quite sure where. She could see he was watching closely, occasionally slowing to look at potential lanes and tracks where he could hide with the car and she knew she couldn't let him. He saw a turning up ahead and turned off his lights as he approached it. Callie knew that the moment he stopped driving he would be able to turn his full attention to stopping her from escaping or making a noise. He would be able to knock her out, or even kill her. She had no illusions about her ability to defend herself – perhaps she would have been wise to take up martial arts or self-defence classes, but it was too late now. She had to take her chance whilst he was still preoccupied.

* * *

They had turned off the road onto what was little more than a rutted dirt track and had therefore slowed a little. Callie slid one hand down onto the seat belt release and as Lambourne turned again into a muddy farmyard track, she simultaneously undid her seat belt and pulled the door handle. Rolling out of the car before the door had really opened, her arm got caught in the seat belt, stopping her from fully falling from the car.

Lambourne slammed on the brakes and grabbed for her arm, but the sudden jerk of the car coming to a halt was enough to release her arm from the seat belt and he was only able to grab the sleeve of her jacket.

Callie pulled against Lambourne's grip, but he had hold of her too tightly, so she cried out in anger, twisted and kicked at the car and in one desperate, ferocious move that tore her jacket, she managed to free herself from his grasp. The sudden release sent her sprawling and winded her. For precious seconds, she couldn't move. She heard him come after her and she hardly knew where she got the strength, but she was up and running out into the lane, Lambourne close on her heels.

With a final burst of speed, she flew out into the lane and stopped as headlights dazzled her and there was a screech of brakes.

"Fuuuuck!" she heard Jeffries shout as the car skidded to a stop, inches short of hitting her.

Miller was out of the car and running round the front of the car as Lambourne careered out of the opening, and seeing Miller and Jeffries, turned and ran.

"Go!" Jeffries shouted at his boss. "I've got her." Jeffries ran to Callie, who had sat down in the middle of the road, crying with relief. Miller must have realised that Jeffries' days of running after criminals was long gone, or rather his days of having any hope of catching them were. So, after a quick look at Callie, who waved vaguely to let him know she was okay and he should go after her abductor, Miller chased after Lambourne. Jeffries took off his jacket and put it round Callie's shoulders as he took out his phone to let Control know where they were and that they needed support and an ambulance.

Chapter 30

They had the heaters on full blast in the back of the ambulance where Callie sat with a blanket round her shoulders. It was very warm, but she couldn't seem to stop shivering. The after-effects of the drug, she told herself, and shock, but that didn't stop the shivering. Jayne Hales sat next to her with her notebook open, ostensibly to take a statement from Callie, but she was doing most of the talking.

"Good thing you left those messages on the guv's phone or we wouldn't have known where to start looking for you." She had already explained that Miller had switched his phone off whilst interviewing Butterworth and it wasn't until after the evening briefing that he had remembered to turn it back on.

"But how did you know it was Lambourne?" Callie asked between spasms of shaking.

"We didn't," Jayne admitted, giving her a worried look, probably wondering if she ought to get the paramedic back in.

But Callie smiled encouragement and clenched her teeth more firmly together to stop them chattering.

Slightly reassured, Jayne continued, "The techies had analysed the wording in all the posts on the website connected to our victims and spotted a pattern. The killer was changing names and burner phones for every target, but recycled bits of his profile and messages, using the same words and phrases."

"That was clever."

"Nigel helped them with that. Of course, he would have got onto the pattern much earlier if we had got access to the instant messaging app Lambourne used once he had made contact with the victims, but they were encrypted and it wasn't a matter of national security, apparently."

Callie, normally a staunch supporter of civil liberties and the right to privacy, had to concede that the police would have caught the killer earlier if they had had access to the instant messages, and it gave her pause for thought.

"But how did all that lead you to me?"

"The tech department called urgently this evening to say that they were pretty sure that the same person was in contact with someone else and sent us the details. We recognised the photo as your friend Kate, which was just as well as that wasn't the name she was using."

Jayne looked amused, but Callie just nodded her understanding. She was absolutely not going to ask what name Kate had used.

"So we phoned her," Jayne continued, "and she said she was supposed to be meeting him tonight but he had been a no show and someone better had come along."

That explained it, Callie thought. The man with Kate was just a random bar user, not the date from the website. That date was Adrian of course, a little late, but there to meet Kate. She shuddered at how close they had both come to being the next victims.

"We were relieved," Jayne went on, once she was sure Callie was okay, "but then she realised you had gone AWOL and weren't answering your phone. She went outside and rang you again, heard the ring tone and found your phone in the gutter and called us back immediately. The boss charged over there and some witnesses remembered seeing a woman who fitted your description, and whom they took to be drunk, being helped into a car. Fortunately, one of them was able to give us a good description. Caused a bit of a panic, I can tell you."

Callie shuddered. She hated to think what could so easily have happened if Kate had just assumed she had gone home.

"I'm just so glad they managed to track down the route he was taking."

"Well, that was down to you, I reckon. You tried to get out of the moving car, didn't you?"

Callie nodded.

"Your passenger door took the wing mirror off a cab as the driver was dropping off a passenger. He was absolutely livid. He gave chase and radioed all his mates to help. We just had to follow the taxis."

Callie smiled again, but this time it was for real. The thought of the police cars, chasing the taxis, chasing the car she was in was like something out of a cartoon and she was sure it hadn't really been that easy.

"Well, I'm very grateful to them." She sighed and shook her head. "It never occurred to me that Adrian was the killer. I mean, I even knew he'd been through a terrible divorce. But he just seemed boring, petty and ordinary. How can I have been so stupid?"

She looked over at the police car where she could see Lambourne sitting in the back, hunched and defeated, with his hands cuffed and with a grim-looking police officer sitting beside him. Lambourne had a small cut above the eye and some incipient bruising to his jaw. She hoped it hurt. As she watched, the car pulled away, taking him to the police station.

Jayne made herself scarce as Miller hurried over to the ambulance, limping slightly.

"How're you doing?" he asked, concern and exhaustion etched across his face.

"I'm fine," she lied. "What about you?"

"Just a knock." He shook his head impatiently. "It's you I'm worried about."

"Why?"

"You, I, well…" He gave up trying to express himself and gave her a hug instead, which surprised her. She would normally have felt uncomfortable about such a display of affection in front of everybody, but tonight it felt good. It was what she needed, and she couldn't help but close her eyes and sink into the warm embrace, hugging him back as tightly as he held her.

"Boss?" Miller tensed as Jeffries called to him.

Callie could see Jeffries behind Miller's back, gesturing impatiently as he muttered, "For fuck's sake."

This rather broke the mood, for Callie at least, and she pushed Miller away.

"Go," she told him. "You're needed at the station."

"But—"

She could see he was torn between wanting to stay with her, and knowing that he had work to do.

"Go," she repeated firmly. "I'm fine. I need to go to the hospital and get checked over, and have my blood taken to check for GHB before it's out of my system. Now you go and do the interview and make sure you build a rock-solid case against him."

He nodded and with a last look at her, turned away and went over to where Jeffries was waiting to drive him back to the station.

* * *

Jayne was under orders to stay with Callie as she was taken to the hospital in the ambulance. Much as she liked the policewoman and even counted her as a friend after the events of the past few weeks, Callie was pleased to find Kate already at the hospital waiting for her. She must have had an awful time with no idea what was happening and Callie was glad someone had found the time to ring her to let her know she was safe.

"I would never have forgiven myself if you weren't all right," Kate later confessed. "After all, it was me who got you into the situation in the first place."

But Callie didn't blame her friend one bit. She was okay, and the killer was in custody. She just wanted to make sure he stayed there. There was no doubting that he had drugged and abducted her. She had had the blood tests done and was sure that they would prove it. Lambourne would go down for her abduction if nothing else. She just hoped that the interview or the search of his home and office would provide further evidence of his guilt as far as the other victims were concerned, because a good lawyer might get him off the murders and she wanted, needed, to know that he was going away for a long time. A very long time.

* * *

The following morning, after a fitful night's sleep, Callie insisted that she was feeling fine and persuaded a reluctant Kate, who had slept on the couch in case her friend needed anything in the night, to leave. She wanted some time to herself, she said, to think about the previous night, but in reality, it was more because she didn't want to think about it that she wanted to be alone.

Kate meant well, but she was so wracked with guilt and the fright of what could have happened to Callie, that she couldn't stop talking about it. Callie appreciated that different people have different ways of dealing with trauma, but while Kate needed to discuss it, Callie very much needed to put the fear and the horror of her abduction into a little box somewhere deep in her brain to be taken out and examined at a later date when she felt stronger. For now, she needed to do something physical and banal, like cleaning. So, once she was alone, she donned rubber gloves, armed herself with a cleaning spray and sponge and tackled the bathroom.

It was almost lunchtime when the intercom buzzed to let her know that she had a visitor.

As she pressed the intercom button to speak to whoever was at the door, the slightly hesitant "It's me" told her immediately that it was Miller. What she didn't know as she buzzed him in and opened her front door, was whether or not he was on his own. It occurred to her that a video entry system would be a good idea and added it to her mental shopping list, and was relieved when she saw just Miller coming up the stairs.

"Come in." Callie carefully checked the stairs behind him, in case Jeffries was lurking in the stairwell, but the absence of either heavy breathing or swearing indicated that Miller was truly alone.

He stood just inside the door and made no move to come further into the flat. His coat was wet and she realised that she hadn't even noticed that it was raining outside, she had been so intent on her cleaning.

"Can I?" She indicated his coat and moved towards him, hoping that another hug might be on offer.

"I can't stay," he said.

"That's fine. You must be really busy. So much going on." She was gabbling, she realised, and told herself, firmly, to shut up.

"I just wanted to let you know what was happening, and see how you were."

"That's good of you," she said. "So, what is going on? Has he confessed?"

"No, not yet. He's not saying anything, but I've no doubt he will if you're right."

She looked at him enquiringly.

"If he did this to punish women for adultery, he'll want to tell the world about it. Make sure everyone knows why they deserved it, in his mind."

"You're right. He'll want to justify his actions."

"I'm hoping he doesn't save it for the trial, though. It would be good to have a confession before we get there."

"Do you have enough evidence if he does make you wait?"

He nodded, and she let her breath out in relief, not having been aware that she had been holding it as she waited for his answer.

"The car had a foldaway bike in the boot for his getaway, as well as a container of petrol," he said.

Callie couldn't stop a slight shiver at the thought of what might have been.

"And we found fake number plates in his garage. His laptop computer has gone for analysis but they have already confirmed that he used the SusSEXtra website and was in touch with each of the victims under a variety of aliases. We also found a bottle of" – he hesitated – "not sure how to pronounce it but sodium oxybate?" He looked at her questioningly.

"Medical GHB. Used for narcolepsy, I think." She was glad to have something practical to think about. "But I've never had a patient on it. It's very rarely used."

He nodded.

"We're going through the hospital records, but it seems that he used to help out in a sleep clinic."

Callie mentally kicked herself. She had known that, why didn't she make the connection earlier?

"But surely someone would have noticed it missing? It's a controlled drug."

"You would have thought so, but apparently the one bottle they had some time back was out of date and listed as destroyed. The two signatures to the statement of destruction are pretty unreadable, so no prizes for guessing that they could both be him."

"But you'll need to prove that. I could help. Check the previous drug registers–"

"You're too involved." He cut her off, sharply, then softened. "We have people checking them and doing handwriting analyses. We'll prove he took it, don't worry."

Callie nodded. She suddenly realized that what she wanted, more than anything else, was for him to hold her, and looking at him, she thought, for a moment, that maybe that was what he wanted too. She looked away quickly. That would never do.

"Well, it looks like you've got it all sewn up. Thank you for coming to let me know. If there's anything I can do, do let me know," she said brusquely and he nodded and went to leave.

As she opened the door, he hesitated again and spoke in a husky voice.

"Take care of yourself, Dr Hughes."

"I will. Goodbye, Detective Inspector Miller," she said, holding her hand out. "And thank you."

He briefly shook her hand and hurried out. As he left, she closed the door firmly behind him, before, finally, sinking to the floor and allowing herself to cry.

THE END

If you enjoyed this book, please let others know by leaving a quick review on Amazon. Also, if you spot anything untoward in the paperback, get in touch. We strive for the best quality and appreciate reader feedback.

editor@thebookfolks.com

www.thebookfolks.com

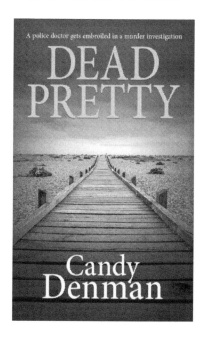

GUILTY PARTY – Book 3

A lawyer in a twist at his home. Another dead in a private pool. Someone has targeted powerful individuals in the coastal town of Hastings. Dr Callie Hughes uses her medical expertise to find the guilty party.

Available on Kindle and in paperback

VITAL SIGNS – Book 4

When bodies of migrants begin to wash up on the Sussex coast, police doctor Callie Hughes has the unenviable task of inspecting them. But one body stands out to her as different. Convinced that finding the victim's identity will help crack the people smuggling ring, she decides to start her own investigation.

Available on Kindle and in paperback

Printed in Great Britain
by Amazon